FOUR EIDS
and a FUNERAL

Also by **FARIDAH ÀBÍKÉ-ÍYÍMÍDÉ**

Ace of Spades
Where Sleeping Girls Lie

Also by **ADIBA JAIGIRDAR**

The Henna Wars
Hani and Ishu's Guide to Fake Dating
A Million to One
The Dos and Donuts of Love

FOUR EIDS
and a FUNERAL

FARIDAH ÀBÍKÉ-ÍYÍMÍDÉ
and ADIBA JAIGIRDAR

FEIWEL AND FRIENDS
NEW YORK

A Feiwel and Friends Book
An imprint of Macmillan Publishing Group, LLC
120 Broadway, New York, NY 10271 • fiercereads.com

Our books may be purchased in bulk for promotional, educational, or business use. Please
contact your local bookseller or the Macmillan Corporate and Premium Sales Department at
(800) 221-7945 ext. 5442 or by email at MacmillanSpecialMarkets@macmillan.com.

Library of Congress Cataloging-in-Publication Data

Àbíké-Íyímídé, Faridah, author. | Jaigirdar, Adiba, author.
Four Eids and a funeral / Faridah Àbíké-Íyímídé and Adiba Jaigirdar.
Description: First edition. | New York : Feiwel and Friends, 2024. | "A Feiwel
and Friends Book." | Audience: Ages 14-18. | Audience: Grades 10-12. |
Summary: The death of a beloved mentor, and the need to save and rebuild
their fire-damaged Islamic Center, bring former best friends Said and
Tiwa back together, rekindling their romantic relationship.
Identifiers: LCCN 2023048760 | ISBN 9781250890139 (hardcover)
Subjects: LCSH: Muslim teenagers—Juvenile fiction. | Muslim families—
Juvenile fiction. | Community centers—Juvenile fiction. | Muslims—
Political activity—Juvenile fiction. | Vermont—Juvenile fiction. |
CYAC: Muslims—Fiction. | Muslim families—Fiction. | Teenagers—
Fiction. | Community centers—Fiction. | Political participation—
Fiction. | Vermont—Fiction. | Romance stories.
Classification: LCC PZ7.1.A1675 Fo 2024 | DDC 823.92 [Fic]—
dc23/eng/20240215

First edition, 2024
Book design by Maria W. Jenson
Feiwel and Friends logo designed by Filomena Tuosto
Printed in the United States of America

ISBN 978-1-250-89013-9 (hardcover)
1   3   5   7   9   10   8   6   4   2

*For all the librarians who fight for
marginalized readers—thank you*

Beatrice: "I had rather hear my dog bark at a crow than a man swear he loves me."

(Act 1, Scene 1)

Benedick: "For which of my bad parts didst thou first fall in love with me?"

(Act 5, Scene 2)

Much Ado About Nothing, William Shakespeare

LET'S GET ONE THING STRAIGHT: THIS IS A LOVE STORY.

I know both the funeral and the fire might be alarming, but I can assure you that despite the rather unfortunate beginnings, the betrayals that would put even Shakespeare to shame, and the regrettable *incident* several Eids ago, this is simply a morbid tale about two doofuses who fell in love over the course of several years.

You may hear other iterations of this story from *untrustworthy* sources. But this is the true account of what *really* happened.

This is a tale of four Eids. And a funeral.

Act 1

THE INCITING
INCIDENT

1

OUT OF THE BLUE

Said

"Can Said Hossain please report to the principal's office?"

I glance up at the speaker hanging off the ceiling in the classroom, wondering if I just didn't hear correctly. But from the way Julian is looking at me with a raised eyebrow, I know that it *was* my name being called to the principal's office.

I furrow my brow at Julian. In all my time at St. Francis Academy for Boys, I've never been called to the principal's office. I've never gotten into trouble. I've been so good, in fact, that I'm on honor roll, and on track for early admissions to the best universities in the country. My parents often use these facts as dinnertime conversation to impress anybody and everybody.

"Can Said Hossain please report to the principal's office *immediately*?"

Mr. Thomas glances at me from his desk. "Said?" he asks, motioning toward the door. He doesn't seem too bothered about the fact that one of his top students is getting called to the principal's office out of the blue, so maybe I shouldn't be either.

Since class is almost over anyway, I gather up my things into my backpack and slip out the door. The hallways of the school are completely empty, but I can hear the sounds coming from different classrooms as I make my way down to the principal's office. The near-silence would almost be peaceful, if worry wasn't gnawing its way into my stomach.

I turn into the main office, and immediately I'm greeted by a familiar voice.

A voice that sounds a lot like my older sister's.

The closer I get, the more sure I am that it *is* her. From the fact that she's loudly trying to convince the principal that his rules are ridiculous, to her long black hair and her bright purple sweater.

"Safiyah?"

Saf turns to me, her eyes wide with . . . well, I'm not really sure what.

"Said!" she says. "Oh, finally. We need to go."

"What's going on?" I glance from her to Principal Carson, who has never looked so uncomfortable. Usually, he has an air of authority about him, the kind that will make any student here think twice about breaking any rules. But apparently just a few minutes with Safiyah can change all that.

"There's been an inci—" Principal Carson is cut off with a small glare from Safiyah, but my stomach drops all the same.

"Ammu? Abbu?" My mind immediately jumps to the worst possibilities.

Safiyah shakes her head slowly. "It's . . . Ms. Barnes." And then, I just know. Even without Safiyah telling me, I know. Because I knew she was sick. I had even written to her. Sent her a get-well-soon card, like that would somehow help her deal with the cancer. But I'd never let myself consider the possibility that she might actually . . .

"I'm so sorry, Said." Safiyah holds out her arms, and it's like my

4

body is working automatically. I walk into her hug. Safiyah wraps me up tightly in her warm embrace, and we stay like that for a long moment. All the while I'm trying to register it—Ms. Barnes is dead. Ms. Barnes, the woman who encouraged my love of reading. Without her recommendation letter, I probably wouldn't have even gotten into this school. And now she's just . . . gone.

"We have to go," Safiyah says as soon as I pull away from her hug. "The funeral is tomorrow morning, and if we leave now we should be able to get back to Vermont with plenty of time to spare."

"But . . ." I shake my head, because Safiyah's words are barely registering in my mind. Ms. Barnes gone. Funeral. *Back to Vermont?*

"Said has classes," Principal Carson chimes in when I've been silent for a little too long. "There's still a whole week left until the semester is over and the summer holidays start."

Safiyah scoffs. "Look at him!" She waves her arm at me like I'm some kind of a painting in a gallery. I blink at Principal Carson, because, really, I'm not sure what he's supposed to be looking at. "You think he's going to be okay going through classes for another whole week? He needs to be back home, with his family. He's distraught."

"This Ms. Barnes was . . . a family member?" Principal Carson asks.

Safiyah glares at him once more. "Is he only allowed to be upset when a family member passes?" she asks. Her voice doesn't rise—Safiyah doesn't shout—but there's this way she has of making it all low and scary. When we were kids, Safiyah used to use this voice on me to make me do all the chores she didn't want to do. I've grown immune to it now—a little bit immune, at least. But Principal Carson is obviously meeting Safiyah for the first time. He shifts uncomfortably in his seat.

"Well, no. It's just, we don't know a Ms. Barnes, and—"

"Check his school records. You'll find Ms. Barnes's letter of recommendation for Said. They were close. She was like a mentor to him."

Was. That's the word that echoes in my head over and over again. Ms. Barnes *was* like a mentor. Because she is no more.

"I just don't know if—"

"We're going!" Safiyah exclaims, throwing her hand up. "I'm taking Said, and we're packing up his things and driving back to Vermont, whether you think his loss is important enough to warrant missing a week of classes or not." She spins around and stomps out the door.

I stand there for a moment longer, because in her anger she's obviously forgotten that she came here to get me.

Principal Carson heaves a sigh. "Said, you can go. I'll send a message to the registration office," he says. "And I'm . . . sorry for your loss."

I swallow the lump in my throat. "Thank you," I say.

SAFIYAH SEEMS COMPLETELY UNIMPRESSED BY MY DORM. OF course, my side of the room is perfectly intact. Everything in its place, and a place for everything. But Julian's side is a completely different matter. There are clothes strewn all over, and his books are anywhere *but* on the little shelf above each of our desks specifically designated for our schoolbooks.

"How does Julian ever find anything in this pigsty?" Safiyah asks, clicking her tongue with disapproval as she eyes his side of the room.

"He gets by," I say, while staring at my own side of the room. I figured I still had an entire week left to pack up for the summer. Now, with grief lodged in my throat like a rock, the idea of putting away all my things seems even more daunting.

Safiyah seems to almost sense this, because she slips past me and begins pulling clothes from my drawers and into an open suitcase.

"When did it happen?" I ask, after a moment.

Safiyah looks up at me, but she doesn't stop in her one-track focus of packing up my things. "I'm not sure. A few days ago, I think."

A few days ago. Shouldn't I have known something was wrong? Isn't there something in the universe that's supposed to tell you when someone you love is suffering? Is . . . dead? But for the past few days, I went about my life like everything was normal. I went to my classes, played soccer with Julian, did my homework. All the while, Ms. Barnes was gone.

"How did you find out?" I ask Safiyah, instead of indulging my guilt for longer. I can feel the pressure in my throat growing, can feel the pinprick of tears behind my eyes. I'm definitely not going to break down in front of Safiyah like this. Not now.

Safiyah stops in her tracks for a moment. "Um, I just . . . someone from home told me." She goes back to packing up my things like she didn't hesitate to answer my question. But I immediately know: It must have been *her*—Tiwa. For all her faults (and she has many), Tiwa, at least, loved Ms. Barnes as much as I do. At one point in our lives, Tiwa would have told me as soon as she knew.

"Okay, all done!" Safiyah says, zipping up the suitcase. "The sooner we get out of here, the sooner we can get to . . . well, the funeral." She glances at me out of the corner of her eye, and there's sympathy written all over her face. She's looking at me like I'm about to break, or something.

7

I duck my head and approach Julian's unkempt desk. "I should let Julian know," I say. "He'll wonder . . . what's happened."

"Can't you just text him or something?" Safiyah asks.

I shake my head, picking up a pen from his desk and unfurling a balled-up piece of paper. "We can't check our phones in between classes. When he gets to our room, he'll be confused."

"Well, I'm going to get your things into the car," Safiyah says, dragging my suitcase behind her. "So, I'll see you there in a few minutes, okay?"

"Okay."

"Don't forget to add a Pokémon drawing to your note," Safiyah adds as an afterthought.

I pause. "How do you know Julian likes Pokémon?"

Safiyah just glances pointedly at the dozens of Pokémon plushies lined up on Julian's bed. "Every time I've spoken to him, he's mentioned Pokémon half a dozen times," she says before slipping out the door, and I realize she has a point.

With Safiyah gone, the rock in my throat seems to grow even larger. I swallow down the lump and tap my pen against the piece of paper. How do I explain to Julian exactly what's happened, when he doesn't know anything about Ms. Barnes?

I had to leave in a hurry because my hometown librarian passed away? But Ms. Barnes was so much more than that. She was my friend, my confidante.

My sister came to drive me back to Vermont early, I scribble down quickly, *because* . . . I stop there, unsure of what to say next. *Because a friend of mine passed away.* It doesn't seem like enough, but I guess it's all the information Julian needs. *I'll see you over the holidays,* I add, and do a quick doodle of Psyduck, which is—for some strange reason—his favorite Pokémon. And just that two-minute drawing lets a strange relief wash over me. Like learning about Ms. Barnes's death had twisted me into a knot of grief, and the ink against the paper was letting some of that grief out.

"YOU SHOULD CRY," SAFIYAH SAYS ONCE WE'VE BEEN ON THE ROAD for a few hours. There's been nothing keeping us company except for whatever radio station gets picked up by the car's frequency. We've listened to everything from country music to heavy metal, and even a talk show about different kinds of potatoes.

"Why would I cry?" I ask.

"Well, because crying is good for you. You shouldn't keep your emotions bottled up like this."

I roll my eyes and stare out my window instead of looking at Safiyah. Ever since she started majoring in psychology at college, she thinks she knows everything. Well, she's always been like this, but it's just worse now because she has the promise of an undergraduate degree to back up her know-it-all attitude.

"Said . . . I'm sorry," Safiyah says softly after a moment. And I thaw a little. She's trying to help—even if she's being completely and utterly unhelpful.

"I'm fine," I say, even as pressure builds behind my eyes. I blink away the tears and keep my eyes trained on the window.

"You should share a happy memory you have of Ms. Barnes," Safiyah says. "She would like that, right?"

Safiyah didn't really know Ms. Barnes, but she's right. She *would* like that. Ms. Barnes was the kind of person who liked to think about the positive things in life. She wouldn't want me to spend this entire drive glaring out my window, being annoyed at my sister, and feeling guilty because I didn't write to her enough during her time at the hospital.

I try to think of a happy memory. "Well, I remember when I got into St. Francis, and Tiwa was annoyed at me. She said she wouldn't speak to me ever again if I decided to go."

"That *doesn't* sound like a happy memory . . ."

"Let me finish," I say. "She was so annoyed at me. But then she went to see Ms. Barnes. She said Ms. Barnes invited Tiwa into her office, and made her tea in her little china cups. That's what she did when she wanted to have a serious conversation. And she told Tiwa about how she had written the letter of recommendation for me, and all the reasons why I needed to go to St. Francis, and all the ways it would help me. And Tiwa was still annoyed, but when she came to our house afterward, she understood. She wanted me to go."

"That's a story about Ms. Barnes? It sounds like it's more about Tiwa," Safiyah says.

I scowl at Safiyah but I know there's some truth to what she's saying.

The thing is, every happy memory of Ms. Barnes somehow feels tied to Tiwa. Even every happy memory of home is tied to her. "It's just that . . . that's the kind of person Ms. Barnes was. She was always making peace between me and Tiwa, always helping us see each other's side. I thought Tiwa would be angry at me the whole week before I left for St. Francis, but Ms. Barnes made sure that didn't happen. She made sure I had the best last week in New Crosshaven."

Because of Ms. Barnes, I knew that even though I was leaving,

I would always have people back home. I would always have Tiwa. I would always have Ms. Barnes. But Tiwa and I aren't friends anymore. And Ms. Barnes is gone. I don't get a lot of time to think about that, though, because the next moment, Safiyah swerves the car so fast that I'm pretty sure I see my entire life flash before my eyes. A car honks in front of us, and misses us by just a few seconds.

Safiyah curses under her breath, and I turn to her with a glare.

"What the hell was that? You could have gotten us killed."

"It's dark," she says. "I didn't see that car coming. It's fine, it'll be fine."

I pinch the bridge of my nose with my fingers. I always knew Safiyah was a terrible driver, but I didn't realize how much worse she might be at night. I check my phone for the time. It's already ten p.m., and we haven't even left Virginia yet. It'll probably be a few more hours until we're in Vermont.

"I think we should pull over for the night. Get some rest somewhere."

"We'll be late to the funeral!" Safiyah says. "It's just a few more hours."

"You're tired," I say. "You've been driving for hours. You want it to be our funeral next?"

Safiyah sighs. "Okay, fine. We'll find a place to stay for the night, but . . . we'll have to be up at the crack of dawn if we want to make it back in time."

I nod, already setting multiple alarms on my phone. There's no way that I'm going to miss my chance to say goodbye to Ms. Barnes. Not even Safiyah's terrible driving can keep me away.

2
WHAT AN ASSHOLE

Tiwa

FUNERALS TO ME ARE LIKE WEDDINGS.

People fly out from far and wide to celebrate someone's life. There's food, music, and family drama—only, after a wedding is over, the guests don't dig up a six-foot hole and shove the celebrant in.

I guess that's the only difference.

That and the fact that at least at a funeral, it's acceptable to be dressed in all black and to wear an unflattering scowl all day.

Do that at your auntie Amaal's wedding and suddenly you're the weird one. At a funeral, there's little judgment. I guess everyone is too busy being sad to judge others and how they look.

Besides, it's not what Ms. Barnes would have wanted. She was all for being yourself and not giving a shit about what anyone thought of you. She would have wanted everyone to show up here as their authentic selves, whether that be wearing a circus costume or a fancy suit and tie. She'd want to know everyone was celebrating her life without forcing themselves to be less than they are.

When Ms. B got her cancer diagnosis last year and had to start chemo, I remember how she'd bought these ridiculous wigs and would wear them without a care in the world. Her favorite was this electric-blue one that kind of reminded me of the wig from that old Katy Perry music video. She'd worn that wig everywhere she could: to my birthday, to the annual New Crosshaven pumpkin festival, and even to the Eid party at my house last year.

Picture after picture of her with her big smile and her bright-blue hair is on the board by the entrance of the funeral home, where everyone has hung up their favorite memories of her.

A stark contrast from the way I imagine she looks now inside the closed wooden casket: her eyes shut, face pale, and head mostly bald with small tufts of unruly ginger locks, like it usually was when she wasn't wearing her wigs.

No more smiles, no more telling me funny stories from her youth, no more life.

No more Ms. B.

I wipe my eyes with the back of my hand and reach out to touch the casket's lid, hoping that when I do it will somehow trigger something in the universe and I'll wake up and this will all have been a really fucked-up dream.

But of course, when I touch it, nothing happens.

I'm still here in this funeral home.

And Ms. Barnes is still dead.

Someone clears their throat. When I look up, I'm met with an annoyed-looking stranger peering down at me.

"Are you done? You've been standing here for ten minutes. Other people want to pay respects too," he says.

I now notice the lengthy line behind him. I didn't realize I've been here for so long.

"Oh . . . s-sorry," I say, swallowing the knot at the back of my throat. It wouldn't help anyone if I started crying in front of this stranger, who's already pissed off at me.

I wipe my eyes again and give Ms. B one final glance, before moving away from the casket.

The room is crowded, filled with people from all over, young and old. A lot of people must have really loved the library—or just Ms. B. She had an infectious personality that made it hard not to want to hang around her all the time.

I recognize a few people from school. No one I'm friendly enough with, though, to strike up a conversation or even give a polite nod to. So I decide to find my own corner.

It's weird to think that I was in this very same funeral home less than two years ago, and yet everything and nothing has changed. The layout is different, as is the paint on the walls, once an oatmeal beige, now a sickly green. The feelings that come with being here have stayed the same, though. I still feel the same squeezing in my chest, the same pit in my stomach, the same urge to hide from the reality of things.

Honestly, I'm tired of funerals.

There are seats all around the room, most unoccupied. There is something about standing at a funeral that makes the whole thing less depressing. Sitting forces you to think, which I guess is the last thing I want to do right now. So when I finally find my seat, I do what anyone does when they want to avoid dealing with their thoughts and emotions: I pull my phone out and turn it on. I'm hoping that while I've been here all morning, something scandalous happened online to some rich celebrity that will take all my attention away.

When my phone switches on, I'm immediately met by four missed calls from my best friend, Safiyah.

I sit up, eyebrows furrowing. Saf usually never calls so early.

I hope everything is okay with her . . . I press the call back button just as the room falls silent.

Saf's familiar ringtone sounds somewhere in the room: the shrill sound of *The Powerpuff Girls* theme song.

But it wouldn't make sense for Safiyah to be here; she barely knew Ms. B. Maybe there's another person with Saf's level of love for the Powerpuff Girls. But that's impossible.

I look up, noticing now how almost everyone in the room is staring in the same direction. At the front entrance.

Strange.

I stand to get a better view, regretting my decision when I see what, or rather who, had caught everyone's attention.

My best friend, Safiyah Hossain, and her brother, Said.

I take back what I said about not being judgmental at a funeral. People are definitely judging. They both look incredibly out of place here.

Safiyah is wearing a bright purple sweater with a print that says *Hello Suckers* in bold and Said . . . well, he's wearing his fancy boarding school uniform. Looking like his usual douchebag self.

Safiyah spots me and smiles, waving frantically as though we aren't at a funeral. Some people turn to look at me now.

I hesitate before I walk over to her, grimacing when I accidentally lock eyes with Said for a brief moment.

When I get to the entrance, Saf pulls me in for a tight hug.

"I missed you so much, T. How've you been?" Saf asks when she finally frees me, as though we don't talk every single day.

She has this creepy serial killer smile on her face. It's weirding me out.

"Uh . . . I'm okay, considering," I say.

Saf nods, looking sad.

"I can imagine how hard it's been. I know you both really liked her," she says.

The *both* she is referring to is me and Said.

I'm almost forced to look at him now. It would be weird if I didn't.

When I do, I'm surprised to see him staring right back. Even more surprising, though, is the expression on his face. His usual disdain whenever we're together is replaced by something new.

His eyes are bloodshot and glassy—he looks like he's been . . . *crying*.

But I don't understand why when he was perfectly fine going off to boarding school and abandoning everyone he knew. He was fine never visiting Ms. B at the hospital, not even when she was at her worst.

Why pretend to care now?

It's too late.

I'm still staring at him when he finally opens his mouth to speak.

"I'm going to go and pay my respects," Said says, turning to Saf now.

She squeezes his hand and pats his back, and he moves past me like he always does these days. Like I'm invisible.

I roll my eyes. *That's* the Said I know and hate.

"What an asshole," I mutter, forgetting Safiyah is here. I usually try to keep my thoughts about her brother to myself when she's around.

"I'm sorry, I tried calling earlier to give you a heads-up," Saf says, looking guilty.

I shake my head. "It's okay. Besides, he'll only be here for a day or two as usual. I'm just so happy to see you," I tell her, but the guilt still hasn't left her face.

"About that—"

"Hi, everyone! Can I have your attention please—the wake will be in the Walker Center. We're all about to head over, so please grab your things and get ready to leave," Clara Sheppard, one of the librarians who worked with Ms. Barnes, announces to the crowd.

"We should leave quickly before the road gets busy," I say.

"Let me just go and get Said first, okay?" Saf replies.

I nod, trying to mask my displeasure at the sound of his name. I guess this is the cost of having my best friend be the older sister of my sworn enemy.

Saf reappears a few moments later with Said. We stare at each other again in silence, my arms folded now to show how displeased I am with having him here.

His glowering tells me he feels the same.

Safiyah clears her throat. "So! The Walker Center . . . I take it I'm driving?"

"I don't mind driving," I say, mostly because I'd rather not die today. Saf drives like she's in a video game and has an unlimited number of lives.

"You sure?" Saf asks.

I nod. Very sure.

I glance at Said, again, expecting a protest. But it doesn't come. Saf nudges him and he looks at me, still scowling.

"Tiwa," he says with a nod.

I raise an eyebrow. Is that meant to be a greeting?

"Said," I reply in the same weird, antisocial manner. He's usually a lot more vocal, but I guess since his favorite childhood librarian died, he might not have much to say after all.

"Tell Tiwa I'll be walking to the Walker Center. Don't want to be the last ones to arrive there with the snail's pace she goes at. I'll see you in a few," he says to Saf.

Clearly Said doesn't realize I have his time today. After all, other than crying about the person you used to know now dead and lying in a casket, funerals are relatively uneventful.

"That's rich coming from the guy weeping at the funeral of the woman he spent the past four years ignoring. Hope you have a lovely walk. With any luck a coyote might eat you on the way and you'll never have to be put through the misery of being driven by me again," I say.

Said turns red, but his expression is unreadable.

"Seriously, guys, we will get kicked out, our slot is over," Clara says, clapping her hands together and gesturing toward the door.

"You're such a—" Said begins, but stops himself at the last second, as though scared that the ghost of Ms. B will rise up and reprimand him.

I smile, victorious. Which only makes him look more murderous.

"That's it, I'm driving. And you're both going to sit in the back seat and not complain about it or each other. Got it?" Safiyah asks.

We both stay silent.

"Good, now hurry up. I have plans after this," she adds.

"Plans? Ishra plans?" I ask, saying the second part slowly.

Ishra is a girl who works in the Walker Center and has been the target of Safiyah's flirtations for years. It became a running joke among us, the one-sided crush she had on her, until recently, when Ishra started flirting back.

Saf smiles, before walking out the door without confirming or denying anything.

I'll dig for more information later when Said isn't around.

Once we get into the car, I do what I usually do whenever I'm about to experience Saf's driving. I pray that Allah protects us against any scars or permanent injuries incurred from this.

When I'm done, I face the other way. I look out the window, trying to ignore Said's close proximity to me, and the stuff I couldn't help but notice in the short glances I got earlier. Like how much taller he's gotten, and how his hair is longer and floppier, and how my stomach turns every time he glances my way.

Like now.

I ignore all of that and focus on my second round of prayers, pleading to God once again that Safiyah doesn't kill us all today.

3

NEAR–DEATH EXPERIENCE

Said

BEING BACK IN NEW CROSSHAVEN IS ALWAYS MORE DIFFICULT than I expect it to be. It doesn't really feel like home, when I spend most of my time these days at St. Francis. It feels even less like home with Tiwa in the car beside me, pointedly staring out the window to avoid looking at me. Just like she's been avoiding me for the past four years.

But she still acts like *I'm* the one in the wrong somehow. Like *she* has something to be angry about.

I exhale and glance out the window, at New Crosshaven passing by in a blur. There are still so many familiar streets and buildings. Places where Tiwa and I used to hang out once upon a time. But so much of it feels unfamiliar every time I come back here. I can't quite pinpoint what's different. Maybe it's just me that's changed.

Being back here always feels like a reminder that I don't really belong anymore. That I haven't really belonged since that first year at St. Francis. And since that Eid party when I came back—the one that changed everything between me and Tiwa for good.

"So . . ." Saf's voice breaks through the near-total silence in the car. I can tell she's trying to cut through the tension in the air, the one that always exists whenever me and Tiwa are in close proximity to each other, but she's trying not to be too obvious about it. "Anyone watching anything good on Netflix?"

"You should watch the road," I advise her. "We don't want what happened on the highway to happen here."

Tiwa shifts in her seat, almost like I've piqued her interest.

Saf scoffs. "That was a one-time thing. It was *dark*."

Tiwa clears her throat. "Did something happen? Are you okay?"

"I'm fine!" Saf says, waving a hand around and almost steering the car a little too far to the right. She gets both hands back on the wheel just in time. "Said's just making a big deal of it."

"We had a near-death experience," I say, and when Tiwa's face falls, I instantly regret my words. I know that as much as Tiwa trusts Safiyah, she still struggles with being in cars. "But I made Safiyah pull over for the night, so everything was fine in the end," I quickly add.

"I wouldn't call it a *near-death experience*," Saf says. "But anyway, I can talk and drive at the same time—Tiwa knows that. I know these roads like the back of my hand."

I *almost* look over at Tiwa, to exchange knowing glances. But I catch myself at the last moment, choosing to glare out the window instead. When we were friends, Saf was often the subject of these shared glances between us. Because as much as we both love Safiyah, she manages to get herself into wild situations and always plays them off like they're not a big deal.

"So, Tiwa!" Saf says again, in a singsong voice this time. "Any plans for the summer?"

"Don't know . . . I'll probably help out around the Islamic Center," Tiwa tells Saf. Her voice isn't laced with the usual distaste it has whenever she speaks to *me*.

21

"That's a good idea. Ammu told me that they were looking for teacher's assistants for the Arabic classes. You'd be good at that," Saf says, nodding along.

I have to bite my tongue from replying to that with something mean. Tiwa has been obsessive about the mosque for the past couple of years. But I can't get over the irony of her acting like she's some do-gooder, when she couldn't even be bothered to stay in touch with me after I left for boarding school. She tries to act like the most pious, good-hearted Muslim in the world, but I know the truth about her now.

"And I'm hoping I'll get the internship at that law firm," Tiwa adds.

"That's the one beside that new ramen place, right? They'd be fools not to give you the job. You're the perfect person for it," Safiyah says. I have to concur—I've never met anybody as bossy as Tiwa. Of course she'd want to be a lawyer.

"What about your summer plans, Said?" Saf says this slowly. And in the rearview mirror, I can see her glancing at Tiwa. Almost like she's easing Tiwa into the fact that I'm back for the summer. That annoys me a little, but I have to ignore it.

"I don't know. Probably just . . . catch up with the schoolwork I'm missing this week. Prepare my college applications." I shrug. I hadn't even thought about the summer and what I wanted to do. I hadn't had a chance. The course load at St. Francis is tough. That's how they ensure that most of their graduates make it into an Ivy League, with major scholarship packets. And with junior year ending, college has been on everybody's mind. I can't really tell Saf what my college plans are, though. I haven't told anyone yet.

"Wouldn't want to spend too long here with people like us, after all. Then your fancy private-school buddies might not take you back," Tiwa says in her sweet-as-can-be voice that's dripping with sarcasm.

I want to reply. I have a million retorts for Tiwa. But I'm not going to stoop to her level. Not today of all days.

Not when we've just laid Ms. B to rest.

I know she wouldn't want this—even if Tiwa doesn't want to honor Ms. B's memory, I will.

So instead of replying, I pick up my backpack from the floor of the car and put it between us, hoping that creating this barrier means we don't have to talk to each other for the rest of the car ride.

I hear Tiwa mumble something incoherent under her breath, and I know that she's insulting me.

I take in a lungful of air to calm myself down as Saf turns onto the road that leads to the Walker Center. I'm thanking God that this miserable car ride will be over soon.

And then I see it.

"What's that?" I lean closer to the window, almost pressing up my face to the cold glass.

Up ahead—there's smoke rising in the air.

"What's *what*?" Tiwa's voice still drips with distaste, but I don't have time for her now. A sense of dread is building inside me.

"Saf? Do you see that?"

"Yeah." Saf's voice is barely more than a whisper. She doesn't stop the car or pull over. She keeps driving, and I wonder if she's feeling the same way I am. Like a rock is lodged deep in my stomach, solid and heavy.

Tiwa shifts next to me finally, peering ahead at the darkening sky.

"Is that . . . that can't be . . . ," she mumbles.

The sound of sirens behind us pulls us back to reality. Saf pulls the car over to the side of the road, and we watch as a fire truck plows past us and toward the building encased in smoke and flames.

A building that I once used to know like the back of my hand.

Tiwa looks close to tears now, and I actually feel a bit of sympathy for her.

The Islamic Center is pretty much Tiwa's life. Has been for as long as I can remember.

Beside me, she unclips her seat belt, pushes the door open, and steps out onto the street, like she wants a close-up view of the Islamic Center burning down.

"Tiwa, wait—" Saf calls out, but it's like Tiwa can't hear her. She closes the door behind her and steps away from the corner and closer to the burning building. Her eyes are glued to the flames rising up.

All I can think is that this is most definitely the worst funeral I have ever been to.

SAID AND TIWA'S FIRST EID

HERE'S WHERE IT ALL BEGAN.

A family of four arrives in the town of New Crosshaven, population 3,992. Known for its famous mural festival, a string of serial killings in the sixties, and of course, the largest Islamic Center in all of New England, the town of New Crosshaven has it all, even its own infamous love story.

On the balcony, the boy across the street watches the moving truck pull up to the driveway.

"SAID! Come and bring mishtis to the new neighbors!" the boy's mother yells from downstairs.

"Coming!" Said yells back. He watches the new arrivals for a moment longer, before turning and thundering down the stairs.

"Here," his mother says, shoving the box of mishtis into his arms. "Go and welcome them to the neighborhood."

Said eyes the box of Bengali sweets. "Didn't they just move in?"

His mother narrows her eyes. "So?"

"So they probably aren't thinking about food?"

"It's the polite, neighborly thing to do. I want them to know we are decent people."

Said rolls his eyes, but he clutches the box tighter and turns toward the front door. "Decent people don't disturb their new neighbors," he mutters under his breath as he swings the door open.

"I heard that!" his mother yells after him, but luckily he is already outside before he can be told off for talking back.

The house on the opposite side of the street stands tall and domineering compared to his own, even though they're identical. Said's heart beats faster and faster the closer he gets to the neighbors' front door. He stands just at the threshold, his breath caught in his throat.

"Said!" a voice calls behind him. Said almost drops the entire box of mishtis on the ground. He scrambles to catch it, just as his sister swoops in and grabs it from the air.

"Hey, give that back!" Said says.

"So you can drop it again?" Safiyah asks.

Said sends her a death glare. "What are you even doing here? Ammu told *me* to greet the neighbors."

"She obviously knew you wouldn't be able to handle it." Safiyah waves an arm over the mishtis. "And see? She was right."

"I'm not a baby! I'm only a year younger than you!" Said cries.

"If you say so." Safiyah rolls her eyes.

Said tries to grab the box back from his sister, but she's holding on too tight. They both pull at either end of it, Said clawing at his sister's arm and Safiyah stomping on his foot.

Just then, the door swings open. But Said and Safiyah are a bit too occupied to notice.

"Hello?" a timid voice calls out.

Said and Safiyah freeze for a moment. They turn toward the sound, still holding on to either end of the box of mishtis. A girl stands there, watching the two of them with wide eyes.

Said feels his face heat up with embarrassment. That's all it takes for Safiyah to swipe the box into her hands. She thrusts it toward the girl.

"My mom made you these," she declares.

The girl blinks at the box for a moment, before accepting it into her hands. "Who . . . are you?"

"We're your neighbors!" Safiyah exclaims, like it's perfectly normal for your neighbors to be wrestling over a box of mishtis on your doorstep. "We live in that house right over there." She points to the other side of the street.

The girl's lips form into an O. But she looks at Said, not Safiyah. "Were you the boy who was watching us move in?"

Said's face burns even more with embarrassment—more he ever thought was possible. Before he can defend himself, Safiyah steps in.

"Yeah, my brother can be really creepy sometimes," she says.

Said elbows Safiyah in the stomach, but the girl just laughs.

"My name is Tiwa Olatunji," she says, holding her hand out like they are in a business meeting.

Safiyah and Said both scramble to grab her hand, making for a very strange and clammy three-way handshake. Tiwa looks uncomfortable the entire time.

Once that's out of the way, Said finally gets a word in. "My name is Said Hossain, but my friends call me S-man. And this is my annoying sister, Safiyah."

"Nobody calls you that." Safiyah scoffs.

"Well, you're not my friend, so you wouldn't know," Said says.

"I'll just . . . call you Said," Tiwa says slowly, right as a voice calls to her from inside the house. Tiwa looks back for a moment and says, "I have to go. Thank you for this . . . ?"

"Mishtis," Said finishes. "They're Bengali sweets."

"Right. Thank you," she says, then awkwardly pauses before adding, "I'll see you around?"

Said nods. "We'll be right across the street!"

Tiwa gives them both a bright smile before pulling the door closed.

"She was nice," Safiyah says, already turning around and on her way home, not caring if Said is following or not.

But Said waits for a moment longer, staring at the wooden door in front of him. So much like his own, but with a gold-painted number that says 1411.

She was *nice*, Said thinks to himself.

HERE'S HOW IT WENT FROM THERE.

Several weeks passed, with countless bike rides, one conker match to the death, and three unfortunate falls out of tree houses, and after going through all of that together, Safiyah, Tiwa, and Said were now obviously the best of friends.

So it's no surprise that when Eid al-Fitr finally rolls around, Tiwa and her family are welcome guests in Said's house.

Like every year in the Hossain residence, the Eid party is celebrated after a morning spent at the mosque. Many Muslim families from across New Crosshaven show up at the Hossains' doorstep, carrying glass dishes of food. Soon, the dinner table is laden with more food than there are people. Laughter fills the house, along with the rich and spiced smell of freshly cooked polau.

Said is the first to the door as the bell sounds, barging past Safiyah and the rest of the guests when Tiwa and her family arrive.

"Finally!" he exclaims, smiling brightly at Tiwa. "I have something to show you in the garden!"

"Said, is that how you greet our guests?" Said's mom says, shaking her head at him.

"As-salaam-alaikum, Auntie and Uncle," Said mumbles.

"*And* Eid Mubarak," Said's mom adds, reaching forward to hug Tiwa's mom. Then she squats down, smiling at Tiwa's baby brother, Timi, and pinching his cheeks lightly.

"This boy gets bigger and bigger every time I see him. You're going to be as tall as me soon," Said's mom says, causing him to laugh as she tickles his chin—temporarily pulling his focus away from Said's pocket, which Timi has been watching expectantly since they arrived moments ago.

Said grins and digs around inside his pocket like he always does whenever Timi is around, pulling out a special sweet that makes Timi's eyes go wide. He almost drops his favorite dinosaur toy as his dimpled fingers reach out to grab the candy from Said's palm.

"What do you say?" Tiwa's dad asks Timi.

"Ta ta," Timi replies—which means "thank you" in Timi speak.

"We got you all gifts for Eid," Tiwa's mom says, holding up a giant shopping bag.

"Oh, you shouldn't have," Said's mom replies, but Tiwa's mom waves her off.

"It's a tradition in our family, we usually do a gift exchange on Eid—similar to Secret Santa. My husband calls it Secret Paaro, meaning 'exchange' in Yoruba."

Said's mom accepts the gifts. "How lovely, we'll all have to join in next year!"

As Said's mom catches up with Tiwa's family, Said discreetly grabs Tiwa's hand and sneaks away. They duck under the arms of guests, creeping through the kitchen, before stepping outside.

"Took you guys long enough," Safiyah calls down from the tree house.

"Sorry, next time I'll magic us here with my superpowers," Said says sarcastically.

"Okay, *S-man*," Safiyah says, before sticking her tongue out and ducking back inside.

Tiwa laughs, but Said just shoots her a glare.

The two of them grab on to the rungs of the rope ladder and begin to climb up to the tree house. The wind sways the ladder here and there, but Said and Tiwa are used to climbing this thing by now. They scramble to stand at the top and dust off their new Eid clothes, before taking their usual seats on the ground.

"Where's the apple juice?" Safiyah asks, staring down at Said's empty hands.

"I thought you were bringing it this time," he says.

"No, I specifically sent you down to get Tiwa *and* the apple juice, but apparently I have to do everything around here," she replies, crossing her arms. "Sorry for my brother's lack of hospitality, Tiwa. He's a bit of a doofus."

Tiwa shrugs. "I don't mind not having any apple juice."

Safiyah shakes her head. "No. An Eid picnic is not complete without apple juice. I'll be right back." With that, Safiyah quickly disappears down the rope ladder.

There's a moment of silence before Tiwa finally asks the question that has been bugging her for the past few moments.

"What's . . . *hospillow . . . tility*?"

"I don't know . . . I'm pretty sure it's something to do with pillows," Said says with a strange sense of confidence.

Tiwa *ahhs*, satisfied with his answer.

Said glances at the entryway of the tree house, searching for any sign of Safiyah, before grinning and pulling out some cartons of apple juice from his sweater.

"Here," he says, handing over a carton to a confused-looking Tiwa.

"How did you manage to . . . fit . . . all those cartons—"

"A magician never reveals his secrets," Said interrupts, then leans in and whispers, "I have a pocket inside my sweater."

Tiwa's eyebrows go up. "Like a kangaroo?"

Said isn't sure how he feels about being compared to a kangaroo but nods anyway. "I guess so," he replies, before taking a sip of the juice.

"Safiyah is probably going to kill you when she comes back. She really seems to like apple juice."

"How's she going to know?" Said asks.

Tiwa holds up her juice box. "Hello? This is going to be very obvious."

"Not if we hide them before Safiyah comes back!" Said exclaims. "I'm not going to tell her, and you're not going to tell her, and . . . juice boxes can't talk."

"What do I get if I keep your secret?" she asks.

"Well . . . you and I get to be best friends forever," Said offers, like it's the most simple thing in the entire world.

Tiwa seems to think about it for a second. Said has been a pretty good friend since she moved to New Crosshaven. He always brings her boxes of Bangladeshi mishtis. Her favorite is the round orange ones called laddoos. And he even showed her his supersecret hiding spots around the town. Now that she thinks about it, maybe Said is even the best friend she's had. So, being best friends forever is a pretty good deal.

"I guess . . . that wouldn't be the worst thing in the world," Tiwa agrees. "But . . . to be best friends *forever* we need a contract."

Said looks around for something to write with, but all he spots is a butter knife that Safiyah had brought up for their picnic. He has the perfect idea.

"Follow me!" he cries, grabbing hold of the knife and making his way down. Tiwa has no idea what is going through his head, but she still follows behind.

Once back on the ground, Said approaches the tree that the tree house rests on.

"This is going to be the perfect best friend contract, because it's going to be here forever," Said declares before carving a misshapen *S* into the wood with the butter knife.

For a moment, Tiwa doesn't know what to say. They've just vandalized a tree. But when Said holds out the knife to her, she grabs it with almost no hesitation. She carves out a perfect *T* beside the *S*, and even adds a + in between.

They stand back, observing their work.

There aren't many things in life that are forever, but Said and Tiwa were written in the stars . . . or rather the bark.

4

FUNERAL HUG

Tiwa

BRIGHT ORANGE FLAMES ENVELOP THE ISLAMIC CENTER, SMOKE pluming in delicate ribbons from the windows, the chimney, and the roof.

Before I can say or do anything, my phone's alarm blares loudly, jolting me out of my trance, forcing my attention away from the burning building and to the phone angrily vibrating in my pocket.

The sound of trumpets rings in the air.

I don't have to check the notification on the screen to know what the alarm is for.

I take my phone out and the notification confirms my suspicion:

TIME FOR ZUHR PRAYER

I customized the trumpets to scare the crap out of me five times a day—once at night. Strangely, it's the only alarm setting that actually wakes me up.

"Jesus, what kind of sound is that?" Said says, clutching his chest and glaring down at the blaring phone in clear shock.

"It's my alarm. It's time for zuhr prayer," I reply numbly.

Said raises an eyebrow. "Between the smoke and the trumpets I was convinced *the end times* Ammu always warns us about had finally arrived," he says breathlessly.

I ignore him, shutting the sound off.

The trumpets no longer distract my brain from the most important matter at hand.

The Islamic Center is burning.

I look away from the twisted scene, noticing Clara ushering people away from the Walker Center on the other side of the road. I see fire marshals and bright red fire trucks surrounding the building, their voices rising over the commotion, telling people to keep away. I suddenly feel nauseous.

"Are you okay, Tee?" Safiyah asks.

Am I? I'm not sure. The Islamic Center has been one of the only constants in my chaos-filled life. And now I'm witnessing it ignite like a flimsy matchstick.

"I need to go home," I say simply.

Safiyah looks a bit surprised by this. "What about the wake?" she asks.

I think the wake has been canceled," I say, gesturing to Clara still evacuating the center.

I can feel Said's eyes on me, and as usual I pretend not to notice.

"I think it's a good idea for us to head home too, to be honest—it's been a rough twenty-four hours," he says.

Safiyah claps her hands together with a nod. "All righty then! I'll drive Tiwa home first, so she can make it back in time for zuhr." As usual, Safiyah's tone and mood never quite match the room.

We climb back into the car and I feel the engine come to life as Safiyah turns the key in the ignition. Even as the car pulls out, I can't help but look at the scene we leave behind: the Islamic Center engulfed in flames, smoke rising up through the entire building, escaping through the top of the minaret and turning the blue sky gray.

The center grows smaller and smaller the farther we go. Until it's merely an orange-gray blip in the sky.

I finally force my gaze away, deciding that's enough masochism for today. I startle a little at the sight of Said next to me. I'd somehow forgotten he was still here.

His head abruptly turns when I look at him, as though I had caught him doing something he wasn't supposed to be doing.

I glance down at the space between us, and Said's backpack is no longer there.

Suddenly the car jostles forward and I almost fly out of my seat.

"Sorry! My bad," Saf says cheerily, as if she didn't just make an attempt on my life.

"Someone should revoke your license before you kill us all," Said mumbles as I reach for the seat belt.

It's only then that I realize that Said and I are a little bit closer than before, our legs almost touching.

For a moment I think about putting more distance between us.

But I don't.

I BARELY GET TO CLOSE THE CAR DOOR BEFORE SAFIYAH IS choking me half to death. Her arms are wrapped around me tightly and I swear I see a white light.

"Saf, I can't breathe," I say, my voice muffled against her sweater.

She pulls away. "Sorry, I just feel like I haven't hugged you in forever."

"We literally hugged thirty minutes ago at the funeral," I say, still catching my breath.

"Oh right . . . well, that was a funeral hug, and this is a best friend hug."

"Or maybe a *sorry the Islamic Center burned down* hug?"

"Probably more like a *sorry I didn't tell you Said is coming home for the summer* hug," Safiyah says.

I glance over at the car, where the devil in question is sitting looking disgruntled.

"The *entire* summer?" I ask, trying to keep my voice low and expression mild.

Safiyah smiles guiltily. "Yes, but you won't even know he's here. He'll mostly be holed up in his room working on college applications I imagine, and when he's not doing that he'll probably be visiting college campuses with one of his weird friends from boarding school."

I nod, trying to seem disinterested in all the details of Said's personal affairs.

Once upon a time I would have been the one helping him with college applications and taking road trips to historic college campuses around the country. We'd probably be applying to all the same schools too. But now I know nothing about his future plans and he knows nothing about mine.

"Sounds . . . fancy," I say, keeping up the charade.

The sound of the car horn loudly disrupts the conversation and we both turn to the car where Said's sneakers are now pressed to the wheel, his body stretched over the headrest.

"Stop talking about me and hurry up!" Said yells out the window.

Safiyah rolls her eyes and turns back to me. "I guess that's my cue. Let's hang out next Friday. We can have a Cookies and Crime sesh."

I nod with a forced smile. "You can tell me all about *Ishra* then. I need details."

"Of course, always happy to oblige," she replies with a wink as she steps back toward her car.

I hear Said mutter, "Finally."

I wait until Safiyah pulls out of the driveway before taking out my keys and going inside.

As I make my way through the narrow hallway over to my apartment, I pass my neighbor Mr. Larson's front door, almost tripping over the plants he has lined up on the floor. We've only lived here for a year, and somehow in that time the amount of plants Mr. Larson keeps has doubled. I once glimpsed the inside of his house on my way to school and it looked like a miniature forest.

I wouldn't be surprised if there was wildlife in there.

I open the door to the apartment, and as expected no one is home.

Like always, I take my phone out of my pocket to text my mom to ask when she'll be home, but when my screen unlocks, I am met with a dozen panicked messages from her about the fire and the wake.

I quickly shoot her a text that I'm fine and home now, while slipping off my shoes, shoving them into the mostly empty shoe rack, and dumping my bag on the ground next to it.

My footsteps echo as I make my way over to the bathroom, immediately turning on the faucet and letting the cold water spill over my hands.

At this point wudu is muscle memory; I just do everything three times.

I begin with saying "Bismillah" and then I wash my hands up to my wrists three times. I wash my mouth and my nose. I then wash my face, from my hair to my chin. I pour water over my hands, washing my arms from my fingertips to my elbows. And then I run my wet fingers through my hair, making sure to reach the nape of my neck. I wipe my ears, and then lastly wash my feet up to my ankles.

I finish with a prayer, feeling like I've washed all the bad luck away—the funeral, Said's arrival, and the Islamic Center going up in flames. It seems misfortune comes in threes too.

Grabbing my scarf and prayer mat, I maneuver them across the floor of the living room and face the qiblah.

And then I start the zuhr prayer as always with the fatiha.

MY MOM FINDS ME ON THE SOFA KNEE-DEEP IN A TUB OF SALTED caramel ice cream when she returns home from work.

I watch her shuffle around, checking the mail and discarding her coat on the kitchen island as her eyebrows furrow at what is most likely the latest electricity bill.

"I see you're enjoying yourself," Mom says as she opens another letter.

"I guess. I'm not even sure I like salted caramel but it was all that was left. We need more ice cream," I say.

Mom nods. "Noted."

"Are those bills?" I ask, watching her face wrinkle in real time as she scans the page.

She looks over at me with a weary smile. "Yep, the thieves at the energy company are at it again. But don't worry, it could be worse."

I pause mid bite, taking note of how her voice goes higher at the end of her sentence.

Before I can badger her about the bills, she's speaking again.

"Wasn't the wake meant to be at the Walker Center today? I hope you weren't anywhere near the Islamic Center when the fire started. One of the other nurses was talking about it. Alhamdulillah, no one was badly injured."

I nod. "Yes, it was, but I didn't go because of the fire and everything. Did anyone come into the hospital?" I ask.

"Just one of the firefighters who had a fall inside," she says.

I feel like I can still smell the smoke, still see the orange flames wrapping around the building and pulling it apart. I blink the image away, closing the tub of ice cream now. "At least the funeral wasn't affected. We still got to say goodbye," I say.

"How *was* the funeral?"

I'm not sure whether to tell the whole truth or only some of it. We've never been the kind of family that really acknowledges or discusses *bad things*. Especially not since everything that happened two years ago. Instead, grief is a permanent guest in our apartment, the elephant in our crumbling room.

And so I shrug. "Like every funeral. Depressing as hell."

Mom gives me an appalled look. "Astaghfirullah. Watch your mouth, Tiwa. Hell is not something to joke about."

I roll my eyes. "Sorry, the funeral was okay, I guess. I'm happy I got to say goodbye. But I don't know . . . I still feel heavy."

"Maybe you need a distraction this summer," Mom suggests.

"I'm already waiting on that law internship, that'll probably distract me enough—if I get in, that is."

"I mean something that isn't academic, Tee, like . . . arts and crafts, you could take up knitting or crochet," Mom says in all seriousness. I raise an eyebrow at her.

"Maybe . . . I'll think about it. I think they have supplies at the Walker Center. I'll head down there once the area is safe and open again."

"Good," Mom says. "The fire marshal that came in said that while the Islamic Center probably won't be in use for some time, the Walker Center wasn't touched by the fire and should be good to use this week. Hopefully this means your father will have Eid in his own house this year." She mutters the last part loud enough for me to hear.

I feel the blood drain slowly from my face.

I hadn't considered what the Islamic Center burning down would mean for Eid.

What it would mean for the party we are meant to be throwing.

What it would mean for our tradition.

Every Eid, a family in New Crosshaven hosts the biannual Eid party. We all get together with the other families celebrating at the Islamic Center. There's food, henna stalls, games, and we even exchange Eid presents at the end in Secret Santa style, which we call Secret Paaro. It's also the only time I ever see my parents in the same place anymore. The only time we're actually some semblance of a family.

This year it's our turn to host the Eid party. It's something Mom has wanted to do since we moved to New Crosshaven, thinking it would make us closer to the community. But now that it is actually happening, *of course* it all goes wrong.

"Do you think Dad would really not come to Eid?" I ask, my voice wavering slightly.

Mom looks at me like she regrets saying anything. "No, no, of course not. I'm sure he'll come, he always does. I shouldn't joke about that anyway."

I frown a little. Her reassurance does nothing to settle my worries.

Ever since Mom and Dad got separated almost two years ago and Dad moved to London, then met his new fiancée, I haven't been sure about anything. Especially not the future of our family.

It's sad to think that a building is the one thing holding my family together. It's like with each day that passes, we're all growing apart, more and more.

And with what's happened to the Islamic Center, my worst fears might actually come true.

5

YOU SNOOZE, YOU LOSE

Said

THE AROMA OF AMMU'S COOKING WAFTS OUT THROUGH THE OPEN window of our house before we've even pulled fully into the driveway. The heady scent of creamy korma mixed with the aromatic polau is more a call to home than anything else. And even though the funeral and the fire didn't exactly help my appetite, my stomach grumbles hungrily now.

Safiyah grins as she turns off the ignition and glances at me. "Clearly, Ammu's been waiting for you."

"Great, because I'm starving," I say as we step out of the car. My eyes automatically drift to the other side of the street where Tiwa's old house is. I still remember the day they moved in, and it still feels weird that Mr. Olatunji's blue Suzuki is no longer in their driveway—instead Mrs. Spencer's white minivan is parked there, a constant reminder of everything that's changed.

When we get inside, Abbu is already settled into his usual seat at the dinner table reading what seems to be a book on gardening, while Ammu is fussing with the plates, moving them around until they're each in the exact same position, their designs matching.

"You know Said's not a guest, right?" Safiyah asks as her way of greeting. When Ammu looks up, it's like she hasn't even heard

Safiyah. Her face breaks out into the widest smile, and she runs over to throw her arms around me.

"Said, finally!" she says, stepping back and looking me over with concerned eyes. "Don't they feed you at that boarding school? How are you thinner every time we see you?"

Safiyah rolls her eyes and plops herself down on one of the chairs, scooping a large spoonful of polau onto her plate.

"Nobody cooks like you, Ammu," I say, more to get out of this line of questioning than anything else. I barely even get to sit down next to Safiyah before Ammu is filling my plate up with polau, chicken korma, and vegetable korma. It's a bit much, but I don't complain. My stomach is still grumbling hungrily, so I dig in just as everyone else does.

"Safiyah messaged us about the fire, was everyone . . . okay? Are you two okay?" Her eyes roam all over us, like she'd missed some sign of the fire before.

"We're fine, Ammu," Safiyah sighs.

"We weren't near it, not really. But it looked . . . bad."

"There were already firefighters there when we arrived. And I don't think anyone was injured," I add quickly.

"Still, we'll have to call around and make sure everything is okay," Abbu says. He exchanges a grim look with Ammu. Last time I was home, Abbu and the other Muslim uncles around town would always get tea at the Islamic Center after jummah prayer. It was their weekly ritual.

"I'll have to check with Qaima about the Quran classes," Ammu mumbles, balling up some rice in her hands absentmindedly. "If we can't use the Islamic Center, I don't think we'll be able to have them anymore."

"Maybe you can ask the school if you can book a classroom over the summer?" I offer. When Safiyah and I used to take the Quran classes back when we were kids, the class sizes were small. There were only five other kids in our class, and one of them was Tiwa.

"I don't think we can afford that, Said," Ammu says with a sad smile. "The good thing about the Islamic Center was that everything was at our disposal there already. But…" She shakes her head and her smile brightens. "That's not something you have to worry about."

"We'll figure it all out." Abbu nods in agreement.

"But how was the funeral?" Ammu asks, her voice taking on an even graver tone. She doesn't wait for either Safiyah or me to answer before she continues, though. "That poor Ms. Barnes. I always liked her, you know. The way she took care of you, and how she recommended you for that school. She's always looked out for our family, so I'm sure Allah is looking out for her." At this, both Ammu and Abbu look up at the ceiling like it's their way of making a personal call to Allah himself, asking him to pay special attention to Ms. Barnes. It's a little ridiculous, but a nice thought, I guess. I think Ms. Barnes would have appreciated it.

"Ms. Barnes would have probably wanted your korma and polau at her funeral," I say, remembering how she loved Ammu's cooking just as much as the rest of us.

"The food at the funeral wasn't good?" Abbu asks inquisitively. "Finger sandwiches?" He scrunches up his nose as if he can't imagine anything as awful as finger sandwiches.

"We didn't even get to eat any because we were late," Safiyah says. "That's why we're starving."

"The wait was worth it, though. I've been dreaming about Ammu's shomuchas all semester. I'm going to eat so many of them this summer," I say excitedly.

"You should spend less time thinking about shomuchas and more time thinking about your education. This is an important summer for you, Said. It's the last summer before college applications. Maybe we can take a family trip out to some of the university campuses in nearby states?"

"You should start the applications as soon as you can," Ammu says before I can even respond to Abbu's suggestion. "Your abbu and I can take a look at your essays and help you with them. Maybe we should hire someone who can look over them too? Someone who has experience?" She says this to Abbu instead of me. Like he has more of a say in my life than I do.

I cut in before they can start making any more wild plans. "I think that I should be okay. I've already started looking at applications and . . . I'm going to tour some campuses with Julian once he gets here. He wants to explore the biology departments across different campuses."

My parents almost look disappointed that I'm so on top of things and don't actually need their help. I can't even imagine how disappointed they'd look if I told them the truth.

"You definitely don't need to hire anyone anyway. I'm here, aren't I?" Safiyah says through a mouthful of rice.

"Yes, you're here more than you are at your university classes," Ammu mumbles loud enough for all of us to hear.

Safiyah sends her a glare across the dining table but turns to me and says, "Not to boast, but I *did* get into my top choice university, and I had my pick of the litter too."

"I'm not sure how that's a 'not to boast,'" I say, but Safiyah just sticks out her tongue at me.

"Okay, okay," Abbu interrupts. "The important thing is the

applications get done. Harvard, Duke, Johns Hopkins . . . they expect the best of the best. If you need help, Said, we're all here."

I know he means it in a supportive way, but I can't help the sadness that washes over me at his words. At this entire conversation, really. Ammu, Abbu, even Safiyah, have pinned their hopes on me going to a top university for premed. In their minds, there's no question about it.

"Thanks, Abbu," I mumble, looking down at my half-finished plate of food. My hunger has dissipated now. At some point, I'm going to have to tell them that I have no plans to study medicine like they all want me to.

That my dreams are different from the ones they want me to have.

"You're not eating!" Ammu exclaims, pulling me out of my thoughts. She starts piling more polau onto my plate.

"Ammu, that's en—"

"This is why you're getting so thin. Turning down perfectly good food!" Ammu says. She sounds angry, but from the way she pats my cheek I know she isn't.

In an attempt to stop her chastising, I look across the dining room for a subject changer, noticing a pile of gift-wrapped boxes.

"What are those?" I ask, gesturing to the pile.

Ammu looks over, her attention successfully diverted.

"Those are the Secret Paaro gifts for this year. We picked the names a few weeks ago, but don't worry, we already picked a name for you—I think you got one of the Salim twins. Ishmael, I believe," Ammu says.

Last Eid I was still trapped in St. Francis doing exams, and so I didn't get to take part in the biannual tradition of swapping gifts on

Eid. I'm pretty sure the Olatunjis started this tradition when they first arrived, and ever since, the community has taken part.

"Thanks, Ammu, I'll probably get him a soccer ball or something," I say, using the opportunity while she's still distracted to dump half my polau onto Safiyah's plate. She cries out with a loud "Hey!" but doesn't put any of the rice back.

Ammu and Abbu don't even reprimand us. For a moment, as I sit there taking in my family around the dinner table, it almost feels like the old days. Before boarding school, before Tiwa and I had our falling-out.

And it reminds me of why I can't tell Ammu and Abbu about animation school. At least, not yet. Because it'll ruin everything.

"And then Gengar just swallows me whole—it was so scary. Word of advice, don't fall asleep playing Pokémon. You'll just dream of weird shit, Said."

"Noted," I say into the phone, hastily tapping the buttons on the controller. "But what does this have to do with what I asked?"

"Oh. What . . . was the question again?" Julian asks. I can hear him hitting his controller as I blow up a car with my rocket launcher.

"How were the last few days of the semester?" I ask, while trying to dodge his gunshots on-screen.

"Boring," Julian complains. "The seniors tried to fill up the teachers' bathroom with bubbles as their senior prank, but Mr. Thomas caught them before they were out the door, so we didn't even get that!"

"They didn't try again?" I ask. I've never known there not to be a senior prank in all the time I've been at St. Francis.

"Couldn't, could they? Placed janitor Joe as twenty-four-hour security in the bathroom so they wouldn't do anything else. I swear, the teachers in that school really have sticks up their butts. It's the last week of school, have some fun, you know?"

I can almost picture Julian's face getting all scrunched up like it usually does when he's ranting like this. It could be a rant about anything—from serious stuff like politics (which is rare) to debating the best-tasting Skittles color (yellow, according to Julian).

"Well, at least that means our prank next year has even more of a chance to be legendary," I point out.

"I've already been thinking about this!" Julian says excitedly. On-screen, I manage to take out two of the people on his team, so I know he's distracted. "I think that we could . . ." Julian's voice dims out as my phone rings with another call. I glance down at the pillow where I'd placed my phone so I would have my hands free to play our game. The caller ID reads *New Crosshaven Library*.

"Julian, can I call you back?" I ask, cutting Julian off midway through his growing list of senior prank ideas.

"Oh, sure. Everything . . . okay?"

"Fine, just have another call I need to take. I'll call you back, all right, and maybe next time you can try to beat me."

"If you didn't distract me with all your questions, I would be kicking your ass!" Julian says defensively.

I roll my eyes, mumble goodbye, and quickly accept the call from the library.

"Hello?"

"Hi, is this Said Hossain? It's Clara Sheppard from the New Crosshaven Library," a nasally voice sounds on the other end of the phone line.

"Yes, this is Said," I say.

"Wonderful! I just called to ask if you could come into the library tomorrow morning. There's something Ms. Barnes wanted you to have," Clara says.

"Oh." My throat dries up at the mention of her, and I sit up straight on my bed. "What is it?"

"I think it's better if you come and see for yourself. The solicitor will explain everything when you get here." Clara's voice is a little too upbeat.

I've never had to deal with a solicitor before. I can't imagine what Ms. Barnes has left me that a lawyer needs to get involved.

"Okay. What time tomorrow morning?" I ask.

"Well, I told the lawyer to be here at ten thirty, so it would be great if you could make it then."

Going out that early means I'll have to skip my late-night FIFA session with Julian, which I've been looking forward to since yesterday. I make a mental note to text him about rescheduling.

"I'll be there," I say.

THE LIBRARY LOOKS EXACTLY HOW I REMEMBER. THE SAME UGLY moss-colored carpeted floors, the same smell of hope and despair, the same blinding overhead light fixtures, and the same tall, wooden bookcases lining the cream walls, alongside the familiar mural of famous book spines. Stepping into this place feels like coming home. Unlike most of New Crosshaven, the library never changes. Even Ms. Barnes's hedgehog pencil case is still perched on the reception desk, watching me walk over.

There's no one behind the desk, and when I glance around, I

realize the library is almost completely deserted. No sign of Clara anywhere.

I look beyond the reception desk to the office where Ms. Barnes used to let me spend countless hours reading and eating cookies from the staff snack cupboard.

There's a note stuck to the office door now. The handwriting is so large that I can see it even from where I'm standing: *Out on my break! Back in 5.—Clara*

On the wall, the clock reads 10:32. Clara must be running late this morning.

I consider waiting by the desk for a moment, but the rows of books pull me in as usual. I wander down the aisles, finding myself in the children's classics section. This used to be my favorite section of the library when I was younger. The green carpet gives way to a rainbow rug, while the cream walls are covered with portraits of the library staff drawn by kids. I spot a few of Ms. Barnes as a happy stick figure with bright-blue hair and can't help my smile.

I scan the shelves and my eyes land on the familiar gilded spine of one of my favorite books: *Alice's Adventures in Wonderland*. Ms. B recommended it to me years ago, and I have thumbed through this very copy in her office a dozen times. I make my way over to it now, and just as my fingers graze the hardcover, it disappears from view.

I stare at the empty spot for a moment, trying to figure out what just happened. And then I see her. On the other side of the shelf, I spot my archnemesis's head. And her fingers are wrapped around my copy of *Alice's Adventures in Wonderland*.

My jaw clenches. "What the hell are you doing?"

Tiwa doesn't even look at me. Instead, she flips through the pages and casually says, "Reading," as though she didn't just steal the book from me.

"I was going to grab that." My voice comes out through gritted teeth.

Tiwa shrugs, still not sparing me a glance. "You snooze, you lose."

I turn around and march to the other side of the shelves, ready to get my book back. But suddenly Tiwa isn't there. When I look around, I realize she's moved on to the adult science fiction section with my book still tucked under her arm.

I stride angrily to where she's browsing through the shelves and grab the copy of *Interview with the Vampire* before she can.

Tiwa's head whips around and she finally meets my gaze, her eyes wide.

"Doesn't feel good when someone does it to you, does it?"

She arches an eyebrow at me. "Excuse me?"

"You stole *Alice* from me," I say, gesturing to the book in her arms.

"I'm pretty sure this book belongs to the public library of New Crosshaven, so unless your name is *library*, I didn't steal anything from you," she says.

Annoyingly, she has a point.

"I'll give you Anne Rice, if you give me Lewis Carroll," I say, figuring that bargaining will probably get me better results than my previous methods.

Tiwa looks up at the ceiling, considering it.

"Hmm . . . no, I think I'm good," she says with an uncharacteristically bright smile.

I narrow my eyes at her. Before I can get in my next insult, Clara appears seemingly out of nowhere.

"There you both are," she says, her smile as pleasant as her voice. "This is Ms. Sanchez, the solicitor I was telling you about." She nods to the woman standing next to her wearing a black blazer and blush-pink blouse.

We barely have the time to exchange hellos before Clara is ushering us all into the office.

"Sit down, and I'll get you all some coffee!" Clara exclaims before shuffling out the door.

I hesitate for a moment, before taking my usual seat in the corner closest to the door. Tiwa sits down several seats away from me, while Ms. Sanchez slips into a chair opposite us.

"Thank you for coming, both of you. I won't keep you long," Ms. Sanchez says with a tight-lipped smile. "The deceased, Mary Louise Barnes, has left you both one item in her will."

I can only blink at Ms. Sanchez in response. I hadn't expected that Ms. Barnes would leave me something. I've never been left anything in a will before. In all the movies and TV shows, will readings seem a lot more dramatic. And they never happen in the public library's cramped office.

"I have the paperwork here for you. All you have to do is sign off that you accept the responsibility."

"Accept the responsibility for *what* exactly?" Tiwa asks, and as though heard by the universe or Allah himself, Clara comes back in juggling a tray of coffee mugs in one hand and a ginger cat in the other.

Laddoo? I stare at the cat with wide eyes, taking in how much he's grown since the last time I saw him.

"Mary left her cat . . . La . . . doo? . . . in your care. I have here a list of instructions handwritten by the deceased as well as the form that I will need you both to sign so I can hand the cat over to you today."

Silence fills the room.

"Both of us?" Tiwa questions.

Ms. Sanchez nods. "Yes, it says here, in the event of Ms. Barnes's death Laddoo should be left to both Said Hossain and Tiwa Olatunji—that is you two, correct?"

"Yes, but—"

"Great! I just need you both to sign the paperwork and then we can hand the cat over," Ms. Sanchez says, sliding the document in front of us.

I stare down at the page, still processing the fact that Ms. Barnes left us her cat, of all things.

Clara sets both the tray and Laddoo down. And as if Laddoo already knows his new owners, he jumps up onto my lap, considering me with inquisitive eyes. I don't even think about it before reaching out my fingers and running them along the fur on his head. He purrs softly before promptly lying down. Like he's decided my lap is his new home.

"He remembers you!" Clara exclaims as she passes a mug of coffee to Ms. Sanchez. I'm not sure if that's exactly the case—Laddoo has always been an affectionate cat after all—but the idea of him remembering me fills me up with a warm feeling anyway.

"I always think about when Laddoo used to run off to visit you both in the Islamic Center," Clara says fondly, before her smile shifts into a frown. "It's such a shame about what happened. Do they have any idea what caused the fire?"

"The fire department says it was an accident that started in the kitchen. But we don't know all the details yet. I think we'll know more later in the week," Tiwa says.

I suspect she found this information out through the usual channels: the New Crosshaven neighborhood watch forum. I make a mental note to ask Ammu and Abbu about it when I get home.

"I'm hoping that Eid can still go o—" Tiwa starts, before Ms. Sanchez interrupts her by clearing her throat and looking at the clock above Tiwa's head pointedly. "I do have another meeting scheduled soon."

I glance at Tiwa out of the corner of my eye, trying to gauge her reaction. We've both been left in charge of Laddoo. We both have to sign the paperwork. Sharing this responsibility with Tiwa is the last thing I want, but Ms. Barnes wanted us to do this.

"I can sign first," I say, grabbing a pen. Laddoo shifts on my lap, like he's unhappy with the slight disturbance, and even Tiwa turns her head to me. I wonder for a moment if she'll refuse, but she doesn't say anything else. I sign on the dotted line, and when I place the agreement down on the table, Tiwa picks it up and swiftly adds her own signature.

I glance down at the orange ball of fluff, who I'm pretty sure has already fallen asleep.

I guess we're now the proud parents of Laddoo the cat.

6

BAD VIBES

Tiwa

Ms. Barnes must be playing a cruel joke on us from beyond the grave.

It's all I can think as I watch Said snuggling Laddoo outside the library. He looks way too happy about this situation. I think it's the first time I've seen him smile in years.

Said catches me staring, and as expected his smile drops. "Sorry, did you want to hold him?" he asks.

"It looks like you guys are bonding. I don't want to break up the party," I reply dryly.

"I remembered you were obsessed with Laddoo when we were kids so I figured you'd want him, sorry I asked," he mutters.

Said seems to forget that while he's been frolicking around with his fancy boarding school friends, I've been here with Ms. Barnes and Laddoo every day.

Something the cat seems to have forgotten too. I watch as the orange cat nuzzles his ears against Said's shirt.

Said bumps noses with the cat and I try not to look too disgusted by Laddoo's betrayal.

"You really shouldn't look at your new cat like that; it might give him a bad impression of you."

Instead of acknowledging him I just ask, "So how are we doing this?"

"Doing what?"

I gesture to the cat he's cuddling and Said looks down at Laddoo. "Oh, yeah, I guess we can have a custody agreement or something, I think that's how co-parenting usually works, right? I can have him at my place and you can have visitation."

I raise an eyebrow at him. He can't be serious.

"Just joking, we can share him," Said says, wearing a small smile at my reaction.

"I can have him on weekdays and you can have him on weekends," I suggest, taking out my phone to make a note of this.

"Shouldn't we get him for an equal amount of days?" Said asks.

"Mathematically speaking, I think it makes more sense for Laddoo to spend more time with the person who has been here for his whole life, not the guy who abandoned him and thinks he can waltz back in whenever he feels like it."

Said's expression sours and he looks directly at me, scoffing. "I left to go to school. I didn't know getting a good education is a crime."

I roll my eyes. Apparently the only way to get a *good* education is to go to a fancy-pants school and turn your nose up at everyone you used to know.

"The crime is that you're an elitist prick."

Said's eyebrows furrow and he looks at me blankly. His confused act only makes me want to hit him.

"*Elitist*—" he begins, his voice rising, but is quickly cut off by the sudden movement of Laddoo springing up and out of his arms.

I see a flash of ginger, and before I know it Laddoo is on the ground, dashing around a corner out of sight.

FOR SUCH A SLEEPY ORANGE CAT, TRYING TO HUNT LADDOO DOWN proves to be a near impossible task.

We search the Walker Center for what feels like the hundredth time and there's still no sign of him anywhere.

"We've been parents for all of an hour, and we've already lost our cat," Said says breathlessly.

"Well, *I* didn't lose him," I mutter loud enough for Said to hear.

He scoffs. "Maybe if you weren't being so hostile, Laddoo wouldn't have run away. He could tell you were bad vibes."

I slam the storage cupboard full of cleaning supplies that I was searching through and turn to Said once again.

"If anyone's bad vibes it's you. Laddoo could probably smell your pretentiousness and decided he didn't want to be near such a snob."

Said squints at me. "One, I'm not a snob. I'm so far from one actually that my friends at school call me Mother Teresa. And also, Laddoo can't smell pretentiousness. His only concerns are when he can eat, when he can nap, and when—" Said cuts himself off mid-sentence and his eyes widen. "Wait, I think I know where Laddoo is."

"Where?" I ask.

"The Islamic Center," Said says, like it's the most obvious thing in the world. When he senses my confusion, he continues, "The prayer room."

This time *my* eyes widen. Of course. If there's anywhere Laddoo would be, it would be there. Growing up, I saw how Laddoo used to circle around the groups of people seated in prayer. The aunties loved to shower him with attention, feeding him their rice, petting him, and giving him orange laddoos—the South Asian sweet he's named after.

It would make sense that Laddoo was in the prayer room right now, seeing as when he wasn't with Ms. Barnes, he seemed to always be there, enjoying the benefits of being the New Crosshaven Muslim community's honorary Muslim cat.

If Laddoo isn't there, then I'm not sure where else he could be.

I nod. "Okay, let's go find him."

When we get outside, I realize that I wasn't prepared to see the Islamic Center again; it looks like a skeleton of its former self.

The basic structure still stands, but almost everything else has been devoured by the fire, leaving behind a blackened exterior and charred remains. This is where Imam Abdullah leads prayer five times a day, where Said's mom teaches Arabic on Thursdays and Sundays, where we have Eid parties twice a year, and where I come after a rough day in school and need someone to confide in.

I spot the kitchen at the back, completely destroyed. I know that's where the Eid decorations are usually kept, and I wonder if anything is at all salvageable.

"Do you want to wait here? I can go in and look for him?" Said asks.

I finally look away from the building and turn to Said. He looks strangely sympathetic.

I shake my head. "Let's go in together."

Said looks around. "I'm not sure exactly how to go inside. There doesn't seem to be an entrance anymore."

I follow his gaze over to where a large wooden archway used to be, but is now just two metal cylinders that vaguely resemble a door. It's sectioned off with caution tape that reads FIRE LINE: DO NOT CROSS.

"After you," Said says, gesturing ahead. Clearly happy for me to risk my life first.

I glare at him but move forward anyway, ducking under the caution tape and stepping over the rubble, toward the entrance.

I hear Said's footsteps behind me as I stand in the crumbling foyer. I scan the floor by the staircase leading up to the prayer room, frowning at the soot-covered steps and the lack of structure beneath them.

"Laddoo!" I shout. Only silence greets me. "Laddoo!" I repeat louder.

"Let me try," Said says.

I sigh. What makes him think that his voice will suddenly summon the cat?

"Laddoo!" he shouts. There's a beat of silence, before I hear scuffling coming from overhead.

"Traitor," I mumble under my breath, while Said beams like he's won some amazing prize.

"Like I said, bad vibes," he says, before striding forward and balancing his weight on the first step. When it doesn't give out under him, he nods at me and moves on to the next step. I follow behind, while eyeing the staircase suspiciously.

Said leaps up, taking two steps at a time, while I follow behind, treading carefully. When I climb onto the middle steps, I feel the ground wobble beneath me. A crack sounds nearby. I can hear crumbling underneath, like cement breaking apart.

For a moment, I freeze. My heart beats rapidly. The ground shifts again, jolting me to the side, and I let out an involuntary gasp. Before I can move, a pair of strong hands grab ahold of my waist and I'm lifted up. Next thing I know, my feet are planted firmly on the ground again and I am face-to-face with a concerned-looking Said.

"Are you okay?" he asks, his big brown eyes staring at me intently, boring holes into my skin. I notice then that this is the first time in a long time that I've actually *looked* at him. Usually, and rarely these days, when we are in the same room I try to avoid contact altogether. He's changed. I hadn't noticed it before, but now that I do, I see all the subtle changes.

The lines on his face are harsher, his jaw squarer like he's constantly grinding his teeth, his skin a darker bronze—probably due to the fact that he moved from the icy, unpredictable weather of New England to the heat in Virginia. He also smells different. Said used to smell like some concoction of Axe body spray and lemon shampoo, but now he smells of something different. Something *sweeter*.

"Tiwa?" Said calls my name, and I realize that one, I'm still staring at him, and two, his arms are still circling around me.

I quickly move back, slipping out of his arms and avoiding his gaze once again, feeling dense heat pricking my face and neck.

"I'm fine. Let's just focus on getting to the next floor before these steps finally collapse and we die," I say.

He's silent for a moment, still looking at me, and I try not to stare back.

Looking at Said is like looking directly into the sun: It's painful, makes me feel hot and uncomfortable, and I get burned each time.

Finally, I hear him sigh, muttering something about me being *extremely unpleasant* under his breath as he quickly jogs up the rest of the steps and I trail behind him carefully, ignoring his lingering musky scent and the unsteady rhythm of my heartbeat.

We get to the floor where the prayer room is located and I am shocked to see that the hallway looks almost exactly the same. They must have reached the fire before it could spread to this floor, and relief spreads through me. The wall is lined with colorful posters and a giant message board, all unsinged. From the outside, it looked so much worse. I assumed all of the center would be crumbling and ash covered.

This is still salvageable. Maybe this won't mean the end of this year's Eid plans. There is hope.

Something nearby pulls me from my thoughts. The familiar sound of paws scuttering about echoes through an open door of one of the rooms.

"Laddoo?" I call out to more scuttering sounds, followed by a muted *meow*.

I watch as Said dashes into the room the sound came from. "Found him!" Said's voice comes from the distance, before he emerges with the fluffy ginger cat in his arms and a relieved expression on his face. I feel the same relief inside. It isn't until this moment that I realize how tense this whole situation was.

"Where'd you find him?" I ask, moving close and scratching Laddoo's ears softly, glad not to have lost or killed Ms. Barnes's cat so soon.

"He was over by his usual spot in the prayer room, waiting for an auntie to come and feed him sweets no doubt," Said says, a noticeable fondness to his tone.

"Typical, risking it all for candy," I say. Laddoo loving laddoos. It was partially why we'd named him after the sweet in the first place. That and the fact that laddoos are orange. In our eleven-year-old minds, it only seemed to make sense to name the cat that. We'd taken the task of naming the kitten way too seriously, and for some reason, Ms. Barnes kept the name. Maybe that's why she'd given him to us both. Because we named him.

"Wouldn't you risk it all for candy too? I can't say I blame the guy—I think I'd run into a burning building for less," Said says thoughtfully, stroking Laddoo's head.

I raise an eyebrow. "Of course you would. I, for one, have some self-preservation."

"Is that so?" Said asks, glancing at me sideways.

"Yes," I say confidently.

"Remember the time you accidentally set your entire arm on fire? I believe your reasoning was, *I want to know if fire is truly as hot as the scientists say*," Said says, making his voice high-pitched at the end, mocking me.

I feel my face burn. "That's one example, and I was *twelve*," I say.

He gives me a look like he's been challenged to a duel of some kind.

"Oh yeah? Remember the telephone incident—"

"Don't you dare bring that up," I say, eyes wide as I shove my hand over his mouth and feel the vibration on my palm as he chuckles lightly.

"Fine, I won't mention it." His voice comes out muffled.

My hand is still covering his mouth as I look up at him sternly. "Promise?"

Said looks down at me, his eyes boring into my skin once again, making my palms sweat.

"Mhm, I pinkie swear," he says seriously, his voice gruff, vibrating once again against my palm. To make his point, he holds up his pinkie like he always does. I'd forgotten about that weird habit of his. Of him seeing the interlocking of pinkies as a blood oath.

It's then that I realize once again how close we are. How easy it was to slip back into old habits. I drop my hand and I don't bother honoring my end of the promise. Instead, I pretend none of that happened, attempting to fake an interest in the art pieces hung about, while beside me Said clears his throat.

The poster in front of me is a drawing titled *Yunus and the Lonely Whale* and is an illustration of a giant whale washed up on the shore, and a boy nestled inside the whale's stomach holding a candle.

I've seen this drawing before, countless times over the years. And each time it renders me speechless.

Of course, of all the paintings in the room, the one I happen to find myself in front of is Said's. I see his name scribed below in light-blue ink.

"I remember this. I can't believe they still keep this up here after so many years . . ." Said says.

I'm not surprised that it's still up here after so many years. For one, his mom does work here, and two, his art is probably the best art up in the hall. The rest are mostly stick-figure drawings from kids who come here often. Said's looks like something you might find in a gallery of some kind.

Despite not being a fan of Said as a person, I do like his art. It is much nicer than his personality. I imagine, if his art was all over the Islamic Center, it would be enough to distract people from the toasted exterior. Though, they might fall to their death on the stairs.

That thought gives me an idea.

"Do you still draw?" I ask him.

He looks at me, and as seems to be the case today, his gaze singes my skin and as usual I don't feel the burn.

Then he nods hesitantly. "I do sometimes I guess, why?"

This lights up my brain even more, all my ideas and hope swimming in my mind.

"I want to save the Islamic Center, and I think you can help."

7

I'M A KNOBHEAD, AREN'T I

Said

I BLINK AT HER. "SAVE THE ISLAMIC CENTER?"

"Yes," Tiwa says.

"Who are we saving it from?"

"We're not saving it *from* anyone, we're just saving it," Tiwa says, ignoring my bamboozled expression. "Barring the charred walls and the destroyed kitchen, the Islamic Center is still salvageable. I think we could even still use it for Eid this year."

I look around at the crumbling interior and all I can see is Tiwa's delusion. I raise a questioning eyebrow at her, but it's like she's not even registering me.

She continues. "Remember when the Stevensons' flower shop was going under because Mr. Stevenson had an accident and was in the hospital?"

I have no idea who the Stevensons are but I nod anyway.

"Well, at that time this local artist called Palette painted this amazing mural of tulips outside the shop. The entire town rallied behind them and helped raise funds so they could keep afloat until Mr. Stevenson was all better. And with all the tourists who come to New Crosshaven to visit our murals anyway, having Palette's mural up helped business even more. I think we could do the same thing with the Islamic Center, and I think you could help us do that. Think about if you painted something like this now. It would help people see just how important this place is. You could make a mural, and we can try and raise funds toward repairs, and showcase the mural on Eid day. It's going to be perfect."

Tiwa looks so excited, like I've already agreed to this plan and everything is set in stone.

"Is it even safe to use the Islamic Center for Eid?" I ask. "The tape outside and all around the building seems to suggest it's closed for good."

Tiwa frowns but continues, undeterred. "Fine, we'll use Walker this time, and make sure that the Islamic Center is fit for purpose by next Eid."

I look around at the art covering the walls. At the painting that's apparently made her decide she needs my help.

"Why not use that Palette guy? He clearly already has experience saving buildings in this town."

Tiwa narrows her eyes at me. "He's not in town anymore. He's gone off to LA. Besides, I like your art more anyway."

My cheeks warm, but I'm still searching for reasons to say no.

Because all I see in the Islamic Center is a place I barely recognize anymore. The drawings on the wall are signed with names of kids I've never met and the old ablution room has been replaced by a new Arabic classroom. Even the things that are the same are somehow different. The green-and-gold carpet shaped to look like floral-patterned arches are worn and stained, and smell like they've been here for a little too long; the same box of *My First Book of Dua* books they always made us read as kids rests next to a pile of headphones to help people listen to the khutbah.

It feels like this place has changed so much, morphed into something unrecognizable. Or maybe it's me that's changed. I'm the unrecognizable one in this situation, while everything and everyone has moved on without me.

"I don't know . . ." I mumble, even though I know and the answer is *no*. "I drew this so long ago and . . . it doesn't feel right."

What I really mean is I'm not the same person who made that painting. That version of me no longer exists.

The change in Tiwa's expression is immediate. Her eyebrows scrunch together and her face settles into a look of pure annoyance.

"What's that supposed to mean?"

"I mean, I haven't been back in this place in years. Just because they kept my art up on the wall, doesn't mean I have to help save it."

Tiwa scoffs, and I can see the hurt on her face. A part of me feels bad.

"Your mom literally teaches here and you don't care?"

"Of course I care—"

"Well, you have a funny way of showing it," she says. "It seems that the only person you care about is yourself."

I have a feeling we aren't just talking about art here.

I don't even understand why she'd want my help with saving the Islamic Center, if I'm so selfish. Especially when I'm not a part of this community anymore. The only time I come to this mosque now is when Abbu and Ammu force me for Eid every once in a while, and even then it's a struggle having to pretend I remember the various uncles and aunties who comment on just how much I've grown and ask about what boarding school life is like. I'm basically a stranger here.

Tiwa has been throwing accusations like this at me since I got back from school. I'm about to ask her what she means, but she cuts me off.

"Fine, let's just take Laddoo and go," she says. The familiarity that was between us just a few minutes ago is completely gone, and I feel a tinge of regret. But I know I shouldn't. I don't owe Tiwa anything, and I don't owe her community anything either.

"Who should take Laddoo first?" I ask as the orange cat squirms in my arms.

She sighs, resigned. "You can have him for now. I'm not sure we even have space in our apartment. I'll need to warn my mom first. I'll pick him up in a few days or something."

"Okay." I nod.

On the way back down, Tiwa doesn't even look at me once. She walks down the steps precariously and I follow behind. When we get outside again, the summer breeze is grazing my skin and making Tiwa's braids swing behind her.

The regret I was feeling earlier grows with each step, and I want to make things between us better somehow.

"Tiwa, wait—"

She turns back to me sharply and my throat dries up.

"What?" she asks.

I want to ask her why she hates me so much, but I can't bring myself to ask. So instead I just say the first thing that pops into my head. "Tell your mom I said hi."

Tiwa looks confused, like she was expecting something more, and then without another word, she turns away from me once again, leaving me outside the crumbling Islamic Center with our new cat and my thoughts.

I look down at Laddoo once again. "I'm a knobhead, aren't I, Laddoo?"

And Laddoo meows in agreement.

AMMU IS MORE EXCITED ABOUT SEEING LADDOO THAN I WOULD have imagined. When I walk in the front door, holding the ginger cat in my hands, she lets out what can only be described as a squeak of delight.

"It's Laddoo, Ms. Barnes's cat?" I explain, even as Ammu grabs him out of my arms and begins to scratch his tummy.

"Of course I know Laddoo. Is that why you went to the library? To get him?" Ammu asks finally after she's given the cat way more cuddles than I would deem necessary.

I nod slowly, but don't add the part about having to share custody with Tiwa.

"Well, some mail came for you while you were out," Ammu says, pointing at the kitchen counter with a bunch of envelopes, magazines, and packages stacked on it.

I make my way over, sorting through letters addressed to Ammu and Abbu, and even a few packages for Safiyah, before I find a large brown packet with my name printed on it. I recognize the St. Francis school logo stamped on the top of the envelope.

Ammu finally puts Laddoo down on the floor and shuffles to the stove. She stirs a pot of khichuri that's almost done, and adds a sprinkle of red chili to the beef curry. All the while, Laddoo follows behind, watching her every move like Ammu is his new best friend he can't bear to be parted from. I suspect it's because Laddoo knows Ammu is the one most likely to feed him in this house.

"Aw, are you hungry, Laddoo?" Ammu says, almost like she can hear me. She crushes up some rice between her fingers, and leans down to let him lick it off.

I roll my eyes and rip open the packet. I expected the summer homework that the school had already emailed me about, but when I see the contents, my stomach drops.

"Anything exciting?" Ammu asks, somehow managing to tear her eyes away from her new favorite member of the family.

"Just . . . some homework from school," I say with a shrug. Ammu has always been good at picking up on when I'm lying but I've gotten better at it in the past couple of years, especially with being away.

"Make sure you focus and get it all done. Maybe do it early, before Eid preparations start," Ammu suggests.

"I will . . . I'll get started right away, actually." I pass her a smile, tuck the envelope under my arm, and hurry upstairs.

In my bedroom, with the door closed, I sit down and empty the contents of the package onto my desk. There is homework—I didn't lie about that—but there's also the university file that I'd been working on with the school guidance counselor, Mr. Robinson, for the past year.

I flip it open. It still has the familiar notes that Mr. Robinson had written up from our meetings, and the flyers and leaflets of the various arts universities we had talked about. But there is a brand-new leaflet for the New York School of Animation, with updated information for this year's application.

I open up the leaflet and thumb through its contents. There are new images of the school in the middle of New York City, and pictures of some of the famous alumni who have graduated from there. I spot some of my favorite animators from Pixar, Disney, and even Studio Ghibli. I try to ignore the way my heart hammers loudly at the sight of them. I can too easily imagine myself in their places one day.

I turn to the last page of the leaflet, the part where Mr. Robinson has left a note in his neat handwriting: *This summer is probably your best chance to work on your art piece for this! It's very competitive and I want you to really give it your best shot, Said.*

My eyes scan over the application process as listed. Most art schools want a portfolio that you build up over a few months. But the New York School of Animation is different. They only want *one* piece of work. Something that really showcases who you are and what you can do. I'm not sure how exactly I'm supposed to work on a piece like that while hiding that I'm even applying to this school from my parents.

I pick up my phone and text Julian: *Are you busy right now?*

Julian's reply is almost immediate. *Nope, free as a pidgeot liberated from the clutches of a poké ball*

I roll my eyes and instead of texting back, I hit video chat. Julian answers on the first ring.

"Said! Long time no see!" Julian exclaims. He's lying back on his bed, his mass of curls half tied up, half hanging down on his shoulders.

"I literally saw you last week," I say. "And are you still in bed? It's five p.m."

"It's the summer, dude. Five p.m. is basically dawn in the summer."

Somehow, I don't think Ammu would agree with Julian's logic.

"I just got mail from school," I say.

71

"Gross. I never open mail from school." Julian scrunches up his nose. "I get my little brother to open it and give me the highlights reel."

"If I asked Safiyah to open my mail, she'd probably use it to extort me or something."

"I can definitely see that; she's threatened me on multiple occasions when she visited St. Francis," Julian adds. "What did the school send you anyway?"

"Some homework, but also my university file," I say. "Mr. Robinson wants me to work on my art piece this summer."

Julian's expression sobers at the mention of university. "Have you told your parents yet?"

"No." I sigh, picking up the miniature rickshaw figurine on my desk. I want to tell Julian I've tried, but I know I've gotten nowhere close to even trying. "And I'm not sure how I'm going to work on my application without them knowing. I don't even know *what* I'm going to work on."

Mr. Robinson and I had discussed a few different possibilities back in our meetings. I'd suggested something to do with soccer and Mr. Robinson had looked at me as if I had kicked a soccer ball into his face. He suggested something to do with St. Francis but that had made absolutely no sense to me. St. Francis was school, no matter which way you spun it. And the idea that it defined me in some way made me more uncomfortable than anything else.

"I'm sure your parents will be more chill about it than you think," Julian says. "I told your mom last year that I was thinking about becoming a beekeeper after graduation. She was totally on board with it."

I lean back in my chair until it almost tips over, fiddling with the wheels on the rickshaw. "They probably thought beekeeping is a branch of veterinary sciences. There's no way of making art seem like a viable career option to them."

"You have to tell them at some point. You don't want to be a balding middle-aged man, trapped in an office still trying to live up to your parents' expectations and regretting all your life choices, like my dad."

"I know. I *will* tell them," I say. The difficult part is figuring out the how. "Anyway, it won't matter if I don't come up with an idea for my application. Mr. Robinson and I have been going back and forth about it all year, and I still have nothing."

"I can help!" Julian says. He finally sits up, and the screen wobbles as he moves his phone around to a new position. "What do you need to do?"

"I have to submit one art piece with the application. And it has to be personal to who I am. But it also has to stand out and show them all the things I'm capable of," I say. Just saying it out loud makes it feel like an impossible task.

"What about the school art prize you won that time?"

I remember that art prize and the piece I illustrated for it. It was an interpretation of the Mad Hatter's tea party, but with my family members as guests instead of madcap woodland creatures. I was so proud of it back then. So were my parents. They even sent a photo of it to everyone they know—which is a lot of people across multiple continents. I still get messages about it to this day.

I shake my head. "It needs to be bigger, I think, and more recent. My art style has changed a lot since then."

"What about New Crosshaven?" Julian asks.

"What about it?"

"Dude, you never shut up about that place. *New Crosshaven has the best pastry shop in the world*—"

"—because it does," I mutter under my breath.

"—*New Crosshaven is* so *artistic that there are no other towns that can compare.*" Julian goes back to his normal voice as he finishes mimicking me, and raises an eyebrow. "You love that place, and you're there now. Perfect time to do something about the town."

"I don't sound like that," I grumble, but Julian isn't wrong. I may not have been back here in years, but New Crosshaven is kind of what inspired me to become an artist in the first place. Growing up, the murals that often popped up around this town made me see everything in a different light. It made me realize just how powerful art could be.

"I could do something about the town, I guess. But I'll still need to figure out—" I cut myself off, suddenly remembering the conversation I had with Tiwa earlier that day. The one that ended as horribly as any conversation could end.

"You need to figure out . . . ?" Julian prompted.

I shake my head, because I'm still trying to make sense of it all. Tiwa wanted me to paint a mural to help rebuild the Islamic Center. But a mural could also be my application for art school. It would definitely stand out, and it would show the school exactly who I am.

"Julian," I say. "You are a genius."

SAID AND TIWA'S
LAST EID TOGETHER
Three Years Ago

WHERE WERE WE? AH YES, THE LAST EID. WHERE IT ALL WENT wrong.

A LOT CAN CHANGE IN FIVE YEARS. A NEWCOMER BECOMES A seasoned local. A resident becomes an occasional guest. And both go from best friends to total strangers.

No longer the naive adolescents they once were, making blood oaths in tree bark and swapping secrets over juice boxes, Said and Tiwa now find themselves under the influence of timeworn resentment and pubescent hormones.

"Said! Go and help your auntie bring the cake in from the car," Said's mother yells from the second floor of the Islamic Center.

Said looks up at the ceiling, trying not to drop the heavy box of Eid gifts in his hands that his mother made him carry over from the Walker Center next door.

"Next she'll want me to paint the walls magenta," he mutters under his breath as he lugs the box over to the empty table in the middle of the ground-floor lounge.

"You heard her, Said, go and get the cake—I'm hungry," Safiyah says from where she's sprawled out on the couch, eating Malia Auntie's shomuchas.

"Why can't you go get it? It's not like you're busy. Besides, you're older than me. Shouldn't the eldest do the most labor?"

"That's where you're wrong, Said. I'm very busy food testing so that all the Eid guests don't get sick. It's a difficult job but someone must do it," Safiyah says through a mouthful of shomuchas.

Said rolls his eyes, but nevertheless turns around to do his mother's bidding. He walks past the front doors, noting how more and more people are filing in for the Eid party. Soon, the lounge area will fill up with guests eating, drinking, and laughing in their finest Eid clothes, while the aunties cook in the adjoining kitchen.

Said spots Nazifa Auntie struggling with the cake by the trunk of her car. He quickly rushes over, grabbing the cake from her hands.

"Oh, thank you," says Nazifa Auntie. And while Said tries to balance the heavy cake all on his own, she gives him a once-over.

"Have you gotten taller?" Nazifa Auntie asks.

"A little," Said replies, even though it's a lie. His school uniform barely fits him anymore, and since coming home for Eid during spring break, he's hit his head on his doorframe more times than he can count.

"I'm just going to put this inside," Said says, turning around and retracing his steps toward the lounge. The journey back is more tumultuous, not just because of the wobbling cake, but also because of the emerging crowds making their way up the stairs to the main hall.

Somehow, Said manages to get the cake all the way into the

lounge. Once he sets it down on the table, he takes a step back and lets out a breath of relief.

The cake in front of him is grander than he had originally thought. It's shaped exactly like a mosque, with a dramatic dome, lots of peaks, and two minarets made from icing sprouting from the base of the cake.

"Isn't this cake kind of blasphemous?" Said asks to no one in particular.

"I like it," Safiyah answers, stepping close and inspecting the cake with a keen eye. "It's cute. I like the way it slants just a little. It gives it a homemade feel."

Said tilts his head, noticing the cake's slant too.

"It's like the Leaning Tower of Pisa—*The Leaning Mosque of New Crosshaven*," he jokes.

"Okay, now that's blasphemous," Safiyah says, hitting the back of his head lightly. "If you don't want it to resemble the ruins of Pompeii, I'd suggest moving it to a place where some doofus won't knock it over."

"I'll move it to the pantry, then," Said mumbles, rubbing the back of his head now.

"Put it in the fridge in the pantry. That way the icing won't melt. But make sure to take it out in an hour so that the guests aren't eating frozen cake."

"Okay, boss," Said says dryly.

"Good, and do it before Tiwa comes, please. She's recently gotten really into baking sweet treats ever since that librarian you're friends with started giving her lessons. But unfortunately, they're more like poison treats. I told her that she could bring her cake here, but I'm going to have to take one for the team and eat it all so that we don't end up with food poisoning as party favors," Safiyah says.

Said goes still at the mention of Tiwa—his former best friend who he often tries and fails to forget.

"You're so brave," Said says sarcastically, trying to bury the nervous waver of his voice. Since getting back days ago, he's been lucky to have avoided seeing her. Tiwa has been on vacation with her family, *or so he had heard*. Not that he was keeping tabs on her or anything.

"I'll go and do that now, then," Said says, wanting to get away before Tiwa arrives in general. "After that I'm going to pop over to the library to see Ms. Barnes for a few minutes."

It wasn't like he could hide from Tiwa forever, but at least for now he could.

"TIMITOPE, WHAT DID I SAY ABOUT LITTERING? I'M SO SORRY," Tiwa's mother says, looking and sounding embarrassed as she pulls the now eight-year-old Timi forward. She picks up the trail of candy wrappers on the floor and stuffs them into her handbag.

"It's honestly no problem, Mrs. Olatunji," Safiyah says, smiling down at the young boy. "I can get him something to put the rubbish into as he eats?"

"Don't encourage him, dear, he's already had too much candy today," Mrs. Olatunji says, which makes Timi's face screw up in disagreement. "Where's your mother, by the way, Safiyah? I brought over some extra rice and stew for the tables."

"You're too kind, Auntie. My mom is upstairs on the second floor in the hall. She's wearing a golden sharee, you can't miss—" Safiyah is interrupted by a loud yelp from the entrance of the lounge.

Standing there in the doorway is Tiwa, who is carrying a large stack of brightly colored cupcakes, and her dad, who is carrying what seems to be a tin of banana bread.

"I dropped one of my cupcakes on the floor," Tiwa says in a sad voice.

"Oh no . . ." Safiyah says, trying to sound sympathetic.

"You still have twenty-nine cupcakes left," Tiwa's dad says, looking a little relieved that there is one less cupcake to eat.

"I made thirty for the thirty days of Ramadan this year, though. Now it's meaningless."

Tiwa's dad awkwardly smiles at Safiyah and then turns to Tiwa and pats her head. "There, there."

"You're not helping, Dad," Tiwa says. "But it's fine, people will still enjoy the rest."

"Can I have a cupcake?" Timi asks, reaching out for one.

"NO!" Tiwa's mom's eyes widen as she smacks his hand away. "I mean . . . Timi has eaten so many snacks already. He needs to have some proper food upstairs first."

Tiwa nods slowly. "Okay then . . . more for everyone else down here. Dad, do you want one?"

Mr. Olatunji gives his wife a panicked look, and Safiyah quickly steps in and takes the cupcakes from Tiwa. "I'll take them to the table over there. Why don't you clean up the smushed cupcake and we can go and get some food too—I heard Nazifa Auntie hired an ice-cream truck this year. It seems she's really going all out for her Eid party."

Tiwa's eyes light up with excitement. "I'll clean up right away. Where are the cleaning supplies again?"

Safiyah glances at the closed door of the closet with the cleaning supplies. "I believe . . . they're in the pantry over there." She points to the opposite direction of the closet.

"They keep the cleaning supplies in the pantry? That's so weird," Tiwa says, but she doesn't find it too weird, because she continues with a shrug, "Okay, I'll be right back!"

Safiyah keeps her eyes trained on Tiwa as she makes her way toward the pantry. But as soon as Tiwa is out of sight, Safiyah looks around the lounge, as if she's on a mission. Finally, she spots Said outside in the line for the ice-cream truck. She doesn't waste a moment before sprinting up to him.

"Said!" she calls as soon as he's within earshot. He whips his head around, eyes wide as Safiyah bounds toward him.

"What? Is everything okay?" Said asks.

"The cake! Did you get it out of the fridge in the pantry? You have to do it now!" she says breathlessly.

"Has it been an hour al—"

"The cake will be too frozen if you don't take it out right now, and you'll ruin Eid for everyone," Safiyah says, frantic.

"I knew you liked cake, but not this much," Said mumbles as he steps out of the line, away from Safiyah, and toward the pantry.

"I'll get you an ice cream," Safiyah calls back to Said.

"I want sprinkles too!" Said yells as he turns the corner.

He strides over to the pantry door, pushing it open with a sigh. The last thing he expects is for a voice to shout, "Hey!" as he enters.

"Oh, sor—" The apology dies on his lips when he sees who it is. Tiwa stands in the middle of the pantry, looking at Said with the same surprise he's feeling. The last time Said saw Tiwa was months ago when he was home for Christmas break. It's been longer since they've spoken. At this point he can't remember which one of the many things they stopped speaking over. Seeing her now, his instinct is to pull her in for a hug like they always used to when he was home, but they don't do that anymore.

"What are you doing here?" she asks him, folding her arms.

He looks over at the fridge and the cake now out on the table next to it.

Said's eyebrows furrow. "I was told to come in here and get the cake from the fridge . . ."

"Oh, well, I saw it in there and took it out. Cake isn't meant to be in the fridge, makes it taste funny," Tiwa replies, and Said remembers what Safiyah had just said about Tiwa being some kind of baking connoisseur now. Not that he made it a habit to remember all the small details he could about Tiwa's life given they were no longer on speaking terms.

"Wait, what are *you* doing in here?" he asks.

She gives him the same look she gave him during the Christmas break. Like he was the last person on earth she'd rather be speaking to.

He hoped his face told her the same, even though that would be a lie. His traitorous brain always wanted to see and speak to her.

"I'm looking for cleaning supplies," she says in a flat tone.

He raises an eyebrow. "In the pantry? Wouldn't they be in the supply closet or somethi—"

"What's it to you?" she asks, suddenly defensive.

"I was just trying to help," he says.

"Well, I don't need your help. Never have, never will."

Her words sting but he doesn't let it show. "Leave then, or at the very least move out of the way, so I can get the cake and not ruin anyone else's day."

"I'll leave when I find what I'm looking for," she says, stepping back farther into the room.

Said steps closer. "I guarantee you, it's not in here. So stop wasting your time, and go."

Tiwa steps back once more, her voice rising. "I told you, I don't need your help! You're the one who should leave. I know you're good at that."

Said narrows his eyes at her. "You're unbeliev—" He begins stepping closer, but he's interrupted again by her sharp tongue.

"And you're an assho—" Tiwa starts but doesn't get to finish because her final step back results in her falling right onto the table behind her and into the Eid cake.

Said lunges forward, trying to break her fall, but only ends up falling into the cake with her.

Suddenly, the door of the pantry flies open and an alarmed-looking Safiyah bursts inside, accompanied by the prying gazes of some of the Eid party guests behind her.

"What happened? I heard a crash!" Safiyah says, eyes wide in alarm, as if she hadn't been listening through the door the whole time.

Like two surprised deer caught in headlights—*the headlights in question here being the confused glares of the aunties and uncles*—Tiwa and Said lay frozen on top of the former *Leaning Mosque of New Crosshaven*, covered in frosting and shame.

This Eid, often referred to by the Muslim community as *cake gate*, would not soon be forgotten. Of all the chaos of that fateful Eid, three events cemented it as being one for the books:

The ice-cream truck; the case of the disappearing shomuchas (to this day no one has quite figured out where they all went); and last but certainly not least, Said and Tiwa's infamous fall into the Eid cake.

The pair may have started in tree bark, but they ended in frosting.

8

COOKIES AND CRIME

Tiwa

THE CREDITS ROLL AT THE END OF THE MOVIE, AND I HEAR THE sound of sniffling down the line.

"Are you . . . crying?" I ask, sitting up on the couch.

"No . . ."

"I can hear you, Dad," I say, fighting the urge to laugh.

"Okay, fine, I was crying, but that's because it's an emotional story about the plights of friendship and the importance of family," my dad says, and I almost can't believe that this is the same heartless man who thought that Bing Bong dying in *Inside Out* was hilarious.

"*Bride Wars* isn't an emotional story, Dad. If anything it's a horror movie about the plights of codependency."

"You might be right, Tee dear. I'm probably emotional because it hit too close to home. Do you know how stressful planning a wedding is? And I'm not even doing the planning."

"Sounds horrific," I say with as much care in my voice as I can muster. I stand, knees clicking as I hold the phone close and wander into the kitchen.

"Honestly, you haven't even heard the half of it—"

"What time is it over there, by the way? Is it already midnight?" I ask quickly before he can go off on a whole tirade about *the wedding*.

Hearing about your dad getting married to someone who isn't your mom is always going to be weird. It's not that I'm not happy for him or anything, just that I like to pretend most days that things aren't as different as they are, and the wedding is one of the many things that bursts that bubble.

"England is only five hours ahead, Tee, I'm not in Australia," Dad says in a low chuckle.

"Might as well be," I mutter, grabbing a lemonade from the fridge while balancing the phone between my shoulder and my head. "You know, Safiyah told me that English people eat *baked beans* and *Yorkshire puddings* with every meal. I can't tell if she's misinformed or not, but I also wouldn't be surprised if it were true. Some of the foods you describe just sound dreadful."

I try not to make a face as I remember the dish Dad had sent me a picture of, which consisted of congealed cow blood, mushy tomatoes, and burned mushrooms. He assured me that the food over there tasted better than it looked. I'm still not convinced.

"I'm not surprised. Safiyah emails me strange pictures that she calls *British memes*, whatever that means. Maybe if you visited some time, you could see for yourself instead of getting all your information from Safiyah," Dad says. I can hear the caution in his tone. How hard he's trying not to overstep and go into dangerous territory for us, aka, bursting the bubble. ". . . But anyway, how have you been? Anything new going on in the land of Tee?" he continues, changing the subject before I can.

As a family it seems we've all gotten too skilled at dodging the Olympic-sized elephant in the room.

"Um, I'm fine, mostly," I say, which isn't a complete lie. I'm doing okay, a lot better than I was last year or the year before that, anyway.

"Your mom told me about the fire in the Islamic Center. I'm sorry, I know that place means a lot to you," he says, with a note of sorrow in his voice, and I feel something sink inside. The Islamic Center used to mean a lot to him too, I hope it still does.

I was hoping he wouldn't find out about the fire just yet. At least not until I came up with a solid plan—which I technically had until *Said the Selfish* ruined it.

"The fire wasn't that bad; I'm sure they'll be able to rebuild the damaged parts of the building in no time, and we might even be able to still celebrate Eid there," I say, my voice wavering as I embellish the truth a little.

Okay, maybe not a little. A lot. But it's for the good of the family.

"Are you sure? Your mom said it looked pretty bad. She isn't sure if our family can still host Eid or if it could still work there—"

"We can—we will," I immediately interject. "I mean, if we can't host Eid in the Islamic Center, we could still hire the Walker Center," I add desperately. "Or we can use the apartment or, I don't know, someplace else. But it's all fine, I promise. Everything will be great! I've already come up with a plan to help raise spirits and ensure that this year's Eid is as good as it always is," I say, lying through my teeth once again.

I hear Dad sigh over the phone. "Listen, Tiwa . . ." he begins, his voice low and heavy, and I feel hope plummet to the depths of my stomach. I've never liked hearing Dad call me by my full name. He usually calls me Tee—I'm only ever Tiwa when he has something serious to say.

I remember the ghosts of *Tiwa* past, moments where Dad would say my name and the worst news would follow.

Tiwa, your grades are slipping again . . . or *Tiwa, your mom and I still love each other very much, but change is inevitable . . .* or *Tiwa, I'm so sorry, he didn't make it—*

My name is the bringer of bad news, it's always seemed, or maybe it's just me. I'm the bad news. After all, the first year that our family gets to host the town's Eid, the Islamic Center just happens to burn down. My bad luck is catching.

I hear him breathing out over the line and my muscles grow tense as I wait for the bombshell to drop. Is someone else dead? Is he moving to Australia this time instead of London?

"I guess I'll see you soon?" he finally says, his voice no longer heavy.

I feel like I can relax again. "Oh . . . Yeah, I'll see you then," I say, recovering from the sudden emotional whiplash. I quickly hang up before he can ask any more questions about the logistics of my so-called *Saving Eid* plan or decides he does indeed have bad news to share with me.

I fall back onto the sofa, exhausted. Lying for the greater good of the Olatunji family is a lot more taxing than it seems. Well, it isn't technically lying if I do somehow come up with a way to save face and in turn save Eid.

All I have to do is make sure there really is an alternative place for us to host Eid this year. Walker hasn't got all the facilities that the Islamic Center does, but it could easily work just the same.

I just need permission to use it first.

Which means paying a visit to the town hall.

My phone buzzes in my hand and I feel my heart stop again and then settle when I see that it's not my dad with bad news. Instead it's Safiyah, which isn't necessarily any less anxiety inducing given my best friend's unpredictable nature.

S: We still on for Cookies & Crime
tomorrow?

I'd forgotten about that. The week has mostly been a blur, with school finishing up for the summer, the funeral, the fire at the Islamic Center, inheriting Laddoo, and Eid potentially being canceled.

T: Yes, but I might need your help
with something first . . .
S: ???

Safiyah doesn't wait for me to respond before following up with:

S: . . . Who are we burying?

I roll my eyes.
Just meet me outside the town hall tomorrow at noon, I type, and then I quickly add: And bring some lemon squares from Abigail's with you.

THE NEXT DAY I MEET SAFIYAH OUTSIDE THE TOWN HALL AS SHE'S nursing a box of Abigail's lemon squares in her hands and looking up at the large building with disgust.

"No matter how many times I see the town hall, I'm never quite ready for how bright and hideous it is," Safiyah says as I approach her.

I look up at the colorful structure before us. Every inch is filled with some kind of mural-inspired design, greens, purples, and browns meshing and clashing together.

"Me too, it's actually quite nauseating," I say, feeling my head swim a little as I look up at it.

"It looks like one of those My Little Ponies threw up all over the bricks or something. I know we're meant to be the *town of murals* or whatever, but this is just plain wrong."

I laugh, pulling my eyes away from the sight, glancing back down at the box of lemon squares. "Thanks for getting those, by the way," I say.

"What exactly are they for? I thought we were just going to the mayor's office."

I nod. "Exactly, and I need tools of persuasion. Eid is just around the corner, I need the Walker Center, and lemon squares are how I get that."

Safiyah still looks confused. "Does Mayor Williams like lemon squares or something?"

I shake my head. "No, they're for Williams's secretary, Donna. They're her favorite."

Safiyah's eyebrows raise. "How in the world do you know that?"

I look back up at the nausea-inducing building and I shrug. "Let's just say this isn't my first rodeo. Anyway, let's go inside. Donna leaves for lunch in approximately sixteen minutes."

The inside of the building is less aggressively colorful than the exterior, though there are still murals and paintings everywhere. There's a giant wall filled with a timeline of New Crosshaven murals over the last few decades, from the first mural of a flying horse drawn by an anonymous artist in the fifties to murals as recent as last year.

The whole wall is basically a mural of murals. Maybe if Said had agreed to my mural idea for saving the Islamic Center instead of being so self-important, ours could've been up here someday too. Immortalized on this mural wall.

I blink up at the wall. *Maybe it still can.* I don't need Said to make a mural.

In a town of murals there should be no shortage of artists.

Another thing to add to my agenda for today.

The mayor's office is on the sixth floor at the top of the building, and as we go up in the old creaky elevator, I swear I hear the shaft get stuck a few times. Nevertheless, we make it out in one piece and head through the double doors of the mayor's office waiting room, where Donna is seated behind the desk typing (as expected) and already nibbling on a sandwich.

"Hi, Donna!" I say with as much enthusiasm as I can muster. Donna's head shoots up, and her sandwich falls out of her hand.

"Oh, it's you again," Donna says coldly. "Listen, Tiwa. I am very sympathetic to your *situation*, but as I told you when you dropped by last week and the week before that, it takes the mayor's office several months to process local legislation changes. When there's an update, I'll email. Until then, stop visiting."

My false smile falters a little. "It's not about that today," I say awkwardly.

Donna's furrowed eyebrows ease up. "Thank god. What is it, then?" she asks, her eyes searching for the time on the clock. Twelve minutes left until her lunch break. I need to make this quick.

"I need an urgent appointment with the mayor," I say.

Donna nods before licking her finger and pulling up an appointment form. "When for? We have appointment slots for Tuesday, Wednesday, and Thursday next week."

I clear my throat, stumbling over my words now. "I, um, I need a slightly *more* urgent appointment than, um, those."

Donna sighs, typing something on the keyboard and squinting at the screen. "Well, I might be able to squeeze you in on Monday . . ."

"Could you maybe squeeze me in for today instead—preferably this afternoon?" I ask, to which Donna lowers her cat eyeglasses at me, glaring at me once again.

I nudge Safiyah and she finally thrusts the lemon squares forward, placing them on the raised part of Donna's desk.

Donna eyes the lemon squares and then looks back at me, her eyes narrowed.

I feel my heart beating fast in my chest as she slowly raises the telephone up to her ear and then says, "I'll see what I can do."

As expected, lemon squares are enough to bribe even the coldest of people. They could probably create world peace if Abigail's could make enough of them.

An hour after handing Donna the bribe in dessert form, Safiyah and I are sitting outside the mayor's office waiting to be called in for our urgent appointment while the smell of lemons wafts in the air.

"I should've eaten a few of those squares—I was tempted to before, but now I'm having regrets," Safiyah whispers, holding her stomach while watching Donna in the corner of the room eating the snacks blissfully.

"We're going to have cookies at your place, remember? This meeting won't take long," I say, even though I've never done something like this before and can't know for sure how long it'll actually take. I just hope it doesn't take as long as my other town hall request has taken, otherwise there won't even be an Eid to celebrate.

"If you say so," Safiyah mutters, sinking into her chair just as a voice sounds from above.

"Tiwa, Tiwa Ola . . . tunji?" The deep timber of Mayor Williams's voice rings out as he steps from behind his office door.

I stand quickly. "Hi, Mayor Williams, that's me," I say.

He nods with a smile and his eyes crinkle only slightly in the corners, the rest of his skin frozen and waxy like gallons of Botox have been pumped into it.

"Come on in!" he says, and I look back at Safiyah.

"I'll be quick, promise," I say hurriedly and Saf gives me a thumbs-up, whispering *loudly*, "Good luck!"

I follow Mayor Williams into his office, the door closing behind me with a click.

"Take a seat," he says, gesturing to the one in front of his desk.

I move to sit down as he takes the chair opposite me on the other side of the wooden table. He swivels to the side and clicks the computer's mouse, and I can see the blank page he pulls up reflected in his glasses.

"So, Tiwa Olatunji. How can I help you?" he asks, his lips tugging upward. His smile seems a little menacing, and I think it's because it looks like the corners of his mouth are being held up with imaginary strings.

I clear my throat, trying to focus on the reason I came here: the Islamic Center and Eid.

"So as you, um, probably know already, the Islamic Center burned down earlier this week and so my community's Eid celebrations will need to take place somewhere else. As you can imagine, spirits are low right now and so I had two requests."

"Yes, I was so sad to hear about the unfortunate incident. We're working very hard to find out what caused the fire," he says.

"Oh, thank you, Mayor Williams," I say.

"No problem, Miss Olatunji. What were your requests?"

I sit up and begin trying to order my thoughts. "Well, firstly I was wondering if we could use the Walker Center for Eid? I will make sure to have everyone in and out on time and I'll arrange the cleaners and—"

"Of course, I am more than happy for you to use the Walker Center, especially given the fire. You'll just need to fill out one of the hire forms, and I'll have Donna process it ASAP," Mayor Williams says, interrupting me.

"Thank you," I say, feeling a weight lift from my chest and shoulders. That was easier than expected.

"And please do let me know if I can help in any other way to make things easier going forward," he continues, still wearing that scary, plasticky smile.

"The other thing I wanted to ask is about potentially creating a mural in honor of the Islamic Center. I thought it could be a really nice gesture to the community and raise morale, while also bringing in even more tourists, seeing as this time of year is when people visit for the mural festival," I say. "I don't currently have an artist in mind, but I saw the mural wall downstairs and I thought it could be really cool to use a local artist."

Mayor Williams crosses his hands over each other and leans forward with a sigh.

"That sounds like a wonderful idea, Miss Olatunji—you know I always love a mural. I just had one commissioned for the local park. But I'm afraid that having one on the site won't be possible."

I raise an eyebrow. "I thought the damage wasn't that bad—there's space on the sides of the building. If it's the artist thing, I can look for someone, you won't have to do anyth—"

He interrupts again. "That's not the problem, Tiwa. I'm afraid we can't have the mural on the Islamic Center site because it will get in the way of our building plans."

"Building plans?" I repeat.

He nods. "Yes, we have just signed off on the building of apartments in that area. It's part of my move to ensure there is adequate housing for everyone in New Crosshaven."

I'm still trying to process what he's saying. He can't be talking about knocking down the Islamic Center, can he?

"What do you mean, building apartments?"

There's a grave expression on his face—then again maybe it's just his face.

"We've discussed it at length and we believe that one community center should satisfy the citizens of this town. Unfortunately, that does mean what's left of the Islamic Center will have to be demolished."

I feel sick.

"What about the Muslim citizens of New Crosshaven? Don't we get a say in what happens to our center? If you care so much for the citizens of New Crosshaven, why not rebuild the center?"

"I'm sorry, Tiwa. I can see that the Islamic Center meant a lot to you, but there just aren't enough Muslims in this town to justify keeping the center when we could bring in more residents. You must see how this makes sense, right?" he asks.

I don't respond at first. I can't bring myself to speak. Nothing about this makes any sense.

How is demolishing the Islamic Center something that is meant to make sense?

I almost ask him this very question, wanting to shout in his face and demand that he care about the community he's taking from me, but I remember that Eid is so soon, and I still need a place to host it. Making him rescind his offer to let us have the Walker Center benefits no one.

I nod numbly, and he claps his hands together.

"Right, let's get you the paperwork, then."

"I've always hated that man. He literally looks like a creepy mannequin," Safiyah says, biting angrily into a peanut butter cookie.

We're back at her place, seated on the couch eating cookies and watching a disturbing crime show about a serial killer who likes to eat his victims' feet. I can't even concentrate on the cookies or the feet, I just keep thinking about the fact that in a few weeks the Islamic Center won't even exist anymore.

"I mean, who even elected him as mayor—I should be mayor," Safiyah continues, her voice muffled as she shoves a chocolate chip cookie into her mouth now.

"What a scary world that would be," Said mutters as he comes through from the kitchen.

"Rude!" Safiyah says, pointing a cookie at him accusatorily. "I'd make a great mayor. Heck, I could run this country. When I'm in charge, I'll get rid of low-rise jeans," she says decisively.

"Why low-rise jeans?" Said asks, his voice coming closer.

I feel tense, choosing to ignore his presence and continue focusing on drowning in my misery.

"Because they're disgusting. I don't need to see all of *that*," Safiyah says.

I hear Said's low annoying laugh now directly behind, and I realize I can't distract myself anymore.

If it wasn't for Said, I could have proposed the mural to Mayor Williams properly. Maybe then he would have seen it as something that could make the Islamic Center worth saving.

Or maybe he would have still demolished it.

Maybe nothing I did could have saved it.

"Hey!" I hear a smack and I turn as Safiyah hits Said's hand away from the jar of cookies between us.

"Ow! What the hell, Safiyah," Said says, rubbing his hand.

"That's what happens when you try and take my snacks from me. Go and get your own."

Said glares down at her. "But you took all the cookies. How am I supposed to get something that doesn't exist?"

Safiyah shrugs, taking a bite of another chocolate chip cookie. "I don't know. Use your single brain cell and figure it out or something. I'm trying to relax, drink my apple juice, and have a *private* conversation with Tiwa, so go," Safiyah says, shooing him away.

I notice Said's face twitch at the mention of apple juice. He glances at me, and I look at him and I have to stop myself from reacting. Once upon a time, *apple juice* had a different meaning to us. Our code word meant that we'd go somewhere to speak in private. His eyes linger on me and I force myself to look away.

There's a pause and then I feel movement as Said reaches between us and grabs a handful of cookies before Safiyah can stop him. Said moves away quickly, dropping into the armchair in the corner, beside a sleeping Laddoo, and away from Safiyah's death stare.

He leans back into the chair and turns to face the TV, ignoring his sister's gaze burning holes into him.

"Said—" Safiyah starts.

"Shh, I'm trying to watch the feet killer," Said says.

Saf throws a cushion at his face, but Said ducks and it misses, almost hitting an expensive-looking vase.

"Anyway, where were we?" Safiyah says, turning back to me. "I'm sure we can figure out some other way to honor the Islamic Center, like releasing doves into the air or hiring one of those blimps—"

Safiyah is cut off by Said clearing his throat loudly.

"*Or* maybe we could create a petition, and you can go around door to door and get our neighbors involv—" she continues, only to be cut off once again by Said clearing his throat even louder than before.

We both turn to find him looking at us, or rather at me. I feel a strange flutter in my chest as we lock eyes once again.

"What?" Saf asks, visibly irritated.

Said blinks at me, and then finally looks away, staring at his sister this time.

"I don't mind helping with that mural thing, by the way," he says so low that I almost think I've misheard him.

"What?" I let slip.

"I can help with the mural for the Islamic Center. You need an artist for it, right?" he asks.

"I thought you weren't interested in painting a mural for the community?" I say, still confused.

Said shrugs. "Well, now I am. I figured I'm home for the summer and I have a lot of free time, so why not? And . . ." He pauses and glances at me, and my chest is still doing that annoying fluttering thing. "I was thinking about it, and my memories here weren't all bad, actually."

I do nothing, say nothing. I just wait for him to finally utter the words *April Fools'* even though April was months ago and Said doesn't look like he's trying to prank me.

For some reason, he actually wants to paint the mural . . . and for some reason, I'm considering his offer. Ms. Barnes would probably be delighted at the idea of us working together. Between Laddoo and this, it seems that somehow, her plan to bring us together is working even from the afterlife.

I feel a tug in my chest at the thought of her.

A mural might not change the mind of Mayor Williams, but it might help everyone else in town see how important the Islamic

Center still is. That, along with the petition idea Safiyah suggested, could be enough to stop the demolition plans. I just (a) need to figure out how to actually create a petition, and (b) I need to find a way to be near Said again without wanting to hit him squarely in his douche face.

I'm not sure that I can even trust Said, but it's not like I know any other artists or can pay an artist for that matter. At this point I'll have to accept all the free help I can get.

I sigh. "When can you get started?"

9

PALS BEFORE GALS

Tiwa

PETITIONING IS A LOT HARDER THAN IT LOOKS.

A day after the *Save the Islamic Center* plan was hatched, I'm armed with petition forms printed out from the New Crosshaven local governing website and a renewed sense of hope.

In theory it all seems pretty straightforward.

1. Print out a standard form that people around town can sign.
2. Once said form reaches more than one hundred signatures, submit it to the town hall.
3. The powers at the town hall (namely Mayor Williams) review it and then that's that. We have our Islamic Center back.

Only, in reality, petitioning requires more than just printing off forms and getting signatures. It involves actually knocking on more than one hundred doors and speaking to neighbors I've only ever seen in passing or smiled at awkwardly in the bread aisle at the supermarket.

And as someone who isn't all that fond of other human beings or wide-scale social interaction, this feels like my worst nightmare. This whole ordeal might have been less anxiety inducing if it wasn't for the fact that Safiyah was abandoning me last minute.

"I'm not abandoning you," Safiyah says while trying to use a straightener to curl her hair in the small standing mirror in the corner of my bedroom. She arrived sometime this morning so that she could scour through my wardrobe for clothes.

"What do you call this, then? I think the dictionary definition of *abandonment* definitely covers leaving your friend of many years to face the town—alone I might add—while you go on a date with your crush. What happened to pals before gals?" I say, sitting on the floor by my bed with two clipboards in my lap, and a ball of yarn and a crochet hook in my hands as I watch the traitor get ready.

I'm *mostly* joking. I'm happy for Safiyah, really. The part of me that isn't joking is the part scared shitless about the prospect of facing up to all my neighbors alone.

"Firstly, I can't believe you actually said *pals before gals*, and secondly, it's not a date," Safiyah says, applying ChapStick to her lips now. "I'm helping Ishra with her college applications."

"I thought you guys were the same age?" I ask as I attempt to crochet a line.

"We are. She just took a gap year to look after her grandma and save for college, and now she needs help with applications," Safiyah says. "But don't worry, you won't be alone. I have arranged backup for you."

"Who?" I mutter.

Safiyah hesitates before answering and I know immediately who it is.

"Said—but before you protest, you should know that I told him to be on his best behavior."

It's bad enough that I have to spend time with him because of the mural, and now this? I wonder what Safiyah offered him in exchange.

"Whatever, I guess beggars can't be choosers," I say.

"That's the spirit, Tee," Safiyah says, before standing up and turning to face me. "What do you think? Do I look like I'm trying too hard? I want to seem like I stumbled out of bed like this, and happen to look flawless but with zero effort."

I take in Safiyah's bouncy curls, the unhinged expression on her face, and the overly steamed summer dress she swiped from my closet, and I nod thoughtfully.

"You've succeeded, totally effortless," I say.

She breathes out, relieved. "Thank goodness. I'm going to head off; good luck with the petition and try not to maim my brother. My mom will miss him dearly if you kill him."

I roll my eyes at her. "Okay, I'll try. For Auntie."

"Thank you," she says, and then adds, "I told Said to meet you by Walker at noon by the way."

"Sounds great," I say dryly.

Between being stuck with Said and the prospect of hours of forced social interaction with relative strangers, I can already tell that this is going to be a long day.

SAID IS WHERE SAFIYAH SAID HE'D BE: OUTSIDE THE WALKER Center, staring off into the sky. Almost like he's anticipating something.

A passerby might think Said is studying the weather, or watching out for a passing plane. But I know exactly what he's looking for: *the man in the moon.*

Obviously not an actual man in the moon, just a cloud shaped like him.

When we were kids Said would often stare off into the sky, trying to find shapes in the clouds. He used to tell me that if you stared long enough, you might just see something out of the ordinary. For him, it was the moon guy.

I'm surprised at how focused he is, his eyebrows scrunched up as he observes the sky.

I guess it's just a bit weird how much he looks like the Said I knew from when he was ten, pulling the same concentrated expression while watching the clouds.

"Just so you know, it's creepy to stare at people," Said says, not breaking his intense staring contest with the sky.

I startle a little, not expecting his voice. I'm still at least ten feet away from him. How in the world did he see me?

"What's actually creepy is the fact that you apparently have eyes on the sides of your face now like some . . . *alien,*" I manage, unsure how to land my point.

He snorts and finally pulls his eyes away from above and over to me.

"What a comeback," he says with a sarcastic raise of his eyebrow. His mouth twitches ever so slightly. "I'm not an alien, I was simply multitasking. Not very hard to do for some of us."

I narrow my eyes at him but decide to ignore the jab, though my face still warms. I didn't come here to argue with him. I came here to save the Islamic Center.

I clear my throat and walk over to him, holding out one of my clipboards and avoiding eye contact with him. "Here's the petition form. I figured it would be easier if we did some individually and some together. You take these streets here," I say, pointing down at the list of little neighborhoods dotted around town, "and I'll do these, and then we can meet up on Rosehill Avenue to tackle that side of town together. Is that all clear?" I ask, looking at his forehead.

Looking directly into Said's face only makes me angry.

"Sounds simple enough," Said says, and again I feel him watching me.

I nod, looking down pointedly at my own clipboard. "Okay, I'll see you in about an hour or so."

"See you then," he says.

"See you," I reply again, not wanting Said to have the final word.

"Later," he adds.

I look up at him finally, trying not to let my annoyance show. His expression is neutral, but behind his eyes, I can see that this is a game to him too.

"Yes, at Rosehill Avenue," I say, stepping back now.

"Mhm, the very place," he replies, moving away too.

"In an hour," I say.

"Yes, the very time," he agrees, pulling out his earphones and slipping them in his ears before I can say anything else. "Bye, Tiwa." He smiles smugly before walking away.

I sigh, looking down at my clipboard filled with rows of empty lines that need to be filled by the end of the day.

"And so the nightmare begins," I say to myself as I turn in the opposite direction, making my way over to the first street.

Forty-five minutes later, I have managed to knock on thirty-two doors, of which twenty-nine actually answered and signed.

Petitioning is not as bad as I'd expected. Still kind of scary but not as much of the nightmare as I'd expected.

"Good luck, dear, hope you get all the signatures you need!" Miss Lewis from number 9 Thorngrove Avenue says, handing me back the clipboard.

"Thanks, Miss Lewis," I reply, trying to make my smile inviting and appreciative.

I've been smiling so much today my face is hurting; it's clearly a sign I wasn't built for this.

When the door closes, I look down at the board, counting the signatures.

Thirty-five signatures down, plenty more to go.

I step over Miss Lewis's rosebushes to door number ten and ring the bell twice.

"Coming!" a gruff voice says from behind the door.

The muscles in my face protest as I put on my winning smile once again.

After a few moments of silence, I hear shuffling before the door finally opens and I'm greeted by a familiar face I recognize from the mosque.

I feel myself relax a little. The last few neighbors weren't Muslim, and so it took a little more explanation and convincing to get them on board. This should be quicker.

"As-salaam-alaikum, Auntie," I say brightly.

I wait for her to respond with the usual *wa-alaikum-salaam*, but it never comes.

Instead she squints up at me, watching my face with a bemused expression.

I clear my throat awkwardly. "As you might already know, the Islamic Center burned down earlier this week, and Mayor Williams has decided that he wants to knock the remaining parts of the building down in order to build new apartments. We are collecting signatures for this petition to put a stop to this and to ask for the Islamic Center to be rebuilt. If you just sign here, you can help get this issue taken to the people in charge at the town hall and hopefully get them to overturn the building plans," I finish reading from my mental script, holding out the clipboard and pen to the confused auntie.

At first she does nothing, just holds on to the doorframe and glares at me unblinking. Then she nods, taking the clipboard from my hands and reaching out to sign.

"Are there any Muslims involved in this project?" the auntie mutters gruffly.

I can't tell if she's asking me or talking to herself, but I feel my shoulders tense and an uncomfortable feeling settle inside.

"Y-yes, um, there are Muslims involved," I say quickly.

I'm not sure why I don't just tell her that I'm involved—that I'm Muslim. I thought it was obvious, especially as I'm pretty sure we've run into each other at the Islamic Center before.

"Here you go," the auntie says, handing me back the clipboard without looking at me.

When she goes back inside, I try to shake off the weirdness I feel as I continue down the street, looking for more neighbors to sign the petition.

The next few houses go well; I see another face from the mosque, an auntie who I remember making mishtis during Eid last year. She greets me enthusiastically and asks how I've been. I even feel the weirdness inside begin to shrink as I knock on number fifteen. This time I'm met with another familiar face from the mosque.

I pull on my smile and take a deep breath getting ready to recite the same lines, but before I can get a word out, I see the neighbor's face twist into a distasteful grimace.

Next thing I know, the door is slamming shut in my face.

10

DESSERT TO GO

Said

I approach Rosehill Avenue ten minutes late, and I don't see Tiwa anywhere.

I got here first.

I smile triumphantly, until I hear Tiwa's voice in the distance. She's in the middle of a conversation with one of the neighbors. Even from where I'm standing, I can hear Tiwa's high-pitched voice and see her strained smile.

I knew I would be much better at this than Tiwa. She's not a people person at all.

I remember in sixth grade, Tiwa always made boys in our class cry because she kept on scowling at them. Josh Donnelly, who was her seatmate that year, even migrated all the way to the other side of class because she made him cry one too many times.

Even now, her smile looks unnatural. I'm too used to her scowling at everyone. Especially me.

She clearly needs my help, and my dazzling personality, so I make my way over to her.

Over her shoulder, I spot the person she's speaking to. It's an older auntie, wearing a blue salwar kameez. She looks as comfortable having this conversation as Tiwa. But then her gaze flickers over to me, and her expression changes.

"As-salaam-alaikum!" the auntie says, a sudden smile on her face.

Tiwa whips around to look at me, her eyebrows furrowed together.

"Wa-alaikum-salaam, Auntie," I say. "My frien—my colleague, Tiwa, and I are just collecting some signatures for our petition to save the Islamic Center. I'm sure you've heard by now about the unfortunate fire, and how Mayor Williams is planning to demolish the building to make apartments. We're trying to do everything in our power to get the Islamic Center rebuilt. It's such an important part of our community."

The auntie nods sympathetically, before reaching out for my clipboard. Almost like there was no question about her signing the petition.

I look at Tiwa with a victorious smile.

"It's so amazing that you're taking charge of this," the auntie says as she hands back the clipboard. "Not many people care about the Islamic Center, or the small Muslim community in this town."

"Don't worry, Auntie, we're doing everything that we can," I say.

"Bahut achchha kaam kar rahe hon. Shabbash!" The auntie ruffles my hair. "Bye, beta," she says before closing the door. I blink for a moment, wondering why she assumed I spoke Hindi, why she barely even glanced at Tiwa throughout the entire conversation, and why she didn't even say goodbye to her.

But as we turn away toward the main road, Tiwa is glancing down at her clipboard, like she doesn't care about the auntie's strange behavior. "How many houses did you get through?"

"Pretty much all of them," I say. "You?"

"Yeah, a good amount. But . . . there were a few who didn't sign. And there was even one person who slammed the door in my face." At that, Tiwa just rolls her eyes like she doesn't care.

I stop in my tracks. "Someone slammed the door in your face?"

Tiwa pauses too, until the two of us are face-to-face. "Yeah, but . . . it's not a big deal." She shrugs. "There was even an auntie who asked if I was Muslim. It happens sometimes."

I can only blink at her, confused. Nobody slammed the door in my face, and nobody assumed that I wasn't Muslim. In fact, one of the uncles invited me into the house for a cup of tea, and an auntie even asked if I was single so she could set me up with her daughter.

"What do you mean, it happens sometimes? Like . . . it happens at the mosque? With aunties you know?" I ask.

"Sometimes . . ." Tiwa says slowly. "But I think it's probably because, you know, I don't wear a hijab. So it's not easy to tell that I'm Muslim. I try not to think too much about it."

"Well, I don't wear a hijab either," I say with a smile.

Tiwa's eyes narrow at me and my smile widens. "What, you don't think I can pull off a hijab?" I ask. And before Tiwa can give me a death glare that can send me to my grave, I add, "I'm joking, obviously. It's not okay that anybody treats you like that. Especially not Muslim aunties."

"Yeah, I guess. I'm fine. We should really keep going with our petition. We have a lot to get done," Tiwa says. She glances down at her clipboard again, but she's lost some of the intensity in her eyes I noticed this morning. She's obviously not fine.

"Maybe we should take a break and get some food. I'm hungry," I say.

I expect Tiwa to put up a fight, because that's our usual way of doing things, but she just sighs and nods. "Okay, sure. Let's get some food."

WE END UP IN A CORNER BOOTH AT ABIGAIL'S BAKERY, AND I suddenly feel like we've gone back in time to when we were kids. Tiwa and I used to be obsessed with coming to Abigail's to share a plate of pineapple-shaped sugar cookies.

We don't order any sugar cookies to share this time around, though. It would be a bit too weird. Instead, I order halal chicken enchiladas with a side of fries, and a glass of pink lemonade, while Tiwa gets a spinach frittata and a cup of coffee.

"I forgot how good Abigail's food is," I say, through a mouthful of enchilada. It's basically heaven on a plate. Which is exactly why I'm going to drag Julian here when he comes later this summer. He has a bigger sweet tooth than I do, and that's saying something.

"Yeah, though nothing beats her pastries, obviously," Tiwa says.

"Obviously," I agree. "And that's why we should order dessert after this."

Tiwa's lips quirk up, almost like she's trying really hard not to smile. "We still have more petitioning to do."

"We'll take dessert to go," I insist. "And from what I see, we've almost reached a hundred signatures."

"That's why we can't slack off. We need to get those signatures, so we can move on to the next step of the process."

"What else is there to do?" I ask. I'd almost thought it would be as easy as getting the signatures and painting the mural.

"A lot," Tiwa says, sounding a little tired. "The petition only means the mayor has to *consider* it. And I still have to figure out Eid at the Walker Center. So much got destroyed by the fire, and my mom and I will have to get new decorations, ingredients, and lots of other stuff. Apparently, planning an Eid party is very costly."

I hadn't even thought about how the fire must have destroyed more than just the building.

And I knew that things have been bad for the Olatunjis for the last two years. I'd heard from Ammu that that was one of the reasons they had moved away from our neighborhood.

"What about if you did a fundraiser?" I ask.

"For . . . ?" Tiwa asks with a raised eyebrow.

"For the Eid party? In Walker?" I say. "I think everybody would love to contribute and help out. After all, it's all of our Eid party. Maybe we could have a bake sale. We could even ask Abigail if she would be willing to donate a few of her famous pastries."

Tiwa considers this for a moment, before slowly nodding her head. "A bake sale could be a good idea. And I could make my cupcakes."

I have never actually eaten one of Tiwa's cupcakes, but I've heard enough from Safiyah to know I never want to try one.

So I just smile and say, "Sure, maybe we can make them together at my place."

Tiwa raises an eyebrow at the suggestion, so I quickly add, "I mean . . . if you want to, that is."

"I guess," Tiwa says. "It's just like you to want to do a bake sale."

"Why? You think I'm sweet?" I ask with a grin.

"You're not funny," Tiwa says in a deadpan voice.

"What are you talking about? I'm hilarious."

"Yeah, that's why I'm laughing so hard," Tiwa says.

I grab hold of one of the fries on my plate and throw it at Tiwa. It hits her right in the middle of her forehead. That finally gets a smile out of her.

"See? Hilarious," I say.

"Whatever," Tiwa says, glancing away, though the smile stays.

I watch her for a moment, and my heartbeat quickens.

Sometimes, when she isn't being annoying, I forget why I hate her so much.

Act 2

MISCHIEF AND MAYHEM

11
CAKE ISN'T FOR CATS

Tiwa

"Where did you put the vanilla bean paste again?" I call out to my mom from the kitchen.

I stare at the cluttered cupboard where the baking stuff should be, seeing no sign of the jar of vanilla.

"Didn't you use it last?" Mom asks, not once looking up from reading her Mills & Boon romance novel.

"No, you used it to make puff puff a few weeks ago for that dementia patient's family . . . and now it's not in the usual place," I say, riffling through the cupboard and once again coming up empty.

I hear Mom sigh loudly, followed by the sound of her book closing and her feet padding across the living room into the kitchen.

She casually reaches into the same cupboard I've been searching through for the past ten minutes, brings out the jar of vanilla bean paste, and hands it over to me.

"It was right in front of you the entire time. You disrupted my book for nothing. Sergio was just about to ask Marianne for her hand in marriage," Mom says.

I stare down at the jar of vanilla paste with shock and mild confusion. Somehow Mom has this alarming ability to pull lost objects out from nowhere.

"Who is Sergio?" I ask, placing the jar in the bag of baking ingredients I'm packing with me to take to Safiyah's house.

"The Italian CEO love interest in my book. I hope that's everything you need. I'd like to spend my day off without further disruption," Mom says, eyeing my very full bag of supplies with a raised eyebrow, and I feel her judgment.

"I take baking very seriously," I say defensively.

"I can see that," Mom says. "I just thought you were going grocery shopping with Safiyah for the bake sale tomorrow, but you look like you're stocking up for the apocalypse . . . Should I be concerned?"

"No apocalypse here, we're only shopping for the ingredients we don't have. I wanted to pack what I could instead of wasting money buying two of the same thing."

Mom nods. "That's smart. I've taught you well," she says just as the sound of the downstairs door buzzer rings out in the apartment.

I chuck the rest of the ingredients in next as Mom goes over to answer the door.

"Hello? Oh hi, dear. Yes, I'll just buzz you in, Tiwa is almost ready," I hear Mom say.

"Is that Safiyah?" I ask.

"Yes, I thought you said she was coming at twelve."

I nod, looking at the clock, which has only just passed eleven thirty. She's early, which is very un-Safiyah-like. Out of the Hossains, Safiyah and her brother are night and day when it comes to timekeeping.

"Maybe the apocalypse *is* coming . . ." I say. It's the only explanation I can think of for her unusual punctuality.

I slip into my shoes just as a sharp rapping sounds at the door. This time I go to answer it.

I'm greeted by Safiyah, which is expected, and Said standing next to her, which is unexpected.

This explains why Safiyah is early for once.

"Hey, Tee," Safiyah says with a smile.

"Hi, Safiyah . . ." I say, reluctantly shifting my gaze away from Saf. "Said," I finish with a curt nod.

His expression remains still and neutral as he nods back at me. "Tiwa."

Safiyah looks back at him with a surprised face like she'd forgotten she'd come here with someone.

"Oh, I forgot to mention, Said is coming with us to the store. He needs special art pens or something for the mural," she says, which explains his presence.

Before I can respond and ask what the plan is for today, I hear Mom's bright voice behind me.

"Said? I thought I heard your voice—long time no see. How have you been?" Mom asks. She looks more pleased to see him than I am—which is probably accurate.

His face changes from neutral to warm. It's clear he's also more pleased to see her than me.

"Hi, Auntie, I'm good, just been busy with school and all," he says with a shrug.

Mom's eyes light up at the mention of school. "Oh yes, you go to that fancy boarding school now. In Virginia I think your mom said it was?"

"Yes, that's right," Said replies quietly, cheeks dusted with pink.

"How wonderful! I hope that's been okay? Are you eating well? Making friends?" Mom continues to prod, leaning her hand against the doorframe, getting way too comfortable.

I for one could do without hearing all the details about Said's boarding school escapades. I've managed to avoid them for years, and I don't plan to break my ignorant bliss any time soon.

He nods, clearing his throat before he speaks again. "Uh, yeah, I've been good. I mean, it was hard in the beginning, but then it got better. I'm eating well, and I've made a few friends. Actually, my roommate, Julian, is staying with my family this summer. He'll be here around Eid."

"Oh, how love—" Mom begins, but I interrupt before she can ask any more questions about Said and his new life.

"We should probably get going now. We have *a lot* to bake," I say quickly, avoiding Said's gaze now. "See you later, Mom!" I finish as I grab my stuff and quickly shuffle Safiyah and Said out the door before my mom can ask any more questions that I don't want to hear the answer to.

WE GET TO THE STORE FIFTEEN MINUTES LATER, THANKS TO Safiyah's speedy driving.

Said goes off on his own to find his art supplies while Saf and I scour through the baking aisle.

"Oh, look! They have crescent moon cookie cutters! If we can find a star cookie cutter, we could make some really nice Islamic-themed cookies," Safiyah says, holding up the metal shape.

I pause to consider it, eyeing the pricey tag attached to it. Our budget is limited, and Safiyah's ideas have been a little too grand to fit the thirty dollars her mom kindly donated.

"I like that idea," I start. "But I think we could make them without the cookie cutters. It could help to cut costs."

"If you say so," Safiyah says with a shrug, putting them back on the shelf.

"Oh, remind me to get mayonnaise," I say. Safiyah screws up her face in response.

"Mayonnaise?" she asks. "Don't tell me you put that in your cakes."

"I don't usually, but Ms. Barnes always did. And her cakes were the best," I say. I feel a dull ache in my chest at the realization that I'll never have a cake made by Ms. Barnes again.

Safiyah doesn't look convinced. "If you say so," she says as we move along the shelves. Safiyah stops again, plucking out a stack of heart-shaped cupcake liners.

"We could use these for the cupcakes to show the love we have for the community," Safiyah says.

I look at the price tag first, before reaching out to grab the much cheaper circular paper cupcake liners. "Cute, but I think we can probably only afford the basic kind."

Safiyah sighs and puts them back. "This is why I need a summer job," she mutters.

"So you can buy heart-shaped cake holders?" I ask.

She nods. "Exactly."

We move farther down, heading toward the end of the aisle.

"Speaking of hearts . . . you never told me how your date with Ishra went," I say, giving Safiyah a sideways glance.

"That's because it was disastrous," Safiyah says. "Apparently I'm terrible at being a lesbian."

I laugh. "How can one be terrible at being a lesbian?" I ask seriously.

"Well, I think being able to talk to girls is in the job description, and I definitely failed on all fronts."

"What happened?"

Safiyah dramatically pauses and turns to me. "Nothing. Absolutely nothing."

"Nothing?"

"Yes, nothing. I couldn't even speak to her. She kept asking questions about my life and how college is going and I choked. Could barely mumble out a reply. She probably thinks I'm very weird, or worse: creepy! I just kept looking at her and not answering." Safiyah groans, and covers her face with her hands. "I am such an embarrassment."

"No, you're not. You're slightly ridiculous at times, yes . . . but definitely not an embarrassment. Everyone chokes sometimes. I'm sure it isn't as bad as you think."

Safiyah shakes her head. "It was terrible, Tee. Probably even worse than I'm remembering. But anyway, let's just change the subject. I'm planning on wearing a disguise for the rest of the summer and avoiding her at all costs—starting tomorrow, of course. I didn't think it would be appropriate to wear a disguise to the store."

"Good thinking," I respond, trying not to laugh at the ridiculousness of my best friend.

As we round the corner, I spot the back of Said's all-too-familiar head in the distance, by the arts and crafts section, inspecting paint pots on the shelf and holding what seems to be a set of brand-new paintbrushes in his hands.

He has this look of deep concentration, like he's trying to solve a difficult equation.

Said seems to be taking the mural more seriously than I thought he would. Which shouldn't be surprising seeing as he's always taken his art seriously. It's one of the things I always loved most about him.

Not just his art but how into it he is. I used to watch him draw for hours while we were supposed to be doing homework.

I almost want to watch him draw again.

As though he can feel my eyes on him, he looks up sharply, like he's been electrocuted by my gaze.

I look away quickly before I'm caught red-handed, pushing the shopping cart into the next aisle hastily as Safiyah follows behind, still moping about her date with Ishra.

"What's next on the list?" I ask Safiyah, ignoring my racing heart.

She pulls out the crumpled sheet. "Eggs. We need two dozen of them."

"Eggs," I repeat with a nod, before making a beeline for the eggs and away from my Said-infused thoughts.

A FEW HOURS AND SEVERAL BATCHES OF BROWNIES LATER, Safiyah is fanning away the smoke in the kitchen while I'm attempting to decorate the cupcakes.

"Tiwa, I mean this with love . . ." Safiyah says, hovering over me now. "The art on that cupcake looks like something out of a Stephen King novel."

I take in the tray of cakes with lopsided frosting half-dripping off the tops, and the smiley face I tried to pipe on the top of one, which looks less like a smile and more like a monstrous grimace.

"It's not that bad . . ." I say, trying to convince both Safiyah and myself. "I'm sure if I add sprinkles it'll look less . . ."

"Terrifying?" Safiyah offers.

"Less like a sad cupcake," I finish. "Listen, neither of us are exactly

Pablo Picass—" Saf starts, but she is interrupted by Said's voice in the corner.

"True, you're both terrible at art," he says, with a half-eaten cupcake in one hand and Laddoo in the other. "Especially you, Safiyah. Remember the time you drew Aasif Uncle for your art project at school and made him cry?"

"I didn't make Uncle cry; he was allergic to the wax in my crayons," Safiyah replies.

"Sure," Said says, biting into the cupcake with a smile.

Safiyah walks up to him and grabs the cupcake out of his hand. "Don't eat our cupcakes! They're for the fundraiser tomorrow," Safiyah says.

Said freezes, and then looks at the cat. "The cake was for Laddoo. He was hungry."

"I'm sure he was. Tell Laddoo that cake isn't for cats," Safiyah says, glaring at Laddoo.

Laddoo meows a retort.

"Shouldn't you be helping out anyway?" I ask, recalling that this was his idea in the first place, yet I haven't seen him since we got back from the store.

He looks at me now. "I was working on the mural sketches—I think I have a few ideas already. But I'm down here now, ready to save you guys from yourselves," Said says, before moving forward to inspect my handiwork. His face screws up when he sees the smiley face I'd attempted to draw. "That is just messed up," he says, shaking his head.

"It's supposed to be a smile," I mumble with a frown.

He tilts his head, inspecting my face briefly. "I can see that. The cupcake kind of smiles like you," he says.

I narrow my eyes at him.

"Since you can clearly do better, why don't you finish the decorations," I say, before placing the piping bag in his free hand.

Said places Laddoo on the ground and pushes up his sleeves. "This is how *not* to terrify people. Watch and learn."

About an hour later, the kitchen counter is filled with rows of baked and decorated treats.

I step back with Said and Safiyah, admiring our handiwork.

I have to admit, the cupcakes definitely look better with Said's swirly designs on them. Not that I'll say it out loud.

"Not so bad for the work of three brain cells," Said says.

I raise an eyebrow at that. "You have more than one brain cell, Said. You should give yourself some credit," I say.

"You're right, I am a genius," Said says.

"That's not exactly what I said . . ."

"Because I'm a genius, I knew what you meant," he replies.

"If delusion helps you sleep at night, then so be it," I say.

"Mm, yes, that and chamomile tea," he says with a wide smile.

I roll my eyes and check the time on my phone.

It's nearly evening and I still have to get back to do my late asr prayer and start maghrib, not to mention the call I have scheduled with my dad.

"I should get going. I have a call with my dad," I say. "When and where should we set up for the bake sale tomorrow?"

"We can meet outside Walker just before the lunch rush. It's the most central place in town, and most people would have to pass by to get their lunches. There are some tables and chairs in the basement of the Walker Center that we can use. Me and Safiyah can also take the baked goods in Safiyah's car. I can even swing by Abigail's to pick up the stuff she said she'd donate," Said suggests, and I'm a little taken aback by his offer.

His investment in Eid is a good thing; I should stop being so suspicious about it.

"Thanks, Said," I say, shifting my gaze away from him. "I can meet you guys there?"

"That works. I'll make sure that Said doesn't eat any more of the cupcakes," Safiyah says, which garners a glower from Said, but he doesn't defend himself, probably because Saf is right.

"Are you sure you don't want to stay for dinner? Mom is about to kick us out of here so that she can warm up the food," Safiyah adds, moving the baking equipment over to the dishwasher.

I glance to the side, noticing Said leaving the kitchen, and I shake my head at Safiyah in response.

"My mom doesn't like to eat dinner alone, but maybe I'll stay another time," I say.

Safiyah nods, hugging me goodbye. "Okay, next time bring your mom too."

I hear the sound of the kitchen door opening once again and I turn to see Said return with the ginger cat in his arms and a plastic bag in his hands.

"Here, a farewell gift," Said says, holding the cat out to me.

I blink at him. "What?"

"We both have to pull our weight in looking after Laddoo, so here he is. I took the liberty of preparing a list of his needs and packing some of the cat food and the box he likes to play in. Oh, and he likes to roam around in mud a lot so you might need to bathe him. He hates water, though, so he might try to kill you in your sleep after," Said says, and places the cat in my arms.

"Thanks for the ample warning, Said. I'll try not to accidentally drown the cat during bath time."

"You're welcome," Said says, before rubbing the cat's ears. "See you in a few days, buddy," he says to the cat before leaving the kitchen once again.

"I'll drive you home," Saf says, and I thank her because I am not sure how I would manage to walk home holding my bag of half-used baking stuff, a cat, and the cat's luggage.

We walk out of the kitchen together, Safiyah grabbing her car keys.

"Ammu, I'm dropping Tiwa home quickly, but I'll be back before dinner," Safiyah says to her mom, who is sitting on the couch watching a Hindi soap.

"Tiwa, are you not staying for dinner?" Safiyah's mom asks, looking up at me, or well, what she can see of me behind the big furry cat.

"Sorry, Auntie, I have to head home to my mom, but I'll come around soon," I say.

"Okay, just don't be a stranger. It's been so long since all of us have had a chance to sit down to dinner together, with your mom working so many shifts these days, and Said always away at school. I can't even remember the last time we all got together . . . When was it again, Said?" his mom asks Said, who is lounging on the couch in the corner.

He looks up at me and I feel like I can almost read his mind.

I know the last time Mom and I were over for dinner with his whole family had to be years ago. Definitely before everything happened at home and with Said and me.

I can tell he's thinking about that time, when I'd always be over. When things weren't so weird and tense.

"Uh, I'm not sure," he says, looking away from me and his mom, pretending to be engrossed in the TV.

His mom rolls her eyes and smiles. "Anyway, we must have you over a few times this summer. I'll make sure to cook your favorite meals to entice you," she says.

I smile at her.

I really do miss eating here all the time. Auntie Nabiha makes the best rice—not that I'd tell my mom this.

"Thank you, I'll see you later, Auntie," I say, and then my eyes briefly flicker over to Said, who I notice averting his gaze from me back to the TV. "Bye, Said," I add.

"Goodbye, Tiwa dear," Auntie Nabiha says.

"Bye, Tiwa," I hear Said almost whisper, not looking at me. I notice how pink his ears are.

Safiyah and I make our way out of the door and into her car.

I place Laddoo on the floor by my feet as I buckle up.

"I'm pretty sure my mom wants to adopt you, you know? She never offers to make my favorite food," Safiyah says.

"Of course she wants to adopt me. I'm amazing," I say with a small smile.

"That you are, my friend," Saf says, returning the smile before pressing her foot down on the gas pedal and pulling out of the driveway. "By the way . . . I noticed that you and Said didn't try to kill each other today. I see that as a great improvement."

"I can be civil with anyone because I'm a delight. I just care about making sure the Islamic Center is saved. It's called professionalism," I state, trying to ignore the rising heat in my face.

Safiyah laughs.

"If you say so. Though, I will say, for supposed mortal enemies, you two sure do get along."

12

PLASTIC SMILE

Said

OUR CAR SMELLS LIKE A HERSHEY'S CHOCOLATE FACTORY AS WE pull up to the Walker Center.

Or maybe it's just the fact that I haven't eaten anything yet today that's making everything seem even more appetizing than usual.

I spot Tiwa by the front steps of the building, and, as Safiyah puts the car into park, Tiwa hurries over to us.

"You're late!" she says as a way of greeting, even though it's only two minutes past eleven.

"See, if you had let *me* drive, we would have been here on time," I say.

Safiyah slips out of the driver's seat as if she didn't even hear me, hugging Tiwa hello.

I roll my eyes even though neither of them can see me, and step outside too. Opening up the trunk where we stuffed the tables and chairs, I begin to unload as Safiyah and Tiwa take out the boxes of baked goods.

"Here okay?" I grunt, placing one of the tables near the footpath.

Tiwa finally turns toward me, frowning. "No. Closer to the steps."

"This thing is heavy, you know," I say, but do as I'm asked, carrying the table nearer to the steps of the Walker Center and setting it up with some of the folding chairs. Tiwa and Safiyah follow behind, spreading the boxes of cupcakes, brownies, and cookies around the table.

Tiwa places a bucket in the middle of the table with the word *Donations* written in big black letters, while Safiyah sticks up a cardboard sign in front of the table that reads *Eid Fundraiser*. But considering her terrible handwriting and the red marker she used, it looks more like a threatening note from a serial killer than anything else.

"If it was windy, the breeze could take the amazing smell of our baking all throughout New Crosshaven," Safiyah says happily as she sits down on one of the folding chairs.

"We don't live in a Disney movie, Saf," Tiwa says with a raised eyebrow.

"Yeah, that's not exactly how the wind operates," I add, before sitting down next to Safiyah.

Tiwa remains standing, looking around the nearly deserted area, and I note that her eyes drift momentarily to the shell of what was once the Islamic Center. She turns away but doesn't sit down. Instead, she chooses to pace up and down the area in front of our table.

Five minutes go by. Then ten. Fifteen. And in that time, the hunger pangs only grow and my stomach doesn't stop turning.

Tiwa seems to pace faster and faster with each passing minute, her shoulders tense.

I want to tell her to take a seat. That it's only been a few minutes. But the words die on my lips. Just because the two of us are working together doesn't mean we're friends. It doesn't mean anything I say will actually make Tiwa stop pacing like her shoes are on fire.

Instead, I turn to Safiyah, who has been too busy staring at her phone to pay attention to her best friend's frustration.

I poke her in the ribs.

"Ow!" Safiyah says. She shoots me a glare, but then she finally notices Tiwa and her incessant pacing.

"Tee, sit down, the customers will come. Don't scare them off with your vigorous pacing," Safiyah says, patting the empty chair next to her.

"But it's been fifteen minutes and we haven't seen a soul," Tiwa says. "Maybe this was a bad idea. Should we move our table somewhere else? Where there will be more people?"

"No," Safiyah says sternly. "You just need to give it more time. People will come, I promise."

I glance at the cupcakes on display and I reach into my pocket for a five-dollar bill. "I'll be your first customer," I say, placing the cash in the glass jar and picking up a red velvet one.

Tiwa raises an eyebrow at me as I start to bite into the cake.

"I'm charitable," I say with a shrug, words muffled. This is only half true—I'm also starving.

"Are you going to pay for the cupcakes you stole last night too?" she asks.

"Already paid for them with my awesome decorating skills. You're welcome," I say, smiling at her.

Tiwa rolls her eyes, conceding. "Thank you, Said, for your generosity," she says in a way that doesn't quite feel like she means it.

"Always happy to help," I say, broadening my grin to irritate her. "By the way, these cakes are surprisingly nice. They taste just like Ms. Barnes's."

"That's because I used her special ingredient," Tiwa says, plopping down on the seat on the other side of Safiyah.

"Which is?"

"If I told you, I'd have to kill you," she replies with a small smile.

Before I can respond to that, a person other than us finally appears in front of the table.

"Hi!" says a girl with an oval face and shoulder-length black hair. Strangely, she's looking straight at Safiyah with a smile that seems to take up half her face.

"Ishra? H-hi!" Safiyah scrambles to a stand, nearly knocking back the chair she was on in the process.

"What's going on?" Ishra nods to all the baked goods, while I try to size Ishra up. So this is the girl Safiyah has been crushing on for the past year and a half. My sister has been texting me endlessly about the girl in the Walker Center with the dreamy eyes and amazing laugh, and how when I come back for the summer I need to meet her.

"Um, we're . . . having a fundraiser?" Safiyah says. She glances at me, panic flashing in her eyes, and then at Tiwa. Almost like she's pleading for us to take over this conversation. Even though any random passerby can tell that Ishra is more than happy to have run into Saf.

"It's for Eid this year, since we lost so much in the fire," Tiwa cuts into the conversation. "I'm Tiwa, Safiyah has told me a—ow!" Tiwa rubs the side of her stomach, where Safiyah elbowed her to shut up while keeping her eyes trained on Ishra.

"Yes, Tiwa is my best friend. And this is Said, my brother," Safiyah says. I wave hello to Ishra, and she waves back.

"That's so cool you guys are doing a fundraiser. I'd been wondering what would happen with Eid this year," Ishra says. "I definitely need a cupcake!"

She digs into her handbag and pulls out her card.

"Oh . . ." Tiwa says. "We don't have a card machine, sorry. We can take cash or Venmo, though."

"Ah . . ." Ishra tucks the card back into her bag and gives the cupcakes a longing glance. "I don't have cash on me. But I guess I could download Venmo? It might take me a few minutes to set it up, though."

"Don't worry about it!" Safiyah says brightly. She digs into her own bag and pulls out a five-dollar bill. "The cupcake is on me."

Ishra's cheeks turn slightly red at the offer. "N-no, I couldn't—"

"It's for a good cause," Tiwa chirps in.

"And the cupcakes are really good. I decorated them myself," I add.

"Okay, I guess I'll take one. Thanks, Safiyah." Ishra's cheeks are even redder as she picks up one of the cupcakes with pink-frosted flowers on it. "I'll tell everyone in the library about the bake sale. Maybe they can come out during their break."

"Thanks, Ishra, and Safiyah can walk you into the library," Tiwa says pointedly.

"Y-yeah, I can do that." Safiyah slips out from behind the table, and we watch as the two of them walk up the steps of the Walker Center side by side.

Beside me, Tiwa glances at her phone. Her eyebrows scrunch together as she puts the phone back into her pocket, clearly dissatisfied. I check my phone too. It's five minutes to twelve—we've been here for almost a whole hour—and the only customer we've had is Ishra.

Thankfully, Ishra is true to her word, because when Safiyah comes out of Walker a few minutes later, she's followed by one of the librarians. They both head toward our table, and the librarian gives Tiwa and me a bright smile as she buys one of everything.

"Nothing helps with Mondays more than a bit of sugar!" she says excitedly as we wrap up her cookie, brownie, and cupcake in some parchment paper to take with her.

"See? I told you people would come," Safiyah says, like one librarian is the equivalent of the entire town.

Soon after, though, more and more people show up. Most of them are out for their lunch breaks, or they're aunties who've heard about the bake sale from somewhere.

"I think this might be Ammu's doing," I say, when we've served half a dozen aunties with a few too many prying questions. "I asked Ammu last night if she could post it in some of those WhatsApp groups she's in."

"The power of auntie WhatsApp groups," Tiwa says.

"It's genius!" Safiyah says. "I should have thought of it myself."

While Safiyah is a few steps away and dealing with some customers from the library, Tiwa and I smile at the familiar aunties from the mosque. Tiwa takes their cash, counts it up, and adds it to our bucket, while I wrap up their baked goods and hand them over. It's a good system, and with the two of us the aunties don't manage to linger for too long, commenting on our appearances or asking about school.

But a few minutes into the lunch rush, I notice Tiwa's shoulders stiffen beside me. I follow her gaze to an auntie getting out of a car by the side of the road. I recognize her almost instantly: We'd seen her while collecting signatures for our petition.

I shouldn't be surprised to see her here, but my stomach clenches at the sight of her.

"Do you want to bring a few more of the baked goods over to Safiyah? I can handle the aunties by myself for a bit," I say, turning to Tiwa.

Her eyebrows draw together. "She's taken an entire box full of brownies, cookies, and cupcakes."

"Yeah, but there's more people coming down from Walker and joining her line. See?" I point to the trickle of people walking down the steps and eyeing our little corner table.

Tiwa doesn't look convinced, but she doesn't argue as she fills up one of the boxes with baked goods and makes her way over to Safiyah.

I turn to the next auntie with my signature smile. "Salam, Auntie. What can I get you?"

"Said, we never see you around anymore!" the auntie says with a mock glare. "I told your ammu that you all have to come for a dawat at ours next week. You and Riaz will have lots to talk about, with university applications coming up."

My smile falters a little. "Inshaallah," I mumble, hoping that will get the auntie off my back.

"I'll take two brownies," she says, and I wrap them up and hand them over to her as fast as I can.

The auntie from the petitioning is next in line. Her eyes light up with recognition as soon as she sees me.

"As-salaam-alaikum, beta," she says with a bright smile, like we're old friends.

136

"Wa-alaikum-salaam, Auntie. What can I—"

"This is such an amazing effort. Is this for the Islamic Center?" another auntie asks.

I nod. "Yes, we're trying to raise money to help rebuild it."

Their faces collectively brighten.

"I hope we can get the Islamic Center back. I do not like praying in the Walker Center, there's no place to even do ablution properly. We have to use those tiny sinks," another auntie adds.

"First, the petitioning. Then, this bake sale! I'll have to tell your ammi about what a great job you've been doing. Mashallah!" the first auntie says.

The aunties around her murmur their agreement, but instead of feeling any sort of pride, anger simmers in my veins. Some of these aunties were just being helped by Tiwa. But it's like they don't even see her.

"Actually, it was Tiwa who did most of it. She bought the ingredients, baked, organized everything."

The auntie's smile turns plastic. "Well, that's nice of her to help out."

"The Olatunjis are hosting Eid this year, so really none of this would even be possible without Tiwa and her mom."

"The Olatunjis?" The auntie blinks at me slowly, like she's confused. "I didn't even realize that they were Muslim. So great to have another Muslim family in the community." I can't help but notice that her words don't match the stiffness of her voice. The Olatunjis have been in our community for almost a decade and Tiwa pretty much lives at the Islamic Center. I know that if they were Arab or South Asian or any race and ethnicity other than Black, everyone here would have been clamoring to praise Tiwa for her hard work instead of me. In all these years, I had never noticed that Tiwa and her family get treated differently because they're Black. Even when we're all supposed to be part of the same community. Part of the same ummah. I guess I never had to notice.

I don't press the point any further and instead, keep serving the aunties and collecting their donations with a plastic smile of my own. After a little while, the lunch rush dies down to a trickle of people, and then to none at all.

"I'm pretty sure those aunties came here to collect gossip more than they did for sweets," Safiyah says as she puts away the empty boxes and Tiwa clears the table of its crumbs with some tissues.

"At least they bought up most of the baked goods," I say.

"Hopefully, we've raised enough for the Eid party," Tiwa says with a sigh.

"I'm sure we've raised a lot of money. And if we need some extra, we'll . . . figure it out," Safiyah says. She gives Tiwa a comforting smile. "Right. I'm going to the bathroom in the Walker Center. If the aunties come back, you'll have to handle them."

"How will we do it without you?" I ask, rolling my eyes.

"It's hard, but I'm sure you'll manage," Safiyah says as she shuffles away.

With Safiyah gone and the lunch rush over, an awkward silence settles between me and Tiwa.

After a few moments, Tiwa clears her throat. "Thanks for earlier."

"Earlier?"

"With the . . . aunties?" Tiwa says. She's looking down at her lap instead of at me. "I didn't really want to have to deal with them again."

"Oh, that's okay. I don't mind," I say. I feel like I should say something more. Like how she shouldn't have to worry about them dismissing her, and how bad I feel that before she told me about it, I hadn't even noticed. But anything I could say would feel empty. Not enough. So I opt not to say anything instead.

"Maybe we should count up how much we've collected so far," I offer, reaching for the donation bucket.

"You expect me to trust an artist with math?" Tiwa asks with a raised eyebrow.

I ignore the thrill I feel at being referred to as an "artist" and roll my eyes. "Like you're such a math genius? If I remember correctly, you needed *my* help to get through fourth-grade math."

"Only because Ms. Miller was bad at explaining things!" Tiwa says. She grabs the donation bucket from me and says, "Let's just split up the donations and count them together."

"Okay." I nod.

But before Tiwa can reach into the bucket, we spot Imam Abdullah walking toward us. He's wearing his signature white thobe and a black-and-gold-patterned tupi on his head.

"As-salaam-alaikum, Tiwa," he says with a smile. "Said."

I'm not sure how he remembers my name after so many years, but I smile and return his salam.

"You're not finished with your fundraiser, are you? My neighbor, Mr. Quraishi, told me about it and I thought I'd stop by," he says, eyeing the donation bucket in Tiwa's hands. "I would have been here earlier, but I had an important meeting with Mayor Williams and was also trying to book a room for jummah prayer in the Walker Center— without much luck. Unfortunately, they only had the computer room left, so I'll have to try another day."

"No, we still have a few things left to sell," Tiwa says. She reaches for the box of sweets and slides it toward him.

"Ah . . . sweet things are not so good for me. Diabetes," Imam Abdullah says. "But I did want to make a donation."

He reaches into the pocket of his thobe and pulls out a check. Glancing at it once with a nod, like he's ensuring everything is in order, he places the check inside the bucket.

"Thank you," Tiwa says. "But you can't just donate without taking something. How about a few sweets for Auntie? Or your kids?"

"Hmm, maybe just a few brownies, then. My wife loves them," Imam Abdullah says.

Said takes the last of the brownies and wraps them up.

"This is a very good thing you two are doing here. There have been so many mosque closures all over the state. I wish there were bake sales in every town in Vermont. Thank you for this," Imam Abdullah says as he pockets the packaged brownies. "Jazakallah Khairan." With that, he turns around, back to where he came from.

"How much did he . . ."

I don't have a chance to finish my sentence before Tiwa fishes the check out from the donation bucket. "Five thousand dollars."

I blink. "Five thousand dollars?"

Tiwa's face breaks out into a huge smile as she looks at me. "Five thousand dollars!"

Before I know it, Tiwa throws her arms around me. "Said, we did it, we raised all the money we need. More than we need!" she says. The joy in her voice is unbridled.

"Yeah," I sigh, letting myself lean into her touch. It's unexpected, strange, to be so close to Tiwa again. But in a good way.

And then, just as quickly as she hugged me, Tiwa pulls away.

"Sorry," she mumbles, looking anywhere but at me. And I run my hands through my hair, trying, and failing, not to look at her.

"What's going on?" Safiyah's voice breaks the awkwardness between us. I have no idea when she got here. We had been so caught up with Imam Abdullah and the check.

"Imam Abdullah came while you were gone. He gave us five thousand dollars."

"Whoa," Safiyah says. "I had no idea Imam Abdullah is so loaded."

"That's your takeaway from this?" Tiwa asks. "He's so generous! His livelihood has been affected by what happened to the Islamic Center and he's still giving us all this money to help with our Eid party."

"You're right, and we should honor his generosity by getting ramen and celebrating this big win!" Safiyah says. "There's that new ramen place on Rosehill Avenue, and I swear their food is to die for."

"Maybe another time," Tiwa says as she begins to pack up her things, still avoiding looking at me. "I have to tell my mom about this."

"We'll pack everything up. I'll call you later?" Safiyah says.

"Okay, thanks, Saf. Thanks, Said." She glances at me, but only for a moment. "See you both later."

With that, she walks away toward her car.

Safiyah turns to me with a knowing look.

"What?" I ask.

"What was that between you and Tiwa?"

"What was what?" I ask, though I have a sneaking suspicion I know what she's talking about.

"The hug?" Safiyah asks. "I don't think I've seen you two hug since you were kids."

I shrug. "We were just hugging because of the good news. A friendly hug."

"Hm, if you say so. That's not how *I* hug my friends, though," Safiyah says. She begins to pack everything up. And as I start helping her load everything back into the trunk of our car, I wonder if Safiyah actually has the right idea about us.

13

MURAL FETISH

Tiwa

THE THING ABOUT SUMMER HOLIDAYS IN THE OLATUNJI HOUSE-
hold is that there is no such thing as sleeping in.

"Tiwa!" I hear my mom call out from some faraway location
(probably the living room). At first I can't see anything. Laddoo
seems to be perched on top of my face. I move him off despite his
meows of protest and then I bury my head beneath my pillow, wanting to block out the early-morning sunlight and the noise. Not even
seconds later, she's calling for me again. "Tiwa!"

I peer out of my sheet cocoon, glancing at the time on the alarm
clock on my bedside table. It's only a few minutes past nine. Of course
Mom would deem this an appropriate time to be up. They should
really pass a law that during summer holidays the morning should be
stretched to at least noon.

Not sure that would stop her, though.

"I'm coming!" I yell before she has the chance to shout my name
again.

I drag myself out of bed, almost tripping over my weighted blan-
ket as I do.

When I finally make my way over to the living room/dining area, the smell of Nigerian-style eggs cooking immediately hits my nostrils and I suddenly don't feel all that tired.

Mom is standing over the stove, stirring the tomato egg mixture.

"Morning, Mom," I say with a yawn.

Mom glances at me. "I take it you slept late again," she says, not even as a question, just a statement.

I nod. "Was brainstorming ideas for the Eid party last night. Now that we have the money and everything, we need to start making orders and figuring out the logistics."

Mom smiles. "My hardworking girl. You need to start sleeping early. It's not good for you, especially doing it every night. But anyway, I called you because you have mail, two letters. I left them on the dining table," she says as she turns the stove off and starts shoveling the eggs onto two separate plates.

Mail? That's weird. I almost never get any mail.

I spot the two letters Mom was referring to, immediately recognizing the blue, red, and gray *LISA Firm* logo, aka the only firm I applied to for work experience for my college application, aka the firm that if I don't get a spot on their two-week summer internship, I might as well kiss prelaw goodbye.

"One of the letters is from LISA," I say to my mom as I scramble to open the letter.

"Who's LISA?" Mom questions in a muffled voice from the egg and agege bread she is now eating at the kitchen counter.

"Laura Ingrid Sutherland and Anderson? The all-women law firm I wanted to do my internship at this summer?" I say, hoping that jogs her memory.

I had told my mom about the internship a few times over the entirety of junior year, the first time when they did the presentation at our careers fair, the second time when I went on a tour of their offices, and the third time a few weeks ago when I applied for their summer internship.

"Oh yes, sorry, old age," Mom replies. "What does it say?"

"I don't know yet, I'm scared to look," I say, holding up the half-opened letter.

"Well, you'll never know until you do," Mom says. "And if you didn't get it, it won't be the end of the world. There'll always be other opportunities, inshallah."

She's right. Without an internship, my college applications might be less competitive than those with mountains of volunteer work and internships, but I could probably figure something out.

Figuring things out when everything blows up is kind of my speciality.

I close my eyes, pulling the letter out of the envelope. Then I slowly open them again.

There's a tense moment before I am screaming. "I got in! I got the internship," I shout.

Mom claps. "Mashallah! I knew you could do it," she says, muffled again by the food in her mouth. "When do you start?"

I scan the letter quickly. "The last two weeks in summer, so I have time."

I feel relief spread through me. That's one less thing to worry about.

I pick up the second letter, and this time there is no logo or address on the envelope. It's just plain and white with no sign of who

145

the sender could be. I open it up with my eyebrows scrunched, reading the first line.

Dear Ms. Tiwa Olatunji,
Your organizer badge for the Walker Center is
ready to collect from the town hall. You will need
to bring this on the day of your event as proof of
permission . . .

It's the permit collection letter for the Eid party at the Walker Center.

"What's that one about?" Mom asks.

I hold it up, showing her. "I have to collect the organizer badge for Walker," I say.

Mom nods. "I can go if you want? After work. You've already done so much with the fundraiser, I want to help," she says.

I shake my head. "It's fine, honestly. I actually need to drop off the petition anyway," I say.

It might also give me the chance to tell Mayor Williams about the fundraiser and mural. Surely if he can see how much support there is, he'll change his mind about the Islamic Center.

Then again, he did seem pretty set on his own plans last time . . . Maybe I do need backup.

Though I'm not sure taking my mom will make Williams see me seriously. I need to be strategic about it.

An idea comes into my mind suddenly. "I'll be right back," I say to my mom, before rushing back to my bedroom. I quickly take out my phone and I scroll to Safiyah's name on my contacts list.

It takes a few rings before Safiyah picks up.

"Do you know what time it is?" she asks, sounding groggy.

"Sorry for calling you so early. I know you don't usually wake up until eleven, but I need to ask for a weird-ish request."

"Go on, I'm awake now I guess," Safiyah replies, followed by a small yawn.

"Is Said awake?" I ask, though the question is more rhetorical than anything. The Said I used to know was always up at the crack of dawn for god knows what reason. At sleepovers, he'd always be up, usually drawing or praying fajr while he waited for everyone else to rise.

"Probably, why?" she asks.

I close my eyes. I can't believe I'm about to do this.

"Can I . . . have his phone number? I need to message him about something."

There is silence at first, followed by the sound of shuffling. I imagine Safiyah sitting up abruptly.

"Who are you and what have you done to my best friend?" she finally says, seemingly recovered from my strange request.

I roll my eyes. "I killed her, blended up her bones, and plan on drinking her remains with the rest of my alien buddies."

"Okay, wow, that's way too dark, Tee," Saf says. "But seriously, I am convinced you have been replaced by an imposter. Still, I'll give you all of my brother's personal details. What could go wrong?"

I laugh. "Thanks, Saf. I will make sure to share his Social Security number with the world."

I hear her tapping, before my phone pings with a message notification.

"There you go, my brother's number. Out of respect for your privacy I will not question why you are scheming with my brother, who I assumed was your sworn enemy, and instead enjoy my blissful ignorance."

I tap onto the highlighted number, adding it to my contacts list begrudgingly.

I've never actually had Said's phone number before, even back when we were still friends—mostly because I did not have a phone until after our friendship blew up.

"Don't worry, he's still my sworn enemy. This is just business," I respond.

"All right, if you say so . . ." Safiyah starts, cut off by some noise in the background. "Sadly, I think I have to go. My mom can hear me talking on the phone and wants me to come down and help her with some chores—this is the consequence of being up early. I will *not* be doing this again."

"Sorry, Saf," I say, feeling bad.

"No need to apologize. I'd wake up at sunrise for you, always."

I decide not to comment on the fact that Safiyah is usually still awake at sunrise due to her allergy to sleeping on time and instead focus on the sentiment behind her words.

I place my hand on my chest dramatically. "Thank you, Saf, that means a lot."

I hear her mom call for her again.

"I'll message you later, duty calls," she says as she finally hangs up.

I stare down at Said's number, hesitating for a heartbeat before taking a deep breath and tapping out my message.

Hey Said, it's Tiwa. Are you free in
an hour or so? I wanted to go to
the town hall to drop off the petition
and potentially get the sign-off on
the mural. I kind of need backup,
seeing as Mayor Williams is kind of
an asshole, and I think he'll be a lot
more open to it if the artist is there
too. Could you bring some samples
of your art as well?

Then I quickly add Okay if you can't! Will completely understand! not to sound as weird as I feel. Though that is probably un-
avoidable given the fact that I'm literally messaging him from an
unknown number.

To my surprise, the three dots indicating that he's typing pop up
almost immediately.

My heart pauses at the sound of my phone's ping as his message
response appears on the screen.

Sure, 10:30?

That was much easier than I thought it would be . . . too easy.

That works, see you then!!! I type out, then I backspace, deleting
all the exclamation points. I'm definitely not *that* excited and I don't
want Said to get the wrong impression, that I'm eager to see him or
something.

Which I'm definitely not. I'm neutral. Completely unfazed by his
presence.

I hit send, and as I'm about to pocket my phone and go back to the breakfast that awaits me, my phone is pinging again.

I'll bring my game face, how can
Mayor Willy say no to this

Below the message is a picture of Said with his messy dark hair and stony expression.

I can't help the smile that forces its way onto my face. I stare down at the picture and message so long, the screen goes dark and I'm confronted with my smiling face in the reflection.

I quickly make my mouth snap back into a line, ignoring the warmth I feel on my face.

Neutral. Totally neutral.

AN HOUR AND A BIT LATER I'M WALKING INTO THE TOWN HALL with Said, petition in hand, this time without my trusted lemon squares for protection.

I feel sweat gather on my brow as we sign in at the front desk. Donna is there as usual, clacking away on her keyboard.

"Mayor Williams will see you soon," Donna says with a tight smile, and I wonder if her stony tone is the result of a lack of bribes this time around.

Unlike before, I didn't need to convince Donna to let me have a last-minute meeting with the mayor. Permits have to be stamped by Williams anyway, so no lemon squares needed today.

I give her a smile, which she does not reciprocate, before taking a seat in the waiting area next to a very pale-looking Said.

"Are you okay? You look like you're about to be sick," I ask, hoping that he isn't actually going to be sick. I'm not sure Donna will be too pleased at having to clean that up, especially since I get sick when I see others get sick, which would just be doubly awful.

I shift away from Said a little.

"So. Many. Colors," he replies, looking around the bright walls of the waiting area, which match the bright walls of the building's exterior. "No wonder there are hardly any birds in New Crosshaven anymore. All the colors from the building probably scared them away." He glances down at my unbothered expression and then at my shirt and adds, "Or maybe it was your clothes that made them feel unwelcome," he mutters.

I look down with him at my shirt and the text written on it: *Ducks Suck.*

"Actually, I think your charming personality scared them away," I reply.

"What did the poor ducks ever do to you anyway?" he asks with a sly smile, ignoring my jibe at him.

The shirt isn't about actual ducks, it's just the name of a toy manufacturing company that I volunteered for hoping it would look good on my college applications. Not sure if UCLA would find *Ducks Suck Ltd* all that impressive from a prelaw applicant, though.

"The ducks simply suck and so I killed them," I say with a shrug.

"How illuminating, Miss Olatunji," the deep, familiar voice of Mayor Williams says from above.

We both look up and he is indeed right there, towering over us with a creepy plastic smile that is a jump scare to look at.

"Would you like to come inside? I'm hoping to have an early lunch," Williams says.

I nod, standing quickly and holding on tight to the petition papers. Said stands seconds later, looking like he's ready to be sick again.

"Good," Williams says, clapping his hands together. "Let's get this over and done with, shall we?"

A few minutes later, we are in his office once again, seated in front of his desk watching him stamp the permit for the Eid Party with careful precision.

I glance down at the petition, my heart in my throat as I go over all the things I want to say to him. All the rebuttals I prepared.

"Right, there we are. A signed and stamped organizer badge ready to use for your Eid party next week. Was there anything else you needed?" Mayor Williams asks.

I slide the petition forward, positioning it directly in front of me, before I look up and clear my throat.

"Yes . . . actually, there was something else," I start, and his eyebrows shoot up with interest.

"Go ahead," he says, mouth stretching into that creepy smile once again.

"Well, um, I wanted to submit this community petition in favor of rebuilding the Islamic Center," I begin, watching as the mayor's smile starts to falter. I try not to let his subtle change in expression deter me. After all, this is good practice for the future when I'm a lawyer and I have to defend my case to rooms filled with complete strangers. At least I know Mayor Williams.

I go on. "We got over one hundred signatures and we raised money through a bake sale that was originally intended to fund our Eid party, but as the amount we raised exceeded our expectations, we thought it could be used toward the rebuilding of the Islamic Center . . . I know you already said that you wouldn't be rebuilding, but you have to see that the community wants this. The Islamic Center isn't just a social community space for the Muslims of New Crosshaven, it's also where we pray, where we have Arabic classes, where we have henna parties. Without it, so many people are losing out on their jobs and their support systems."

Mayor Williams's face is now a line, his eyes blank and his expression unreadable.

Time to bring out the big guns.

I turn to Said, who looks a little rigid as he observes the tense exchange.

"I even brought Said here to tell you about the mural he has planned," I say, nudging Said, who jolts forward a little.

He sits upright and nods. "Yeah, uh, I have this mural I'm planning that represents Islam and the community, and I've brought a few early sketches I've been brainstor—" Before Said can finish, Mayor Williams is interrupting.

"That all sounds wonderful and extremely . . . well thought-out. I appreciate the enthusiasm you both have for the town and its occupants. I'll look over the petition, but unfortunately I don't see our plans changing. Either way, I hope that the Eid party will show the great resources and facilities we already have in the fully functional Walker Center," he finishes, smiling again now that he has crushed more of my hope, and then he adds, "Is that all?"

I nod numbly, feeling my resolve wither away bit by bit the more I stay here.

"Great, you can hand that petition over to me and I'll review it and let you know," he says, giving me one final patronizing smile.

What he really means is, *I have already made my mind up about this and you have wasted your time.*

Once we're out of the town hall building again, Said finally speaks.

"Well, that was a shit show," he says.

"Tell me about it," I reply quietly as we walk on, feeling my eyelids grow heavy with each step.

"I guess we'll see what happens when the mayor reviews the petition, and I'll keep working on sketches for the mural in the meantime just in case. I just know that tonight I'm having some nightmares about Mayor Willy. He looks like one of those *LazyTown* puppets."

If I was in a different mood, I might have laughed at that. Especially seeing as Said's description is scarily accurate. But I can't think of anything but the fact that it seems like the Islamic Center might be doomed after all, and in turn Eid, as we've known it, might be doomed too.

Sure, we could still have small Eid parties in our houses, or even in the Walker Center. But we can't fundraise every year, nor can we expect that the Muslim community of New Crosshaven would want to use Walker, when it isn't equipped for large group prayers and events. Everyone will probably just revert back to celebrating Eid in small clusters.

There will be no more getting together, breaking fasts together for the last time during Eid al-Fitr. No more Arabic sessions. No more community.

And with everything at home, I'm sure that soon the tradition of Dad coming for the Eids twice a year will end too.

When there is no big party with all the community and he has to choose between being alone with Mom or just staying in London, I'm scared he'll choose London—cracking open our family even more. And the crack will eventually turn into a permanent and unsalvageable break.

I don't realize I'm crying until I feel a gust of wind blow on my face, making my skin tighten and the wetness from the tears dry uncomfortably.

"Hey . . . Tiwa, we should sit somewhere, take a breather," Said says, watching me—more specifically, my face. He looks sorry for me and I hate it.

I don't want his pity.

I quickly wipe away the tears, feeling embarrassed that he saw me like this in the first place. I need to pull myself together.

"Yeah, sure," I say, my voice higher than usual, betraying the lies my new expression tells.

"How about the park? We can sit there, catch our breaths . . . talk about our next steps. I think we can figure out exactly what we're doing with the mural. As you can tell, Mayor Willy clearly has a mural fetish, and so we can figure out what makes him tick and implement that," he says, looking over at the small park area across the street from the town hall. It's also littered with bright, blinding murals all around.

"That's actually, like, a very good plan," I say, trying not to sound too impressed. Mostly because I don't want Said to think I rate him highly. He is right about more than just one thing; the mayor does have a mural fetish.

"Of course it is. I'm not just a pretty face to look at, I'm smart too," he says, nudging me as we walk down the street and through the park gates.

I roll my eyes, following him closely behind.

He climbs on top of the balancing bar and walks across it as I go over to the dark blue seesaw at the back where I can sit properly and wallow.

I think about how the mural is all we have left. Are we being too optimistic about the fact that a mural could save our community from extinction caused by the asteroid that is Mayor Williams?

Perhaps we are. Perhaps this is all just pointless.

I feel Said's eyes on me, and I look up. He looks away like I caught him once again.

I watch him jump off the balancing bar and walk over to the seesaw, moving to the other end of the contraption.

"Wallowing?" he asks.

I nod. "Something like that."

"It sucks, but I think it isn't the end. Not yet anyway. We just need a good mural. I've been thinking of different directions to go in. One idea I had was to take a painting by a classic artist and do some kind of Islamic twist on it. I thought it could be cool—I'll make it colorful enough to suit Willy's tastes . . . but also subtle and introspective enough to draw the attention of everyone else."

I stare at him as he talks animatedly about his idea. His face lights up in a way it only ever does when he discusses his art.

It's really nice.

"That would be amazing," I say, thinking about the logistics of it all. "Where would you paint it?"

"I was thinking directly on the Islamic Center grounds, like on the stone in front of the center. So that people would see it when they go by."

"That's actually . . . really smart," I say, still watching his face light up after every word.

He smiles sheepishly, a mischievous glint in his eye. "As I said, I'm handsome *and* smart."

Before I can say anything about that statement, he's sitting on the raised end of the seesaw, and I feel my seat suddenly shift up, almost flinging me into the air.

"Said!" I shout, and he's laughing, like almost catapulting me into space is a funny thing.

"What? I didn't do anything," he says, before doing it again.

I narrow my eyes at him. "Sleep with one eye closed, Hossain," I say, trying to steady myself on the seesaw.

"You mean sleep with one eye open?" he asks.

"Shut up, you know what I mean."

This makes his annoying smile grow even wider. I take this opportunity to plant my feet on the ground, watching his side go up. Before he can catch onto my plan, I quickly jump on the seat again. When he realizes what's happening, Said's eyes fly open and his expression falls, but it's too late. I watch as he falls back and stumbles off the seesaw.

I smile triumphantly. This might not be the victory I was hoping for today, but at least it's a victory.

14

WHEN HELL FREEZES OVER

Said

"I think it's inhumane to be given homework over the summer holidays," Julian complains for the umpteenth time since we got on our video call together. I place the laptop at the end of my bed, beside the pile of homework, my personal essay, and my sketchbook, and adjust my position so I'm actually comfortable.

"Isn't that why we go to St. Francis? To be given inhumane amounts of work that'll eventually help us excel in life?" I ask.

"You sound just like Mr. Thomas when he gives us a million essays to write over every single break," Julian grumbles. But he and I both know that we wouldn't still be at St. Francis if we weren't used to the truckload of work the teachers heap on us at every single opportunity.

I go back to my personal essay for New York School of Animation once Julian's complaining subsides. Despite poring over it for the past hour, I barely have a paragraph written. And even that paragraph doesn't seem up to scratch.

Why My Art Is Meaningful. I stare at the title again, hoping that the words will jump out of me if I look for long enough. But all I have are the most basic ideas, which I know a million other applicants will probably write, about how I started drawing when I was very young and it's always been one of my passions.

"All right, algebra done. Take that, Mr. Dodgson!" Julian says. I glance up from my half-empty page to stare at the grinning Julian on my screen. "Compare answers?"

"You mean, you steal all my correct answers?" I ask. That's usually the way it is when Julian and I do homework together. I help him out with math and he helps me with essays in language arts classes.

"No." Julian scoffs. "Show me, though."

"I've . . . actually been working on my college application," I admit. Julian raises an eyebrow at that. "Your art piece?"

"No, the essay. I know it's not due for a while, but I thought I'd get a head start with it."

Julian shakes his head in mock disapproval. "What will Mr. Dodgson say when his favorite student shows up to school with no algebra homework done?"

"I'll do it, just . . . later," I say. "I guess you'll just have to wait to get the correct answers."

"Or maybe since you're slacking off working on essays, I've become a super genius in math, and I'll be Mr. Dodgson's favorite student," Julian says with a grin.

"Yeah, when hell freezes over," I mutter. It's not that Mr. Dodgson dislikes Julian, it's that his need to make inappropriate Pokémon references whenever he gets the chance gets under our teacher's skin like nothing else. And the more it gets under his skin, the more Julian does it. It's a charming dynamic, really.

"Might be sooner than you think with climate change and all," Julian says. He puts away his algebra work and picks up his physics textbook with a heavy sigh. "Can't believe you're abandoning me to do algebra and physics all on my own."

"You'll get over it, I'm sure," I say, rolling my eyes at his dramatics. Julian picks up his pen and notebook and his eyebrows scrunch as he looks over the problems he has to solve and I go back to staring at my essay.

I pick up the pen, and instead of adding more words to the page, I find myself sketching out one of the mural ideas I had been dreaming up since my conversation with Tiwa yesterday.

To turn a classic art piece into something new and relevant to the Islamic Center.

At first, I try to copy Picasso's cubism style and apply it to my memory of the Islamic Center, but something about it isn't working. I scan my desk for a pencil, and instead my eyes land on the rickshaw figurine Ammu got me one year from Bangladesh. I pick it up, thumbing the wheels of the miniature vehicle as I think. I notice the vibrant patterns dotted around the rickshaw, with birds and peacock feathers on all sides and Bengali words written on the roof.

I pause, another idea forming in my mind.

I sketch quickly, emulating the style of the rickshaw exterior, getting lost in the process, watching as all the parts of the Islamic Center begin to overlap each other in a mess of different shades and shapes.

Underneath the sketch, I write a paragraph about the Islamic Center and my mural. Suddenly, the words begin pouring out of me. I write about New Crosshaven and how much it means to me, and how much the Islamic Center means to the entire community. I write so fast that my handwriting is barely legible. It's like my hand can't catch up to how fast my brain is working.

And I don't stop when I get to the end of my thought process. My hands go over to the other side of the page and begin on a new sketch. It's almost like my brain is on overdrive.

My pen moves quickly over the page, sketching out a reimagining of Henri Matisse's *Open Window, Collioure* where the view from the window overlooks the Islamic Center and some of the people from the community attending maghrib prayer. I can envision the mural already, with soft colors that portray dawn. By the edge of the mosque I draw a tree, filled with bright red apples ready to be picked. And I can't help but think about Tiwa. I wonder what she'll think about these sketches.

"Earth to Said!" Julian's loud voice interrupts my train of thought. My pen hovers over the unfinished shading of the sketch, but I glance up.

"Sorry," I mumble. I had gotten so caught up in drawing, I must not have heard him calling me.

"I thought you were working on your essay. I don't think they'll accept doodles as a form of essay, even if you are applying to art school," Julian says.

"I just got . . . distracted," I say.

"Clearly . . . What exactly are you drawing that it's got you smiling like that?" Julian asks with narrowed eyes.

I didn't even realize I was smiling, but I quickly wipe the smile off my face. I guess it was the apple trees, and the mural and . . . Tiwa.

"Nothing," I say. "Just thinking about art school . . . I guess. I'm working on this mural for my application. It was Tiwa's idea, actually, so we're kind of working together to come up with the mural idea and then I'm going to paint it. I think the New York School of Animation will be really into it."

Julian doesn't say anything for a moment, just stares at me with his lips pursed.

"Tiwa, as in . . . the coldhearted traitor?" Julian asks.

I'd almost forgotten that in my early days at St. Francis, I'd vented to Julian about Tiwa. About the unreturned letters and phone calls.

"She's not coldhearted. Or a traitor. And she's helping me." I shrug.

"Sorry, I just thought you didn't like her. You're always telling me about how she's the reason why you don't go back to New Crosshaven as much anymore," Julian says. "And didn't you say you were dreading seeing her this summer?"

"I was . . . but things have changed," I say. After all, that was before Ms. Barnes died, before the Islamic Center burned down. Before Tiwa and I began to work on the petition and mural together. "Besides, she's Safiyah's best friend. I can't exactly avoid her. They're always hanging out together."

The mention of Safiyah seems to wipe Tiwa completely from Julian's brain. He sits up straight with a strange smile and says, "What's Safiyah up to this summer, then? Do you think she'll be around when I come over?"

I sigh. "Julian, Safiyah's still not into you. You know that, right?"

"Obviously, I know she's into girls!" Julian says defensively. "I'm an *ally*."

"Right," I say dryly, because Julian being an ally has done little to tamper down his crush on Safiyah.

"Let's see what you've been working on for this mural of yours," Julian says, changing the subject.

I glance down at the sketches. I'd been so proud of them only a moment ago, but now I see all their mistakes. The proportions of the mosques are all wrong. The shading is off. There are definitely way too many apples in that apple tree. Instead of showing Julian, I cross out the drawing with my pen.

"I'll have to start fresh, it's not very good," I say.

"Isn't it just supposed to be a sketch?"

"Yeah, but it should be a good one," I say. Especially if I'm going to share it with Tiwa, but I don't say that out loud.

"You are way too self-critical. Probably why they're going to love you at that art school," Julian says.

"I'll have to get in first," I say, flipping over to a fresh page in my notebook.

"I mean, isn't New Crosshaven full of artists or something? Maybe you can find like . . . a mentor or something to look over your application. They'll probably only say good things," Julian says.

"I don't need a mentor. Mr. Robinson is already going to look over everything," I say. But Julian isn't wrong. New Crosshaven is pretty artistic. It is the town of murals, after all. And maybe I can find inspiration for my own mural from the town.

"Let's just get back to work," I say. But in my head, I'm already getting ready for tomorrow. It'll be my research trip around New Crosshaven.

15
SMELL THE ROSES
Said

AMMU AND ABBU ARE BUSY WITH THEIR MORNING ROUTINE WHEN I come downstairs the next morning. Abbu is putting away his lunch for work and sipping on his mug of tea, while Ammu sits at the dining table with a book propped up in front of her.

"Said!" Abbu says when he sees me. "Where are you off to so early in the morning?"

"I was going to go around town. I wanted to have a look at some of the murals," I say. I already have my backpack ready with my sketch-book and pencils.

Ammu puts down her book and glances at me with a smile. Her morning routine always consists of praying fajr, having breakfast and tea, and then sitting down to read at least a chapter of her current book. I feel bad for disrupting it.

"Mayor Williams commissioned a beautiful mural on the corner of Somerset Drive and Adelaide Street," she says, and Abbu nods in agreement.

"We went for a walk one evening and stopped by to see the artist working on it. He wasn't up for chatting too much, though," Abbu adds.

I wonder what exactly Abbu even had to say to him. It's not that

Abbu and Ammu hate the arts. They've always been able to appreciate them. They're Bangladeshi after all, and Bangladeshi people's love of language and literature transcends almost anything else. But they've also always been practical, and there's nothing practical about pursuing art. At least, to them.

"I'll definitely go by there," I say. "I'm also going to swing by to pick up Laddoo from Tiwa's place after, so I might not be home until late."

Ammu's eyes light up at that. "Oh, good! You know, the house just isn't the same without Laddoo." I don't remind her that Laddoo is hardly a staple in our home, considering we only got him from Clara last week.

"Do you want me to drop you off?" Abbu asks as he picks up his keys from the bowl in the kitchen. "I'm going the other way but I don't mind."

These days, any conversation between Abbu and me seems to inevitably land on college applications, and that's not on my list of topics to discuss. So I just shake my head.

"It'll be better if I walk. I wanted to see, you know, how the town's changed and everything."

"Smell the roses . . ." Abbu smiles. "Good. Enjoy it, but not too much. You still have a lot of work to do this summer." With that, he slips out the front door.

I'm about to follow behind but Ammu's voice stops me in my tracks.

"Said, you don't mind dropping something off for me, right?" she asks it like it's a yes or no question, but she's already up from the dining table and getting out a box from the fridge so I know I have no say in the matter.

"Sure, I don't mind."

"Oh, good. It's just, remember your Anjana auntie?"

"Um—"

Ammu doesn't wait for me to respond before continuing on. "Well, she is painting a mural right by Almond Garden. It's supposed to help represent the South Asian community in the area, and I thought it would be nice to show our support by bringing her some food. I was going to give her these during our Arabic class today, but the Walker Center was booked up and I couldn't get a room, and we didn't have anywhere else for the classes." She holds out a box filled with a variety of mishtis. She was hard at work making the shondesh, kalojam, and laddoos yesterday. Ammu is known for her mishtis in this town, so it feels like she's forever making them to distribute to everyone.

"Sure, I can stop by. I didn't know, uh, Anjana Auntie was an artist," I say.

"I mean her *real* job is being a dental hygienist at Pearls Dental Clinic, but she does some art when she has time. It was actually the dental surgeon at the clinic who saw her sketchbook lying around and suggested she should do a mural in town," Ammu says. She's beaming with pride, but I know that if Anjana Auntie's *only* job was being an artist she wouldn't be.

I take the box of mishtis from Ammu and stuff it into my backpack beside my sketchbook. "Okay, I guess I'll—"

"And can you stop by the grocery store? We need some milk, bread, eggs . . ." Ammu pauses, opening up the fridge to peruse. "And cucumbers."

"Okay, mishti for Anjana Auntie. Milk, bread, eggs, and cucumbers for us. Will do. Bye, Ammu." With that, I slip out of the kitchen and open the front door, hurrying outside before Ammu can add any more errands to my list.

Despite all my time away, New Crosshaven never seems to change much. Other than the murals popping up at different parks and intersections, there's little else that's new around town. The shops on High Street are the same as always: local boutiques, florists, grocery shops, cafés. And of course, Abigail's and the dessert-themed murals on its walls that have been there my entire life. What's changed is that I don't quite recognize the smiling faces inside the shops anymore, when once Tiwa, Safiyah, and I used to be regulars around here.

I try to swallow down the weirdness that settles in my stomach at the thought of everything that's different, and everything that isn't, and instead search for the murals around the high street. I spot a familiar one inside an alley between the butcher's and a pizzeria. It's a cluster of bright yellow sunflowers against a faded blue backdrop, each of them bent into different shapes, almost like they're trying to listen to one another speak.

I take out my sketchbook and flip it to a fresh page. Leaning against the wall on the other side, I make a quick sketch of the mural, making notes along the edge of the page as I go. Once I'm done, I slip my phone out of my pocket and take a picture of the sunflowers.

My fingers hover over my phone for a minute as I consider my next move. It feels a little weird to be sending Tiwa photos of this, and to share my ideas with her. It's been so long since anyone has had a part in my artistic process. Usually, art is something I do on my own and then, maybe, I share it with someone. Telling Tiwa my ideas before they're even fully hatched feels vulnerable somehow.

But it's not like I can really do this mural without Tiwa's help, so I send off the picture and type a quick text to follow it up:

maybe the mural could be some
kind of an islamic representation of
Van Gogh's painting?

Tiwa's response comes surprisingly fast: yes! how would you make it Islamic though?

still thinking . . . more murals to see, I type back.

send updates, Tiwa replies.

I pocket my phone, trying to tamp down my grin as I head off in search of the next mural. I guess my day around town will be a little less lonely than I had originally thought.

AFTER A DOZEN MURALS, A QUARTER OF MY SKETCHBOOK PAGES filled, and a lot of texts exchanged, I finally make my way to Almond Garden to deliver Ammu's box of mishtis. Anyone not from New Crosshaven might think Almond Garden should be filled with almond trees, but in reality, it's a small park with a flower garden in the middle that used to be owned by a man called John Almond many years ago. There isn't a single almond tree inside its wrought-iron gates.

The park is buzzing with people when I enter. There's a few kids trying to climb an oak tree in the distance, and a group of women in sundresses having a picnic by the flower gardens. Finally, I spot the woman who must be Anjana Auntie on the other side of the park. She's carefully assessing a half-finished mural on the walled fence, while another auntie is lying on a lounge chair beside her. I approach them slowly, not sure exactly what to expect. Even though Ammu acted like Anjana Auntie was someone I should know, nothing about her seems familiar.

"Um, excuse me, Anjana Auntie?" I ask.

Anjana Auntie turns around, squinting at me as if looking for some sign of familiarity. She must find it, because her eyes light up.

"Said! Your mom had said you were back for the summer," Anjana Auntie says. The woman on the lounge chair glances at me too, taking off her sunglasses and looking me over inquisitively.

"As-salaam-alaikum," she says.

"Wa-alaikum-salaam," I return. "Um, my mom sent some sweets. For support as you worked on your mural." I dig out the box from my backpack, offering it to Anjana Auntie. She takes it from my hand and looks over to the other auntie.

"This is Said, Nabiha bhabi's son," Anjana Auntie says. "This is your Noor auntie. She moved to New Crosshaven just last year."

"So . . . these are mishtis Nabiha bhabi made?" Suddenly Noor Auntie is all about the box in Anjana Auntie's hands and nothing else.

"Do you really think you deserve the mithai when you've just been sitting here sunbathing while I'm doing all the hard work?" Anjana Auntie asks with a raised eyebrow.

I look over at Noor Auntie. She's wearing a full-sleeved red polka-dot maxi dress with a matching red hijab. Not exactly a sunbathing outfit.

"I'm here for moral support, Anjana," Noor Auntie says. "Now come on, you have to share."

Anjana Auntie rolls her eyes but hands the box over. Noor Auntie immediately opens it up, taking out a kalojam and biting into it.

"Said, tell me . . . what do you think of the mural so far?" Anjana

Auntie asks. I turn to properly take in the mural. It's only just beginning to take shape. There are letters from different South Asian alphabets: Bengali, Hindi, Urdu, Gujarati, Tamil, Malayalam, Nepali . . . Each of them is filled with different things. The Bengali letter is green and red with a royal Bengal tiger peeking out of it.

"Wow . . ." I say. "Ammu said you were doing something that was supposed to represent South Asian cultures, but I didn't even know what that might look like. This is amazing."

"Ah, thank you, Said," Anjana Auntie says, waving off my compliment like it's not a big deal. "At least Noor is helping me with the Bengali, when she's not too busy sunbathing and eating all of your mom's mithai. And I'm getting some help from the community for the other alphabets too. There are still a few more to add, but I'm trying to hurry up and get a good portion done before it rains."

I glance up at the clear blue sky and the sun beating down on us. It's a perfect summer day.

"I don't think it's supposed to rain today," I say.

Anjana Auntie smiles. "Trust me, I can sense it and it's going to rain soon. So I better get to it." She picks up her paintbrushes from the ground before turning to me once more. "Tell your mom Noor and I both said thank you for the mithai, and that she's welcome to come and see the mural anytime."

I nod. "I will. I think she'll really love it."

I raise my hand to wave goodbye, turning to leave and then stopping in my tracks when a thought comes to me. "Actually, Anjana Auntie, is it okay if I asked a question about your art?" I ask.

She nods, but continues painting on the fence. "Of course, ask away."

"I've been curious on how exactly you go about planning a mural . . . it seems like a lot of work goes into it."

Anjana Auntie turns to me now, her eyebrow raised. "Are you an artist as well?"

She's looking at me like she can read all my thoughts—it's scary.

"Yes, kind of."

Kind of meaning: It's all I do in my free time.

She nods. "Well, it's actually not as difficult as it looks. I always sketch out the design first and then I find the right paints for it and then I just let go and do it. Honestly, I don't think it's something you should overthink. I won't lie: I was nervous about having to finish this huge mural before the festival starts at the end of the summer, but I always remind myself that murals aren't meant to be perfect."

I've missed the mural festival for the last few years because of school, but it has always been one of my favorite times of year. I remember when I was younger, how the town would fill up with tourists from all over the country, and it would always feel eerily quiet when they left. Kind of like now.

"Thanks, Auntie, I'll keep that in mind," I say. "It's really cool seeing you do this—art, I mean. There aren't a lot of South Asian artists around."

She smiles. "There's more of us than you think. We even have a group for Vermont-based South Asian artists. We try to meet up a couple of times a year to paint and complain about the state of the industry together, if you ever want to join? It's a lot of fun, and there's usually enough biryani for everyone."

I'd never even met another South Asian artist before now. I can't imagine a whole group of them in my state.

"That sounds amazing. I'd love to join sometime," I say, smiling back at her.

"Great! We're going to be unveiling this mural during the festival at the end of the summer. Maybe you can show me your art then and I can give you details about the next meetup."

I nod, feeling a renewed sense of hope. "Thanks, Anjana Auntie," I say.

I wave goodbye to both Anjana and Noor Auntie, and head back toward the front gate of the park. There, I pause for a moment, watching Anjana Auntie at work. Her eyes flick quickly from the sketchbook on the ground where she must have the full mural drawn out and the wall where she's working. Her paint strokes are confident and bold.

As I watch, I can't help but wonder about my parents. If Ammu and Abbu can support Anjana Auntie in her art, maybe somehow I can get them to come around to me too.

ANJANA AUNTIE MUST BE A WITCH BECAUSE WHEN I'M HALFWAY to Tiwa's apartment, it begins to rain. There's no place to take shelter, so I make a run for it, trying to ignore the freezing rainwater soaking through my clothes as I do.

I stumble up the steps to the front door, which is, thankfully, sheltered from the rain, and ring the doorbell.

It's Auntie who answers. "Hello?" she asks.

"Hi, Auntie. It's Said? I've just come to pick up Laddoo," I say through my chattering teeth.

"Oh, you didn't have to come here all the way in the rain. We could have dropped him off," she says. "Come on up."

The buzzer goes off to indicate that the front door has been opened. I hesitate for a moment. I had expected that Tiwa would just hand me Laddoo and I would be off. Pulling open the door, I step inside and climb up the stairs to Tiwa's apartment.

Auntie throws the door open almost as soon as I arrive at the doorstep, like she was waiting to welcome me in.

"Said, you're soaking wet!" she exclaims as soon as she lays eyes on me. "Come inside, sit down. I'll get you a towel to dry off."

"No, Auntie, it's okay, I can dry off when I get home."

"If I let you go home in this state, your mom will never have me over for dinner again. And I wouldn't even blame her," she says. "Come inside."

It doesn't seem like I have much of a choice, so I step inside as Auntie closes the door.

"I'll get Tiwa, and a towel for you. You sit!" With that, she slips from the room and out of sight.

I sit down in one of the chairs by the dining table, setting down the groceries and looking around Tiwa's kitchen, taking everything in. This apartment is so different from the house across the street where she used to live. The kitchen is half the size to start with, and from the fact that I can hear Auntie and Tiwa moving around and speaking through the walls, it seems that this entire apartment could probably fit into the sitting room of their old house.

I get up from my chair, looking at the wall of the sitting room decorated with picture frames. They're mostly pictures of Tiwa and her mom, with a few photos of Timi. I linger a little on the last few photos of him, feeling an emptiness settle inside. I force my eyes away, looking at the other pictures: of birthdays, Eids, Tiwa's middle school

graduation, junior prom. Beside the pictures there's a framed cer-
tificate for Tiwa to commend her for volunteer work at the Islamic
Center. All these framed milestones that I've missed. Milestones that
Tiwa's missed in my life too. It's weird to think about.

"What are you doing?" I turn around to find Tiwa with Laddoo
in her arms.

"I was just looking at your, um, Islamic Center volunteer certificate," I say quickly, feeling my face flush. Tiwa glances down at the
certificate, like she'd forgotten that it was there, and back up at me
with a raised eyebrow. "Were you snooping?"

"No, of course not!" I say. "I was just zoning out, I wasn't looking
at anything."

"But you just said you were looking at my volunteer certificate?"
Tiwa asks, cocking her head to the side.

"Yes . . . when I stopped zoning out, I noticed your volunteer certificate and . . . took note of the fact that you . . . volunteered," I say,
trying to ignore the fact that I've used the word *volunteer* enough
times in the past minute for it to be considered weird.

Tiwa breaks out into a small smile. "I was just joking, you can
look at my volunteer certificate as much as you want. It's a pretty
great achievement. They don't hand those out to just anyone." Tiwa
glances down before adding, "You know you're dripping water on the
carpet, right?"

I look down at the purple carpet and the water droplets staining it
dark around me. "Sorry, it was raining outside and your mom said to
come in and sit down, and . . ." I'm rambling and I can't stop for some
reason. "I'll just take Laddoo."

Tiwa moves toward me, holding out Laddoo. But instead of

174

jumping into my arms, he burrows into Tiwa's shoulders, like the last thing he wants is anything to do with me.

"Less than a week with you and you've already conditioned him to hate me," I say.

Tiwa rolls her eyes. "He's just hydrophobic."

"I don't think so. Pretty sure he loves Safiyah."

"Hilarious." Tiwa deadpans. "If you want Laddoo, you're going to have to dry off. I think Mom's trying to find you some fresh towels."

As if she heard Tiwa mention her, Auntie appears through the doorway with a stack of towels so tall that it almost obscures her head from view. "I was trying to find you a change of clothes but I don't think we've got anything in your size, Said," she says as she sets down the stack of towels on the dining table.

"That's okay, Auntie. I'll change once I get home. It's not . . ." The words *it's not that far* are almost at the tip of my tongue, but it's a twenty-minute walk at least. I'm used to just crossing the street from Tiwa's back to my house.

"It's not a big deal," I finish off, trying to ignore the growing weirdness in my gut. I shuffle toward the kitchen and grab the towel at the top of the stack, using it to dry off in the best way I can. It doesn't do much for the T-shirt and jeans sticking to me like a second skin, but at least I'm not ruining the Olatunjis' carpet anymore.

"Thanks for sending me all those sketches and pictures today," Tiwa says as I finish drying off. "It was kind of like taking a virtual tour of the town, through its murals."

"I think I have some ideas of what we can do for our mural. If you wanted, you could come over and take a look at them tomorrow."

Tiwa blinks at me for a moment, before nodding. "Sure, I could do that."

I nod too, and reach out for Laddoo. This time, he jumps into my arms with no hesitation. I grab my groceries in one hand and carry Laddoo in the other, ready for my walk back home.

"Don't let him run off," Tiwa says, eyeing my precarious balancing act suspiciously.

"I won't. It's not my first time with the cat, you know," I say.

"He has a tendency to slip away without you even noticing," Tiwa says.

"You didn't lose him, did you?" I ask, raising an eyebrow.

"No, of course—"

"He only slipped into our downstairs neighbors' apartment for an afternoon. We found him taking a nap on the balcony. It gets a lot of sun," Auntie cuts in. Tiwa shoots her an annoyed look, and I grin.

"Don't worry, Auntie, I've got a good grip. There's no way he's slipping away from me."

She nods and says, "Give salam to your parents for me, and you'll definitely have to stay for longer next time. Inshallah we'll see more of you from now on."

I can't help but glance at Tiwa, who is looking at her mom.

"Er, yes, inshallah," I say.

If only Auntie knew the reason why we don't see much of each other anymore.

16

I'D DIE WITHOUT YOU

Tiwa

I'VE BEEN FACE-TO-FACE WITH A GIANT SPIDER WEARING A HAT and a wide menacing grin for the past few minutes, and it's more than a little disturbing.

"Is it that bad?" Said asks, watching me silently flip through his sketches for the mural.

I look up at him. "No, no, these are great, it's just . . ." I hold the sketch of the strange spider up higher, squinting at it. "Why does the spider have a top hat and a creepy smile? Is he Willy Wonka or something? And why a spider?"

Said's eyebrows scrunch up together. "Firstly, Mrs. Debbie Downer, the smile isn't creepy—it's just what smiles tend to look like on regular people," he starts, then moves closer to me, pointing at the hat. "And the hat, that's a tupi. I thought it would be nice, you know, since it's a reference to how the spiders protected Prophet Mohammed."

"Oh," I say, not expecting him to say that. I'd forgotten that story. "That is a nice idea. I mean other than the smile, it's a really neat drawing, impressive." I take in the amount of detail in the sketches.

Said had told me that he'd rushed them all, and they weren't quite where he'd want them to be before he started finalizing the final mural sketch. And yet, these look like illustrations that belong in some edgy New York art museum.

Said smiles a little at the compliment and I feel my insides betray me, fluttering at his change in expression.

It seems I can't help liking his smile. Everyone has their weaknesses, I guess, and Said's smile is mine.

"Thanks, I just remembered when I was young and my mom never let us kill spiders because of it. I wanted to incorporate it in somehow, along with the acacia tree from the same story. I've also been doing a lot of research into traditional folk art from Bangladesh and stumbled across this amazing artist Abdus Shakoor Shah and tried to incorporate his style into the pieces, I'm not sure how they all fit . . ." His voice trails off and his expression morphs into his thinking face.

I look back down at the sketches, thinking too. I flip to the next, which is of the tree, then the next, of a young boy stargazing. Each piece seems like it is unfinished, which is to be expected since they are only initial sketches, but it feels almost like each sketch is an unconnected puzzle piece.

Suddenly, I get an idea, and my eyes widen.

"Oh my god, Said!" I say, turning back to him.

"Yeah?" he responds, looking and sounding a little alarmed.

"How precious would you say these sketches are to you, and do you mind if I lay them out on the ground?" I ask him.

He nods slowly. "Not that precious, go ahead."

I don't waste a moment, quickly starting to place each sketch on the floor, side by side. The air from the ceiling fan ruffles the pages, so Said starts to pin them down as I spread them about. Before I know it, his living room floor is covered in his sketches.

"There, perfect," I say.

Said still looks confused. "What exactly am I meant to be looking at?"

I stare at him. "The mural. All these elements represent some cool facet of the community, and together they work so much better, see?"

Said scans the ground slowly, and then nods along. "You might have a point. I didn't think of that."

"Of course. I'm smarter than you, so it makes sense," I say as his eyes narrow at me.

"You're smarter than me? Maybe in your dreams, Tee," he says.

I fold my arms. "Sadly, I don't dream of you, so definitely *not* in my dreams."

He raises an eyebrow and smiles. "You're sad you don't dream of me?" he questions.

"You know that's not what I meant," I say, holding back a small smile.

He shrugs. "Do I, Tee, do I?" he says in a playful tone as he steps closer.

I try to give him my most unimpressed expression and he only responds with a smug look. We continue staring at each other for a few moments unblinking, and I fear that I inadvertently got myself into some staring contest.

Said finally blinks and I finally smile, triumphant.

I turn back to the collage of sketches on the floor. "I feel like there's something missing . . ." My eyes roam over the sketches again. "What happened to the sunflowers sketch you showed me yesterday?"

"I think it's upstairs. I wasn't feeling it anymore," he says.

"Where upstairs?" I ask.

"My bedroom, probably in the trash or in my desk drawer, I don't know."

"Okay, you continue pinning the pages, I'm going to go up and search for it. I think I have an idea . . ."

"Oh no, not more of your genius," he says.

"Oh yes, more of my genius. I honestly don't know what you'd do without me," I say as I start to maneuver myself around the sketches.

There's a pause and then he says, "I'm pretty sure I'd die without you, Tiwa."

Even though it's most definitely a joke, I feel that fluttering inside again. Apparently my brain can't tell the difference between heartfelt and comical.

"Boarding school must have been hard for you, then!" I say without thinking, pausing after saying it. Regret builds. I close my eyes, cursing under my breath.

Before I can try to save myself, Said is speaking. "It was. I kept thinking, *What will I do without Tiwa*, and then I just died. This is my ghost form speaking to you right now."

I turn back to him, and I play off my sudden panic with an eye roll. Only he's staring at me with a strange, unreadable expression.

Like maybe none of that was comical after all.

"I'll be right back," I say quickly, forcing a smile as I climb up and away from the weirdness downstairs.

Said's bedroom is on the right-hand side of the upstairs hallway, only a few steps away from Safiyah's room.

Even though Said knows I'm here, I still feel weird opening his bedroom door and waltzing in. It feels like a violation. Even more so when I slip in and accidentally trip over a potted plant that has been inconveniently situated right next to the door.

Luckily the pot only wobbles a little and the plant stays intact.

I flip the light switch on and the whole room comes into view. The familiar blue-and-white walls, the same posters of Studio Ghibli movies plastered around—his biggest poster obviously being one of *Howl's Moving Castle*. He even has the same race-car bed frame on his desk, and the same rickshaw figurine he's had for years on his desk. The only thing that has changed seems to be his bedsheets. They used to exclusively be *Thomas the Tank Engine* themed, but now they are a more mature and refined navy color.

It's like this room is frozen in time, which makes sense seeing as it basically is.

I stop analyzing his decor and I go over to the trash basket in the corner, which is practically empty. No sign of the sketch there at all.

I move on to his walnut-colored desk in the corner of his room, piled with textbooks and pens. On the cork board in front of the desk he has random sketches he's pinned up and next to those, random photos. Some I can tell are from school, seeing as I don't recognize the people in them but also in some he wears that obnoxious uniform of his.

One boy seems to pop up in most of the pictures: a brown-skinned guy with curly hair and a wide smile. In one picture he's even kissing Said on the forehead, and Said is smiling wide too.

I'm guessing *this* is his new best friend. Or at least his closest friend at St. Francis.

I try not to feel a type of way about it, even though it's hard to look at and internalize the fact that people move on, outgrow you, while you seem to stay the same.

It's not something I'd ever admit to Said. But I sometimes wonder if part of the reason I disliked him so much is because of this very fact. I knew he'd grow past me and this town, and I couldn't bear to witness that. Of course my fears were proven to be true when he more or less showed me that his life here, the people here, don't matter to him. Not when he has his new life ahead of him.

I look away from the photos and go back to what I came in here for. I scan his desk, and I don't see the sketches here either. He mentioned that the sketch might be in a desk drawer so I tug both of them open, feeling relief as I spot the familiar drawing of the sunflowers.

Just as I pull it out, I notice a crumpled up sketch at the back of the drawer. I reach for it, unfurling it slowly. Van Gogh's *Starry Night* with a Said Hossain twist to it.

I'm about to push the drawer closed when something else catches my eye.

Draft #5 of Letter for the New York School of Animation

I lift the sheet up. My eyebrows furrow. Said is applying to animation school? I didn't know that. Then again, I don't know much about him anymore.

It makes me happy to know he's doing that, following his dreams. The world needs more Said art in it.

I find myself reading on. This definitely feels like a violation now, but I can't look away.

The art project I'll be submitting for consideration is a mural I worked on this past summer. As a Muslim, my faith means a lot to me and so when the Islamic Center in my town burned down I got the idea to create art out of it . . .

I pause, reading back the last few lines, a sinking in my stomach.

I snatch the letter out of the drawer, reading it closely, and feeling something begin to wither deep inside.

He got the idea?

I feel a mix of different emotions swirling. Betrayal, anger, confusion. Everything at once, making my head spin and my chest hurt.

I don't take a moment to process before I'm storming out of his room.

I don't have many thoughts, just one.

I'm going to kill him.

I go down the stairs and I'm immediately greeted with Said's bright, traitorous face. It seems like he's about to smile at me, then thinks twice about it, probably registering my expression.

"Did you find the sketch?" he asks innocently, like this whole thing isn't an elaborate ruse. Like he isn't planning on turning around and stealing this from under me. Like how he was just pretending to care and never did in the first place.

I feel so naive for believing him.

"Yes, among other things," I say, holding up the letter now. Said's eyes dart to my hand and the letter in it. At first he just looks confused, so I decide to help jog his memory a little. "I found your letter, the one where you tell your fancy college how *you* came up with this whole mural and saving the Islamic Center plan all by yourself. Wow, I didn't know you were so creative and crafty," I say, my voice shaking, matching the trembling rhythm of my hands as my vision starts to blur. I blink away the tears that want to fall and I see his face morph into a guilty expression, skin draining of color.

"It's not what it looks like. I didn't—" he begins, and I cut him off with a laugh.

"Of course it isn't, it never is what it looks like, is it? I thought it looked like you actually cared. I thought it looked like you were a decent fucking human being."

He looks at me, hurt on his face.

"Tiwa, if you just let me explain—"

"Go on, explain, is this not your handwriting? Did someone kidnap you and make you write this?" I say, waiting to hear what bullshit excuse he has this time.

He looks at me and I see something deflate inside of him. "It's my writing," he says.

And I nod, throwing the letter and the sketch down on the floor with the rest of them. I hate him, I decide. I hate him so much and I hate myself for believing him and spending my summer so far with someone who showed me who he was years ago.

"I'm gonna go," I say as I grab my things. I don't want him to see me cry, and I'm pretty sure I am seconds away from having a full-on breakdown.

I don't look at Said as I turn away and open the front door. I don't wait to see if he is filled with regret. I just leave, stepping out into the light drizzle and cold. Even when it's summer in Vermont, there is still rain.

I'm already past the driveway when I hear a voice call out.

"Tiwa! Wait," I hear Said say, followed by the sound of his feet hitting the pavement as he rushes toward me.

I ignore him, walking faster, but he is quick, catching up to me and then overtaking me. He blocks my path, stopping me from walking any farther.

I'm forced to look at him now. He has an apologetic look on his face.

I sniff, my own face wet both from the tears and the light rain. Hopefully he can't tell which it is.

"Please, just—I do care. The letter doesn't mean anything," Said says, shivering now as the rain slowly begins to soak his shirt.

Out of the corner of my eye I think I see his mom's car pull into the driveway. I need to leave before she asks me why I'm crying, or worse, if I want to stay for dinner.

"Listen, you don't need to explain yourself. I think this whole thing was a mistake anyway, us pretending to like each other. You pretending to care. I think it's best we just go back to how things were before. We were probably kidding ourselves with this mural thing anyway." I hear the car door unlock and I look at him one last time, the distant fluttering inside still stirring when I do. "Bye, Said," I say, before moving past him and leaving him on the side of the road alone.

As the distance between us grows wider, I can't help but think again how I should have never trusted Said in the first place.

17

NUGGET OF ADVICE

Said

I CALL TIWA A DOZEN TIMES BUT SHE DOESN'T ANSWER, AND SHE doesn't respond to any of my texts asking her for a chance to explain. With no other ideas on how to fix my screwup, I trudge into the kitchen and toward the corner cupboard where Safiyah hides her secret stash of cookies inside the box of cinnamon raisin granola. I barely even register Ammu cooking dinner on the stove.

That is, until she stops me from making off with my comfort cookies.

"Said!" Ammu says as I'm digging into the box of granola. "If you have that now, when are you going to have dinner?"

"When I get hungry later?" I ask.

"No," Ammu says firmly, waving around the wooden spoon in her hands dangerously. It's dripping daal all over the kitchen. "Safiyah will be home in a little bit from wherever she ran off to, and your abbu is just finishing up his prayers. We'll eat very soon, so don't spoil your dinner."

I sigh, putting the box of granola back in the cupboard. "Okay, Ammu."

Instead of leaving it at that, she puts the wooden spoon down on the counter and approaches me with concern on her face. "What's wrong?"

"Nothing," I say quickly. I don't know how Ammu has a way of always knowing when something is wrong, but it's uncanny.

"Is it something to do with Tiwa storming away earlier?" she asks with a sympathetic look in her eyes. I feel heat rise to my cheeks. I had no idea Ammu had seen any of that when I came back indoors to find her back home. She hadn't said anything, just asked me to help her take in the shopping.

When I don't respond to her question, Ammu just nods, like she understands.

"You know, when I was your age, I had this friend. Her name was Madhuri," Ammu says. "And we once had this huge fight because we were both up for the valedictorian spot in our high school. She was very competitive, and I guess so was I. And so for our entire senior year, we were constantly trying to one-up each other. We became enemies, really. It was awful. In the end, I became valedictorian and I wrote this amazing speech. It got a standing ovation actually, and people tell me that they still talk about it now. It was one of those speeches that really stays with you. Like Abraham Lincoln's or Martin Luther King Junior's, you know. Maybe one day I'll see if I can dig up that speech—it has to be somewhere in one of the boxes in the basement."

"Uh . . . what does that have to do with Tiwa?" I ask when Ammu finally ends her rambling story.

She blinks at me for a moment, like she'd forgotten all about Tiwa. I half wish I hadn't asked and left things at the end of her nonsensical story.

"Well . . . nothing . . . I guess. But the point is that Madhuri and I made up in the end and the valedictorian thing was silly. Friends always find a way back to each other, so I'm sure you and Tiwa will too." Ammu beams like she's imparted some great nugget of advice.

"But Tiwa and I haven't been friends for a long time. Way longer than you and Madhuri were competing over being valedictorian," I say.

"Well, tell me why you and Tiwa stopped being friends. Maybe I can help," Ammu says, picking up her wooden spoon and going back to the stove to stir the pot of vegetable curry she's making.

I'm not sure if I really want to get into the ins and outs of our falling-out. I've never really spoken to anyone about it in-depth, and considering how Ammu already won't let me spoil my dinner, I don't want to get too deep into a conversation that'll make me wish for those cookies even more. So I decide to keep the explanation short and simple, as I've always done.

"I don't know about her," I say, sitting down on one of the chairs at the dinner table. "But . . . she made it clear that she didn't want to be friends when she didn't respond to any of my letters."

Ammu stops stirring her pot to give me that sympathetic look once more. "Said, you were both kids back then," she says. "All of that was such a long time ago, and if everything with Madhuri taught me anything, it's that life is too short. You don't know if someone you care about will be there the next day, so you need to make sure you tell them when they're there in front of you. When you have the chance. I still regret not telling Madhuri while I could have."

"Did . . . Madhuri die?" I ask, confused.

"Oh, no," Ammu chuckles. "But she moved away to Vancouver and that was that."

"But we went to Vancouver last year, and you didn't mention any friend called Madhuri," I say.

"Oh . . . yes. I knew I was meant to call someone before that trip," Ammu says. She turns off the stove and comes over to the dining table, sitting down in one of the chairs opposite me. "Listen, Said. Friendships are hard, I know that. And there are no rule books to them, which makes it even harder. But you and Tiwa will figure things out, I know that too."

Ammu sounds pretty confident, but considering her own failure at friendship with this person called Madhuri, I'm not sure why exactly.

But something in her words sticks with me. There's no rule book to friendship, but there are rule books for other things. Like card games, despite Ammu's insistence that Uno can be played without any instruction. Or small towns in Vermont obsessed with murals.

"Thanks, Ammu," I say. "This helped a lot, but I have to go take care of something." I stand and hurry up the stairs.

"What about dinner?" Ammu calls behind me.

"I'll come down soon, don't worry!" I shout back before slipping into my bedroom and opening up my laptop. I quickly go to the official website of New Crosshaven, searching for the document with all the town's bylaws. When I finally find it, I download it onto my computer. It's hundreds of pages long, and I definitely don't have the time to go through each and every bylaw to find relevant ones.

I sit back, trying to think what I could search for to find the right clause.

I type in *building* but that gets me over a hundred hits to wade through. I try *petition* and that brings up only ten results. And finally, I find exactly what I'm looking for.

18
A LITTLE BIT OF A NITWIT

Tiwa

"No offense, but I hate your brother. I don't even know how you guys share the same DNA. He is so infuriating and so full of it. Apparently going to a private boarding school turns you into a complete nitwit. I bet they get reprogrammed or something— anyway, I just hate him. So, *so* much," I say, finally taking a breath and looking over at Safiyah, who is seated on my bed with a half-confused, half-scared expression on her face.

It's then that I realize she asked me something and I completely lost track of what.

"Sorry, what was your question again?" I ask her.

Safiyah blinks at me. "Nitwit?" she finally says.

"Yes, he's a nitwit," I say, defending my word choice.

"That's fair, I see that," Saf says with a shrug. "My question was whether your bedsheets were new? I didn't remember you owning anything this . . . bright," she continues, looking down at the tie-dyed-style bedsheets, which contrast greatly with the rest of the room filled with black, gray, and navy decor.

"Oh, right. My mom got them for me for some reason last year, said it would brighten up the room, bring the right sort of energy in, I guess. I didn't need to use them until this weekend when I accidentally spilled my orange juice on my regular sheets, which I wouldn't have done if I wasn't completely blindsided by Said and his traitorous ways and needed an orange pick-me-up while I stayed up every night after his betrayal planning how not to fuck up Eid and still save the Islamic Center somehow. None of this would have happened if Said wasn't such a nitwit. Not the spilled orange juice or the blasphemously bright bedsheets or the headaches I got from always being up so late having multiple existential crises. I hate your brother, Saf. I really, really hate him," I say, realizing now how that simple question led me here.

The orange juice.

"I think I've gotten that now, that you hate him," Saf says. "And I get why you're upset—"

"I'm more than upset. I'm ready to commit multiple crimes against humanity, but I won't because that would be haram and I'm not risking hell for him. You know I should never have trusted him in the first place. It's really my fault for being so naive to think he changed in a matter of days. He was using me all along for his college applications—he never cared. He didn't care about me when he went to school either, stopped answering my phone calls, stopped caring about this town. I should have known that the old Said is dead and he's never coming back."

I slump down onto the bed next to Safiyah, letting myself lie back and close my eyes. Blocking out all of it. I don't want to think about him anymore.

I feel the bed shift as Safiyah lies down next to me.

There's a long pause, one filled with the heavy weight of the future as well as Safiyah's thoughts.

I can literally feel her thinking of what to say next.

"Tee," she finally says, and I turn to her, eyes open again. She's looking at me, clearly concerned.

"You're right, my brother is a little bit of a nitwit—he's a lot of things actually. But he's not malicious. You know I always have your back, and I just think you should consider the fact that sometimes things are simply not what they seem . . . sometimes people make mistakes. All is not always what it appears to be."

"Whatever," I mutter, and then I squint at Safiyah, taking in her appearance now.

She looks . . . different. It's not her clothes, though, it's something else . . .

"Did you curl your hair?" I ask, eyeing her clearly done up appearance. I notice her glossy mouth and eyelined lids next.

"I did. Actually, speaking of that, I need your guidance. Help me find which clothes to steal from your closet. I'm in desperate need of a sundress." Safiyah pushes herself up and waltzes toward my closet.

"A sundress, why?"

Safiyah looks back over her shoulder with a sly smile, momentarily pausing her ambush of my closet.

I immediately know from that look that it's about Ishra. I swear, being friends with someone for this many years is like learning the language of their unspoken thoughts.

"You're going on a date with Ishra?" I ask, eyes wide as I sit up so fast I feel a little bit of whiplash.

"Mhm," she says.

"A *date* date?" I prod.

"Yes," she answers simply, then turns back to my closet.

"What? When? Where? And how did you keep this from me?"

"It happened quite randomly. After the bake sale we started texting here and there and then I bumped into her mom at the grocery store—can I borrow this?" Safiyah says, interrupting herself as she holds up one of the yellow sundresses I got from my aunt on my birthday last year. Of course, it is another unused bright-colored thing.

"Sure. Go back to the grocery thing. What does bumping into her mom have to do with you guys going on a *date* date?"

"Oh right, that. Well, I get to speaking to her mom. Turns out Ishra got into college last year but deferred entry so that she could stay back and help the family and save up and whatnot—and these shoes?" Safiyah asks, yet again stopping the story, holding up a pair of my favorite Mary Janes.

"Yes, stop interrupting the story. I need the details!"

"Okay, okay, sorry! Where was I . . . college, Ishra got into NYU for math—isn't that amazing? She's so smart . . . I think I'm going to take this purse too, it's so cute," Safiyah says.

"Saf!" I say, lobbing a cushion at her head.

She ducks, narrowly missing it. "Sorry! Right, yes. Long story short, she got into NYU last year, therefore she isn't applying to college this year. I've been helping her for no reason essentially, and so with this shocking revelation from her mom, I headed over to the Walker Center where I knew she'd be working at that time and I told her that I know the truth and she tells me that she wanted an excuse to hang out with me. To conclude, I have two dates with Ishra. We're seeing a film today and going to eat some ramen later this week, hence why I'm stealing your clothes."

I raise an eyebrow at her. Before I can ask her any more questions about the whole saga, the shrill tone of my notifications going off stops me.

I look down at the screen, my eyebrows furrowing when I see the email button appear in my notifications. I can see the email's preview before I swipe onto it. Seeing that it's from Donna at the town hall, I quickly click on it, watching as the page loads slowly. *I really need a new phone.* The email comes up and I sit up straighter.

I quietly read, at first expecting it to be some miracle about the Islamic Center and the construction plans being overturned, but instead it's something else entirely.

"You've gone scarily quiet, everything okay?" Saf asks.

I continue reading the email, unblinking. I feel like I'm in some kind of shock.

I look up at her. "It's about the appeal for Timi. The mayor is happy to approve it. It's going to be put to the town hall meeting at the end of this week . . ." I say, reading it over and over just to make sure.

I'd submitted this appeal months ago, knowing that appeals sometimes took up to a year to be considered and seen, and that an appeal relating to local law reform actually being approved was even more unlikely.

With all the bad news, I guess I'd expected the worst to come out from this.

I feel the permanent tight knot in my throat begin to relax, my vision blurring slightly.

"I can't believe it," I say quietly.

I hear Safiyah's footsteps, and then I feel her arms around my shoulders.

I sniff, wiping my eyes before any tears can fall. "I'm going to go to the town hall. Donna says I need to pick my town hall time slot in person."

"Are you sure you're okay to go right now? Why can't they email it like they just did?" Safiyah asks.

"This is Donna's personal email; she says the official approval letter is in the mail but she wanted to give me a heads-up."

Safiyah nods. "It seems the lemon squares worked."

"That they did," I say, standing abruptly now. "You can stay here if you like? I won't be too long, I'll just go and sort out my time slot and I can help you with more outfit suggestions."

"Are you sure you don't want me to come with?" Safiyah asks, the yellow sundress still held up against her torso.

I nod, feeling weird inside, like my lungs are a glass vase ready to shatter, the shards scarring and scraping at me from the inside out.

"I'll be okay. I need the fresh air and thinking time anyway. I'll be back soon," I say as I pull on my sweater and then my sneakers, not bothering to change out of my PJ bottoms.

It's not like I'm there to make an impression anyway.

SOON I'M AT THE TOWN HALL, FEELING SO WEIRD, MY BREATHING is labored. Everything feels like it's in slow motion.

I must have read the email one hundred times on the walk here.

To Tiwa,
This is Donna from the town hall. Apologies for emailing on a Saturday. I shouldn't be sending you this, but given the circumstances, I thought it would only be fair to let you know as soon as approval came through.

. . .

The appeal for the local New Crosshaven bylaw change will likely be approved at the next town hall meeting at the end of the week. The Town Hall meeting is divided into different time slots allocated to each matter. Please come and select your time slot from me as soon as possible.

Best,

Donna

I could probably quote it word for word now. Every single line.

The ugly, bright building that usually assaults my vision and causes my eyes to strain doesn't affect me much today. I'm razor focused. All I can think of is one thing.

I make my way up to the town hall reception area, rushing over to Donna's desk.

The high I'm on deflates as I approach the desk and see no one there.

I look up at the clock. It's Donna's lunch. I should have known.

This is confirmed by the sign next to her computer screen that says *Off to lunch for thirty minutes*. Which means she's in the adjoining room behind her desk.

I sigh. I think about ringing the bell anyway and disturbing her lunch. After all, I just need to choose my time slot and I'll be on my way. It shouldn't take long, right? But instead, my focus is pulled away by the sound of a familiar voice rising.

"You need to calm down, Mr. Hossain," another familiar voice replies, and I turn my head sharply to the direction of the mayor's office and the two figures standing down the hall right outside the office door.

Said and Mayor Williams.

"I *am* calm. I'm just telling you something you don't like. As I said before, Mayor, you have to consider the petition properly. We collected over the number of signatures necessary, and because of that, you're supposed to take this to the town hall meeting for a panel to discuss and decide. With all due respect, Mayor Williams, this is the rule book you signed off on. So surely you agree that due process needs to take place."

I can barely see Mayor Williams's face when Said says that. Said's tall frame covers most of the mayor's face, but the mayor's silence speaks volumes enough.

I feel my heart rattle in my chest as I wait for the mayor to say something.

Said holds up what seems to be printed-out scraps of paper. "Rules are made to be followed, Mayor, you said that before. So do the right thing . . . please," Said says.

I almost can't believe my eyes. Said is here . . . fighting for the Islamic Center, or maybe for himself again, because he needs the mural and therefore needs the Islamic Center. But maybe Safiyah is right and he's just a nitwit, not a manipulative mastermind.

I hear the mayor sigh loudly, his head popping out to the side and his eyes staring at me directly. "I see you brought backup. You two constantly camp out in my office . . . ," the mayor replies, his plastic smile from when I'd last seen him completely gone and replaced with pure annoyance.

Said turns to look at me, as surprised to see me here as I am to see him.

We stare at each other for a few brief moments, but the moments feel like they go on for eons. I feel that same feeling inside but I can't decipher what it is.

Hate, hurt, or some third thing that also causes my skin to heat and my stomach to turn and knot.

He nods at me as if to say hi, and that feeling only intensifies.

Said turns back to the mayor and says: "I don't mind camping out here in protest. I'm happy to go without showering for days on end, and I had a very large breakfast that could keep me going for a while, along with the vending machine snacks and the coffee machi—"

"All right! I'll take the petition to the town hall meeting this week," Mayor Williams says, finally conceding. He rubs his eyes harshly and gestures to the empty desk where Donna usually sits. "Go to Donna for a meeting slot, and let me enjoy my lunch in peace. *Please.*"

Said smiles wide. "Thanks," he says, chipper, which only seems to annoy Williams more.

Without another word, Mayor Williams glares in my direction and then turns and quickly retreats into his office away from his *tormentors.*

Said doesn't look at me again at first. Like he's afraid to. And then, hesitantly, as though ripping off the Band-Aid at last, he quickly turns to me.

"Hi," he says.

I blink up at him, my brain filled with so much I could explode into one million flesh pieces.

My stomach flips.

"Hi," I reply.

I hate how much it's hard to hate Said earnestly when he's right in front of me.

He walks over to me, crumpled pages from what seems to be the town's rule book in one of his large hands.

It's clear he doesn't know what to say, and to be honest I don't either. I'm still angry and don't feel like I can trust him at all.

But when I see him, all of that just fades away and I want to desperately make him smile. It's the most infuriating thing.

I can't quite shake off the impulse to be his best friend, or see him as anything but mine.

"Congratulations on successfully bullying the mayor. It was very impressive," I say, because I can't help myself.

His eyebrows shoot up and he shrugs. "Thanks, it was scary as fuck." He swallows hard and doesn't stop looking at me. I notice the corners of his mouth start to relax, no longer in a stony straight line. "I hope it looked more badass than it felt."

I nod. "It did. Very."

I can tell he's resisting the urge to smile at that. I can tell he's not sure where he stands in this conversation.

It's confusing for me too. Up until thirty minutes ago I was so set on hating him for life . . . again.

But then I see him here and I'm annoyed that Safiyah might actually be right.

"I'm sorry," he says, and then follows up with, "I was never going to send that letter to my school. It's one of my early drafts I'd written in the middle of the night, and as you know from sleepovers, I lose IQ points at night."

It was true he wasn't that bright at night. I remember once we'd played Uno under the covers in the fort he'd fashioned out of his bedsheets, and he'd thought that the Uno reverse card meant that the card he put down with it had the opposite function. So a six would become a nine and picking up two cards would mean donating two instead.

"I'm really sorry. You have every right to hate me. I just want you to know that I'm not pretending to care about the Islamic Center, or you, I care a whole lot, I'm just—"

"A nitwit?" I finish for him, and he finally breaks his resolve, his expression a mixture of surprise and amusement.

"I guess so," he says. "I'll just pick the time slot for the petition then . . ." He scans the reception desk for Donna. ". . . When she gets back."

"I'm waiting for her too. We can wait together," I say.

We have yet another silent staring match that probably only lasts a second or two but feels infinite.

"That sounds good," he finally says.

19

BROWN PEOPLE TIME

Said

I'M SO DEEP INTO MY CURRENT SKETCH OF A RENDITION OF THE welcome sign of New Crosshaven that I don't realize Abbu is calling my name until he's waving his hand right in front of my face.

I quickly take off my headphones and close my sketchbook.

"What's wrong?" I ask.

"Nothing's wrong," Abbu says, his eyes drifting to my now closed sketchbook. "Was that the entrance to New Crosshaven?"

I shrug. "Yeah, just . . . doodling."

Abbu nods slowly. "It was good. Really good."

"Thanks," I mumble, waiting for the other shoe to drop. I know that he wasn't calling me just to compliment me on my sketch.

"So, I'm heading out to Imam Abdullah's for jummah. The Walker Center was fully booked—again—so we're going to pray in his sitting room. I thought maybe you could join me if you aren't too busy," Abbu says.

I blink at him slowly, confused. I can't remember the last time I went to pray jummah. It was probably months, if not years, ago. It's not like St. Francis Academy has an imam, and the nearest mosque to the school is an hour's drive away.

"Uh, I'm not sure," I say.

"Imam Abdullah would probably really like to see you again. He mentioned the bake sale when I went to pray maghrib the other day," Abbu says.

I glance down at my sketchbook for a moment.

"Yeah, sure. I guess I can go to jummah. Let me quickly get changed," I say.

Abbu grins bigger than I've seen him smile so far this whole summer. "All right, I'll be in the car. See you in five."

THE CAR RIDE TO IMAM ABDULLAH'S IS SHORT, AND MUCH LESS painful than I anticipated it would be. For one, Abbu doesn't bring up college applications even once. Instead, he talks about how he's picked up gardening this summer and hopes to serve freshly grown tomatoes at the dawat coming up.

"Since when did you grow tomatoes?" I ask.

Abbu smiles. "It's a hobby I've taken up. Imam Abdullah gave your ammu some carrots from his garden and I thought I'd try to plant some of those too."

I've been so distracted this summer, I hadn't noticed that Abbu was now a full-fledged farmer. He talks about his veggies some more and somehow it segues into him asking about the bake sale and petitioning for the Islamic Center.

When I tell him about the town hall meeting later that day, he actually looks proud.

"Should your ammu and I come?" he asks as he parks the car by Imam Abdullah's house. "There's safety in numbers, you know."

I wonder for a moment if he thinks Mayor Williams and the other town hall politicians would end up starting some kind of a brawl over the Islamic Center hearing.

"I think we'll be okay," I say.

"Right, well. You just call us if Mayor Williams gives you any more trouble. Your ammu and I have had our run-ins with him. We know how to handle him," Abbu says sternly. I'm not sure what methods Ammu and Abbu have for handling Mayor Williams, but I can just imagine. Ammu probably throws him the death glare that used to give Safiyah and me nightmares as kids, while Abbu probably tries to bribe him with mishtis.

"I will, Abbu," I say.

The two of us climb out of the car, pass the dozens of other cars piled around Imam Abdullah's front gate, and ring the doorbell.

The door opens just a moment later, and Imam Abdullah stands in the doorway, his smile visible through his long gray beard.

"Ah, Said. Hossain bhai. You're right on time!" he says, ushering the two of us inside. We slip our shoes off and join the rest of the group in the living room. The place has been set up with a large carpet on the ground. There are a few chairs lined up against the wall, but no couches, no TV. Nothing to indicate that it's a living room at all.

"We had to move some things out to make room for everyone, especially for jummah," Imam Abdullah says when he sees me looking around. "I think you're the last ones I was expecting. One of the benefits of leading prayer in my living room. I can wait for whoever I want to, no set schedules." He beams at me before heading to the front of the room.

Abbu and I sit down on the carpet, side by side with an uncle and his two sons who I recognize. We say our salams, but don't get to say much more before Imam Abdullah begins his khutbah.

He starts off in Arabic, the sound of the words familiar to my ears even though I don't understand any of it. I expect to drift off, but somehow I find myself listening with rapt attention. There's something about the way Imam Abdullah speaks—even in a language I don't understand. It commands attention, but not in a bad way. It almost invites you in.

Finally, he begins translating into English.

"As everyone in town knows, recently our community faced a big blow. Our Islamic Center burned down in a tragic accident. As I reflected on this accident, it brought me back to a time when New Crosshaven did not have an Islamic Center at all. Yes, there was a time when the town had no Islamic Center, and our Muslim population was sparse. It was a sad time, and it was when many felt alienated from their religion. They had nowhere to turn to, nobody to turn to.

"They struggled with their faith in the absence of community. They questioned Islam, if it was right for them. They struggled to pray, to fast, to keep their obligations as a Muslim. Many would say they strayed too far from Islam, but I don't believe that. Allah is the most gracious of them all, and he is understanding of our struggles. And he waits to welcome each of us back whenever we are ready."

I stare at Imam Abdullah, wondering how he delivered a khutbah that felt tailor-made for me. How it feels like he looked right into my soul and into the exact thoughts and struggles going on inside me right now. But Imam Abdullah doesn't look at me. He smiles at everyone and stands up to begin the jummah prayer.

I stand too, raising my hands to my ears as Imam Abdullah says

Allahu Akbar. Somehow, my lips form the words of the prayers along-side Imam Abdullah, my hands and feet follow the motions. It's almost like no time has passed since the last time I prayed jummah.

By the time I turn my head to end the prayer, mumbling, "as-salaam-alaikum wa rahmatullah" under my breath, I feel like I'm back to when I was younger, always going to the mosque with Abbu, praying jamat with my friends and their dads, usually meeting up with the Olatunjis afterward.

And I realize that I've missed all of this more than I had known before this moment: being close to Allah, spending time with Abbu, going to the mosque. And maybe Imam Abdullah is right, maybe I'm ready to be welcomed back.

I CHECK MY WATCH AGAIN AS ABBU PULLS THE CAR TO THE CURB of the town hall.

"You're not late, Said," Abbu says.

"But there's only five minutes until the meeting is supposed to start. It'll take me five minutes just to walk in and find the room where the meeting is taking place," I say, my leg going up and down.

Abbu sighs, parallel parking on the side of the road. Sometimes I wonder how Ammu, Abbu, and Safiyah run on brown people time when I am punctual for absolutely everything. It's like the tardiness genes skipped me somehow.

"Sure you don't want me to come with? I could call work and say I got held up with something," Abbu says.

"That's okay, I'll let you know how it goes," I say, already pushing the car door open and slipping outside. I hurry up the steps of the town hall and toward the reception.

"Hi, I'm here for the town hall meeting?" I ask, looking around for any sign of Tiwa. She's nowhere to be seen. I hope she isn't late to this thing. Knowing Mayor Williams, he would somehow use that to convince everyone why we don't need an Islamic Center.

"Yes, the meeting has already started. It's down the hall to your left," the receptionist says, barely looking up from her computer.

Oh crap.

"Thanks!" I call out quickly, while jogging down the hall. This is what I get for dawdling after jummah prayer to talk to Imam Abdullah and the uncles, and for letting Abbu drive me to the town hall. He had to stop on the way to fill up his car with gas, and then to run errands for Ammu. Which apparently made me officially late.

When I finally spot the door for the meeting room, I quietly twist the handle and push it open. The first thing I see is Mayor Williams at the front of the room, sitting behind a raised podium. There are two men on each side of him, both white.

Rows of red chairs face the podium, and there are only a few people sitting on them, making it easy to spot Tiwa and Safiyah near the front.

I consider joining them, but slide into one of the seats in the back so as not to cause any kind of disruption.

"We're already running over, Mr. Howard. Let's call this to a vote. We still have the Islamic Center issue to deal with," Mayor Williams says, interrupting the man on his right—who must be Mr. Howard. I sit up straight, feeling relief flood through me.

"Fine, I think we've all presented our cases well enough," Mr. Howard says. "All those in favor of passing the road safety sign bylaw say aye."

Everyone except for Mayor Williams mutters aye, with him being the only one opposed.

"So, the road safety sign bylaw has been added. It'll come into effect once we sort out all the paperwork," Mr. Howard says. "Let's take a five-minute recess before reconvening for the Islamic Center issue."

Most people exit the room almost immediately, but Tiwa and Safiyah stand up, hugging each other tightly like they've won the lottery or something. Given their track record, I should have probably guessed they weren't early to the meeting for the Islamic Center.

That's when it dawns on me. I still remember the day Ammu called to tell me what had happened. The hit-and-run, the road sign that could have been there to prevent it from ever happening. Timi.

This bylaw has to be about him. This must have all been Tiwa's doing.

I get up and approach them.

"Hey."

"Hi, Said," Safiyah says, pulling away from Tiwa. Her eyes water, like she's holding back tears, and Tiwa's are bloodshot like she's just been crying. But she's smiling too, so I know it's the good kind of crying. The celebratory kind. "Of course you'd get here right on time."

"Hey," Tiwa says, her voice strangely small.

"Okay, I do have to get going. I'm already late for meeting Ishra, and there's fashionably late which is cute, and then I'm-never-going-on-a-date-with-you-ever-again kind of late," Safiyah says. "Good luck, and let me know how everything goes." She gives Tiwa a meaningful look before hurrying out of the room.

Tiwa and I sit down side by side, silence washing over us for a moment. I'm sure Tiwa is thinking of Timi. *I'm* thinking of him and all I did was catch the tail end of this meeting.

"It's a good precedent," I say finally, breaking the silence.

Tiwa turns to me with a questioning look. "What?"

"That everyone disagreed with Mayor Williams," I say. "Maybe they'll disagree with him again. Clearly he's not Mr. Popular around here."

"Maybe, but none of the town hall committee members are Muslim. I feel like they won't understand," Tiwa says, her eyes downcast.

"They don't have to *understand*, but they have to listen to us, right? So many people signed our petition, they can't just ignore all of us. They're supposed to represent us and our voices so . . . they have to listen," I say.

Tiwa nods, though there's none of her usual confidence in it. I open my mouth to say something more reassuring, but just then the doors open and the committee members and Mayor Williams come back in, along with a small stream of other people from the town— many faces I recognize, some from when I was petitioning, others from dawats and many Eid parties over the years that I've been to. I even spot Imam Abdullah entering in from the back, still dressed in a panjabi from the jummah prayer.

"Now, let's get started," Mayor Williams says as soon as he's sitting behind the podium once more. His eyes land on me and Tiwa for a moment, and he frowns, before looking away. He's clearly not too happy to be holding this meeting.

"There's been a motion raised to rebuild the Islamic Center, which burned down in an accident recently. A few citizens submitted a petition . . ." At this, Mayor Williams raises the petition and passes copies to the elected town hall members. "And the petition has reached the required amount of signatures."

More than the required amount, I want to say, but keep my mouth shut. I'm sure nobody would take too kindly to me correcting the mayor in a public forum like this.

"The issue is that I have reviewed the petition and I have also reviewed the most recent census of our town. The population of Muslim citizens simply does not justify the rebuilding of the Islamic Center. That we had one in the first place is honestly a miracle," Mayor Williams says with a chuckle.

Beside me, Tiwa narrows her eyes in such an intense glare that I'm surprised Mayor Williams doesn't drop dead right then and there.

"I have been consulting with a building contractor who is willing to give us a fantastic deal to come in and demolish the remnants of the Islamic Center, building a block of apartments in its place. They're available to start as soon as next week. It'll serve the population of the town much better than any Islamic Center could, because it'll serve the *entire* population equally," Mayor Williams finishes. He's smiling from ear to ear like he's proud of his ridiculous speech.

"I suppose what poses a problem is . . . What are the Muslim citizens of New Crosshaven meant to do for prayer and community?" Mr. Howard, one of the panel members, asks.

"Well, the answer is simple: the Walker Center. It is supposed to serve the entire community indiscriminately. Our Muslim citizens can book it when they require, same as our Christian citizens, Jewish citizens, Hindu citizens . . . et cetera. It's a shared space to be used exactly in this manner," Mayor Williams says.

Mr. Howard nods his head as if Mayor Williams's point is in any way acceptable.

"Any other questions?" Mayor Williams asks.

I glance around and see Imam Abdullah's raised hand. Mayor Williams spots him too and his face falls into a slight grimace.

"Apologies, Mr. . . ." Mayor Williams begins.

"Abdullah," Imam Abdullah says.

Williams nods. "Mr. Abdullah, I don't believe your name is on the list of pre-approved speakers for this meeting."

Of course he isn't on the pre-approved list; no one is. Mayor Williams made sure there wouldn't be any time for that—not that he'd let us know that anyway.

"I just found out about this meeting yesterday, how could I get on the pre-approved list?" Imam Abdullah says, sounding uncharacteristically angry. In all the years our family has been going to the mosque, I don't think I've never seen Imam Abdullah get angry.

"I'm sorry, Mr. Abdullah, but the rules are the rules. Does anyone who is on the list—apart from the motion proposers—have any last words or questions?" When no one comes forward, Mayor Williams smiles and continues. "If not, let's call a vote. All those in favor of demolishing the Islamic Center and building apartments in its place, say aye."

Beside me, Tiwa's shoulders tense. Even I feel my throat dry up.

They barely presented our case. They barely even glanced at the petition.

Mayor Williams and all his colleagues say aye.

"And those in favor of rebuilding the Islamic Center, say aye . . ." Williams says with a smile that almost seems triumphant as no hands go up.

The decision is unanimous: The Islamic Center will be demolished.

A mumble of dissent spreads through the room, but it's quickly shut down by Mayor Williams slamming his gavel and silencing everyone.

Everything seems to slow down, and my chest aches. All that work. The petitioning, all my sketches, our plans for the mural . . . and it resulted in nothing. Just like that, in a meeting that barely lasted fifteen minutes, these men who understand nothing about our religion took away our safe space. Our community.

"Are you okay?" Tiwa asks. Somehow she looks more put-together than I feel.

"I just . . . can't believe it," I say. "I really thought that . . . they'd listen. I mean, we got so many signatures. We went over the amount required for the petition. And then the mural? It was a really good idea."

"I know," Tiwa says with a sigh. She slumps back in her chair, looking more tired than I've seen her maybe ever. "We tried, Said. At least nobody can say that we didn't try. And at least we'll have our Eid party. That's something, right?"

"I guess. Imam Abdullah will have to lead prayers from his living room for his entire life now," I say, thinking about the tiny space. "How will he entertain his guests when it's not prayer time? He doesn't have a living room anymore."

"And the women will have to find some other place to pray. I'm guessing Imam Abdullah's living room isn't big enough to host us," Tiwa says.

"What will we even do for Eid prayer?" I ask.

"Maybe we should take over Mayor Williams's house for that one."

"Then he'd reconsider."

Tiwa chuckles, but there's no mirth in it. "Yeah, maybe."

"Excuse me?" I look up to find the woman from the reception staring at Tiwa and me with an especially annoyed look on her face. "Meetings for the day are over and we're closing up this space, so . . ." She makes a motion like she's shooing us away.

"We're leaving, Donna, don't worry." Tiwa rolls her eyes.

We walk out of the meeting room and through the corridors of the town hall. I'm still having a hard time believing that we're really losing the Islamic Center.

"So . . . I guess you can stop working on the mural," Tiwa says as we get to the front entrance. She's looking down at the ground instead of up at me. "I mean, we won't really need it anymore."

"Yeah," I mumble. It's dawning on me that the end of the Islamic Center means that Tiwa and I don't have to work together anymore. At the very start of the summer, that thought would have filled me with joy. But now, it burrows a hole in the pit of my stomach.

"Hey, do you want to get dinner or something?" I find myself asking. Tiwa turns to me with a questioning expression and I realize what that question sounded like. Blood rushes to my face and I quickly try to explain myself. "I mean, Safiyah keeps mentioning that new ramen place and I've been meaning to try it out all summer. But all the mural stuff kept me busy, and then my mom was always making me run errands, and I didn't have lunch because I went to jummah prayer with—"

"Okay." Tiwa interrupts my rambling train of thought. She looks at me with a hint of a smile in her expression.

I hold her gaze for a beat too long. Then I say, "Okay. Let's go then."

20

TABLE MANNERS

Said

THE RAMEN RESTAURANT IS ONLY A FEW MINUTES' WALK FROM the town hall.

"It looks pretty full in here," Tiwa comments as we slip inside the door covered in colorful Japanese lettering. It's a pretty small restaurant, with low lighting and soft J-pop playing in the background. There's a miniature fountain toward the back, which means the music is accompanied by the gentle sound of trickling water.

Tiwa is right—the restaurant seems to be full of people, though you wouldn't know it from first glance. It's not filled with loud conversation or sounds of clinking cutlery. It's quiet and atmospheric.

"We're only two, I'm sure they can squeeze us in," I say, approaching the host.

"Table for two?" the host asks. He's a man wearing a sleek black suit and a smile.

"Yes," I say.

He nods, picks up two menus from his podium, and indicates for us to follow him. Tiwa and I walk behind him as he weaves through the restaurant. I look around at the secluded booths separated by partitions. At the couples holding hands, or smiling at each other over their bowls of ramen. I can't help but notice that there are no groups larger than two in the whole restaurant.

A weird feeling burrows in my stomach. Has Safiyah been recommending a couples' restaurant this entire time?

"Here you are," the host says, stopping at a table toward the very back of the restaurant.

"Er, thanks," I say. Tiwa and I slide into our seats, facing each other, while the host hands us our menus. He sets a tealight candle on the glass candleholder in the middle of the table, and the scent of vanilla fills our little corner of the restaurant. I try very hard to ignore the single rose in a vase on the table between us and instead open up the menu. Pretend like I'm reading it, while really I'm trying to hide that my face is flushed red from the embarrassment of this all. I'm going to kill Safiyah when I see her.

Tiwa picks up the menu too, and we both page through it in silence, while the ambient sounds of the restaurant continue around us. Somewhere in the distance, though, I hear a familiar voice. I lean my chair back, peeking out past the partition, and nearly topple out of my chair when I spot my sister.

"Are you okay?" Tiwa asks as I grip the table, trying to find my balance.

"I'm fine," I say, unsure if I should point out that Safiyah is here too. I decide against it. We definitely don't need my sister to make things even more awkward between us. Instead, we descend into silence again.

"Um, I like your new haircut," Tiwa says, breaking the silence after a few minutes.

"I thought with Eid coming up, it might be a good idea. It was getting a bit unruly," I say, not mentioning that Ammu basically forced me to get the haircut.

"Well, it looks nice," Tiwa says. She's looking at me expectantly, and I feel like I should say something nice about her too. I study her closely, trying and failing to avoid looking at her face. Maybe I can compliment her hair? But it's the same as always . . . I would compliment her shirt, but she's wearing her usual plain dark funeral colors. She might think I'm making fun of her, when I'm definitely not.

She's still looking at me, and I realize I've spent a bit too long silently studying her.

"I like your posture," I blurt out, panicked. "It's . . . good, straight. No slumping."

Tiwa snorts out a laugh at that. "Thanks, I guess?"

Before I can say anything else ridiculous, the waiter arrives to take our orders. Relief floods through me. At least nothing can go wrong while we're giving our orders. Or that's what I think. But the next minute, our waiter launches into a list of menu items specifically created for couples.

"We have a number of dishes perfect for sharing between two. Our most popular would be the heart-shaped sushi, made with rice and salmon. Our chef's special is a ramen sharing bowl for two," the waiter says, looking between us knowingly.

I don't know where to look—at the waiter, who continues prattling off different menu items meant for couples, or Tiwa, who is studying her menu like it's the most fascinating thing she's ever read in her entire life. I just know that I have to put a stop to this madness.

"I'll just have a chicken ramen," I say, interrupting the waiter. "For one," I add quickly, in case he gets the wrong idea.

"And I'll have a prawn ramen, also for one," Tiwa says, following my lead.

"All right . . ." the waiter says, inputting our orders into his tablet. He sounds a little disappointed that we didn't choose any of the dishes he listed off. "I'll just bring out your complimentary chocolate strawberries to share in a minute, and—"

"No thank you!" I cut in.

The waiter blinks at me. "Sorry?"

"I'm allergic to strawberries, so that won't be necessary," I say.

"Well, we do have an alternative option. Marshmallows dipped in chocolate?" the waiter says, looking from me to Tiwa like he's hoping she'll have a saner reaction.

"Marshmallows aren't halal, so we'll have to turn that down too," Tiwa says.

The waiter nods. "I'll just take your menus, then." He reaches his hand out and Tiwa passes him her menu. I grip mine, though. How will we get through this dinner without hiding behind our menus?

"I might want dessert," I insist. "I'll just keep it."

"Dessert is a different menu, sir, I must insist . . ." the waiter says, prying the menu out of my hands somehow. I look at it longingly as the waiter walks off with both menus.

"I didn't know you were allergic to strawberries," Tiwa says when I turn back toward her.

"I'm not, actually . . ." I say.

Tiwa raises an eyebrow, and I feel heat rise up my cheeks. "So, why did you say you were?"

"I don't know. He was talking so much and I panicked," I say.

Tiwa smiles, and I try to ignore how that makes my heart skip a beat. The light from the candle flickers between us, casting a golden glow on Tiwa's skin. I know I should say something more to break the silence between us and the fact that we're holding each other's gaze for a little too long, but my mouth is dry, and my stomach is doing somersaults.

Coming to this restaurant was definitely a terrible idea. I glance at Tiwa's face, and how close we are. Or maybe it was the best idea ever.

Just then, the waiter returns carrying a bowl of ramen in each hand, and I'm relieved at how fast the service is. He places one in front of me, and one in front of Tiwa.

"Just let us know if you'll be needing anything else," he says, before shuffling off.

Tiwa and I both dig into our bowls immediately.

"This ramen is amazing," Tiwa says after her first bite. "Safiyah's recommendation was actually good."

"You thought it wouldn't be?" I ask.

"Well, Safiyah's tastes can be weird. Remember the time she told us to go to that pop-up ice-cream shop in the town square? And she said to try their mustard-flavored ice cream?"

I wrinkle up my nose at the memory.

"I feel like I can still taste it," I say.

"This one, though, we'll have to give her the credit," Tiwa says.

"I think she did more research on this one than the mustard-flavored ice cream," I say. When Tiwa gives me a questioning look, I lean forward and whisper, "Safiyah is here."

"Now?" Tiwa asks.

I nod. "I think on the other side of the partition."

We fall silent once again, but not because of any awkwardness this time. It's because Tiwa is leaning to the left, trying to hear Safiyah's voice through the partition. Her eyes widen when she hears Safiyah's laugh, followed by Ishra mumbling something indecipherable.

"She's on her date with Ishra?" Tiwa whisper-shouts, her eyes wide.

"*That's* why her recommendation is actually good this time around. I'm pretty sure she would scare Ishra off with her *usual* recs."

"I agree. She couldn't risk having a mustard ice cream incident on her date. Even I haven't forgiven her for that yet."

"Do you think Safiyah will invite her to the Eid party at our house this year?" I ask.

"I hope so," Tiwa says with a sigh. "And maybe she can even invite her to help Mom and me with all the setup for the party in the Walker Center, seeing as she works there. We'll need all the help we can get."

"Yeah, because we know Safiyah's idea of helping is sitting and ordering everyone else around," I say, rolling my eyes. "I can help too, though, if you wanted." I glance down at my half-finished bowl of ramen instead of Tiwa when I make the offer. I'm half afraid that she'll turn me down. Because what if this summer was just a fluke, and with us no longer working on the mural, we just go back to the way things were?

"Mom would love that," Tiwa says. "Since you came around the other day to pick up Laddoo, she keeps asking about when you'll be coming back to visit."

"I can come and help with whatever you need. And I can bring Laddoo back to you too."

"As long as he doesn't eat all the Eid food," Tiwa says sternly.

"I'll have a talk with him," I say. "It's about time he learned some table manners."

"I'll have you know that Laddoo has plenty of table manners. I trained him myself," Tiwa says.

"Figures," I mutter, and in response she flings a noodle at me.

The noodle hangs from my head, dangling across my face, and I sit in shock.

Tiwa bursts out laughing at that, and I raise an eyebrow at her.

"Think this is funny?"

"I think it is hilarious," she replies, eating her prawn noodles with a massive smile on her face.

"Sleep with one eye open, Tiwa," I say, pulling the stray noodle off.

She's still laughing at me and I can't help but smile back at her. There's a noticeable shift between us, and I feel lighter than I have all summer.

Somehow, even between the rose, the candle, and Safiyah on a date on the other side of the partition, the awkwardness between us fades away. Almost like we're friends. Just the way we used to be.

Act 3

THE BOILING POINT

21
A SLOW SINKING
Tiwa

"WHAT ABOUT THIS?" MOM ASKS, HOLDING UP A BRIGHT CANARY-yellow jumpsuit.

I try not to make a face at the suggestion.

"When have I ever worn yellow?" I ask rhetorically, because we both know the answer to that.

Mom rolls her eyes. "Tiwa, it's Eid, not a funeral. You can't wear black to every occasion, especially not a celebratory one and especially not when we are the ones hosting. We want our guests to feel the warm, bright Olatunji energy!" Mom declares, holding the yellow abomination toward me as if to illustrate her point. "Just try it on, you never know. You might like it."

I eye the jumpsuit warily. It looks like a tiny, misshapen version of a sun, and as I reluctantly take the hanger it drapes on, I feel like Icarus.

Mom smiles but it doesn't quite reach her eyes. "Please, just try it on for me? We can always pick out a backup option in case this one doesn't work out," she says. I sigh and mumble a *fine*. It's not like wearing yellow will kill me. Besides, I know the reason Mom is being pushy about this is because she's nervous. She knows some of the other aunties in the community look down on her not only for being a single mother, but also not looking like them, and she thinks some-how this Eid party might change their minds about us.

I'm not sure I care what they think.

Mom takes out her shopping list and nods. "Okay, next up on the list, we need to get the basket for the Secret Paaro gifts and also the tablecloths, disposable utensils, and decorations. Some lovely kids from the neighborhood volunteered with setup and they'd need to start at the Walker Center tonight. I can't believe it's only three days away . . ." Mom says as we move from the jumpsuits section of the store and over to the home, kitchen, and hardware section.

"Saf and Said offered to help out too," I say as she pushes the shop-ping cart over to the shelf with plastic plates and cutlery.

"Wonderful, you have all been so helpful with everything—oh, I almost forgot I still need to get Auntie Tope her Secret Paaro gift. She's so hard to shop for. That woman doesn't like anything."

This reminds me, I need to get my Secret Paaro gift for Safiyah's mom too before Eid.

She might like some kitchen stuff. I glance around the section, searching for something that could be a gift for her, but instead my eyes focus on the art supplies shelf. Specifically on the carved wooden paintbrush set.

I peer over at my mom, who is preoccupied with counting the dis-posable tableware, and shuffle over toward the paintbrushes.

The brushes have handles in different shades of purple and teal, all different heights and for different purposes, I assume. I don't know much about the differences between a flat brush and a thicker one, but I've seen Said use all of these at some point.

Something tells me he'd really love this set—especially the colors.

Would it be cheating to give two Secret Paaro gifts? Probably, but I guess there is nothing inherently wrong with it.

"Tiwa," I hear Mom call behind me. I turn to her and she is holding up a blue dinosaur-shaped cooking ladle. "Do you think Auntie Tope will like this?"

"I don't know," I say, unsure of why Mom thinks I'd be an Auntie Tope expert.

"I think she'll like it, and if she doesn't, what can I do? I don't have time for her wahala." Mom mutters the last part under her breath.

It seems the universe is playing a joke on her, giving her Auntie Tope as her Secret Paaro match, seeing as they both barely even tolerate each other's presence.

I stare at the place Mom got the ladle from. It seems to be a whole shelf dedicated to dinosaur-themed kitchen utensils, which is very niche but also quite endearing. I feel a heaviness settle in my chest when I think about why it is so endearing in the first place.

"Timi would have loved these," Mom says, holding up a dish towel with tiny velociraptors dotted around in a pattern.

"He really would have," I say, nodding in agreement. Timi's room used to be full of dinosaur memorabilia. Posters of fossils, figurines, and his *T. rex* stuffed toy he'd never go anywhere without.

When Timi died, Mom couldn't bear the thought of throwing it all out but she also couldn't bear the thought of keeping it. And so his things sit in Dad's attic in London, untouched. Waiting for the day Mom is ready to acknowledge the awful thing that happened that tore our family apart and destroyed our world forever.

I'm even surprised that Mom is mentioning him now. Timi is a no-go topic at home. She doesn't know about what's been happening with my petition to get the bylaw passed, and that it finally did, at the town hall, or at least if she does, I didn't tell her and we haven't discussed it. To be honest, I don't really like talking about Timi either. It just brings back memories I'd rather forget. I can't bring Timi back, but at least with this bylaw it feels like I'm doing something good.

"Timi always loved this time of year, remember? He especially loved Secret Paaro. He'd always make us those homemade tokens for a free hug, or a free massage. It was really sweet," I say quietly. I almost feel desperate to talk about it, talk about him, now that Mom has thrown me this very rare bone.

Mom doesn't say anything in response, just nods quietly, her eyes glazed over and distant.

After a few quiet moments, she finally tears her eyes away from the dinosaurs, pulls on a smile, and says, "Let's get going. We still have a lot of things to get from this list today."

I feel a slow sinking but I nod anyway.

Mom still isn't ready to speak about what happened two summers ago; I can tell she still blames herself for it all. Blames herself for letting him go out with his friend to play soccer in front of the house. For not telling him to be more careful. For not hearing the initial screams when the driver swerved onto the pavement.

For not being powerful enough to have reversed time and stopped this all from happening in the first place.

It was no one's fault but the driver's, and yet Mom won't forgive herself. I hope someday she can find a way to.

"Sure, I'll catch up to you. I just need to find a present for my Secret Paaro match," I say.

Mom nods and pushes her cart away without another word.

The heaviness from before doesn't shrink, or move, or leave. It stubbornly stays put, making it a little hard to breathe.

I wonder if maybe the heaviness has been there all this time, but I only noticed it now that Mom mentioned Timi . . . maybe.

I grab a nice floral apron for Auntie and then I look down at the paintbrushes in my hand. I place them both in my basket.

SAID AND TIWA'S FIRST EID ALONE

TWO YEARS AGO

IT WAS THE WORST OF TIMES. IT WAS THE WORST OF TIMES.

Even Dickens himself couldn't have written a more devastating series of events, nor could anyone have predicted what would happen over the course of one year.

Everyone had heard of the unfortunate tragedy that befell the Olatunji family that summer. Grief spread like wildfire around the town of New Crosshaven and beyond, as news of the accident and Timi's passing broke.

It was clear that nothing would be the same in the aftermath.

THE SHRILL TONE OF THE TELEPHONE IN THE LIVING ROOM sounds for the umpteenth time and Tiwa decides that enough is enough.

"Go away," Tiwa says to the ringing phone, and when that doesn't work she throws one of the cushions from the couch at the inanimate machine. It crashes down on the floor, pulling the cord out of the wall along with it. The sound finally stops. "Better," Tiwa mutters, and then goes back to her curled-up position on the sofa where she has been all morning.

It has been like this ever since *it* happened two weeks ago. The incessant calls have been endless, family members and friends constantly trying to check in.

She imagines it will only get worse with the Eid party later today.

In the distance she can make out the familiar sound of her mom shouting at her dad about how useless he is and her dad in turn shouting back at her about how unhappy he is.

The noise from the telephone has now been replaced with the sound of her parents arguing.

She buries her head in the couch pillows. It's not like she can exactly throw a cushion at her parents for them to stop. Based on past experience, they'll eventually grow tired of yelling at each other and instead go back to quietly grieving and not speaking or looking at the other. The house will soon fall silent, but it never lasted; eventually the tension will rise and fill the entire house once more.

Tiwa isn't sure what she hates more, the noise or the heavy silence.

Suddenly the house falls still, and Tiwa hopes that the arguing has finally stopped. But instead of the usual quiet she has come to expect after these arguments, she hears the sound of the door opening and footsteps descending the stairs.

"Tiwa, dear, you need to get up and start getting ready. We need to get to the Islamic Center in an hour for the Khans' Eid party," she hears her mom say from somewhere in the room.

Tiwa unburies herself, rolling over to look at her now. Her mom stands opposite from her, fully dressed in her Eid clothes, her arms folded, her face pale and tired-looking.

"I'm coming," Tiwa mumbles.

"Good, and hurry, we're already running late because of your father. He insists that he needs to bring some more rice when we all know there will be plenty of rice at the party," her mom says with an eye roll, walking out of the room while muttering to herself about the pointlessness of it all.

Tiwa can't tell if her mom means the rice or her dad.

Getting up feels impossible, let alone making the journey to her room. Her bones feel like lead and her head feels too heavy for her body to carry. She feels a part of this sofa now. Leathery, old, worn away, and unmoving.

She wonders if this is what it feels like to be dead. No longer able to feel anything, do anything. But she knows she isn't dead. Timi is. He's the one who isn't here anymore.

He's gone, while she and her family are trapped in this twisted reality.

She closes her eyes, whispering a prayer under her breath and asking Allah to give them all strength.

TIWA CAN HEAR THE LAUGHTER AND JOY POURING OUT OF THE Islamic Center before she's even at the front door. The cheerful shouts of "Eid Mubarak" fill the air.

She and her parents slip through the entrance, watching the celebrations from the edge of the room. At first, nobody notices that a new family has joined their midst. Until one of the aunties nearest to them turns, her eyes widening as recognition flashes in them. Slowly, more and more people turn toward them. The laughter ceases. So does the joy. The shouts of "Eid Mubarak" disappear into thin air, leaving behind an emptiness that Tiwa doesn't know how to fill.

"Tiwa!" Safiyah's voice rings out from the crowd. Tiwa glances around until she spots the familiar face, pushing through the aunties and uncles and hurrying toward her.

"Hi, Auntie and Uncle," Safiyah says, coming to a stop in front of them. "Eid Mubarak!" She throws her arms around Tiwa, and it's the first moment of comfort Tiwa has felt in a long time.

"Hi, dear, Eid Mubarak," Tiwa's mom says, smiling at Safiyah. "I hope you and your family are well. Is your mom—"

Before she gets the chance to finish, one of the aunties approaches them with a strained smile.

"Eid Mubarak," she says. "I heard about what happened. I'm so sorry for your loss."

Tiwa's mom's face falls.

"Eid Mubarak, Amina," she mumbles.

Amina Auntie places her hand on her heart, exaggerated sympathy on her face. "It's horrible to lose a child, especially a son. The entire community feels your loss. But take heart that he at least passed during the holy month of Ramadan. Allah will take care of him, so you don't need to worry."

All of them wear identical expressions of disbelief. Tiwa's mom's face changes from downcast to angry, her jaw clenched and her eyes narrow.

Safiyah glances at Tiwa, noticing how nauseous Tiwa looks. Safiyah turns back to Amina Auntie with a tight smile.

"Amina Auntie, it's horrible to lose *any* child, and of course Allah will take care of him as he will take care of us all, but that doesn't change what a devastating loss this is," Safiyah says.

Amina Auntie looks shocked and appalled at Safiyah's words. She opens her mouth to reply, but Tiwa's mom cuts her off.

"I think I'm going to go outside for some fresh air," Tiwa's mom mumbles. She turns around and swiftly exits the Islamic Center. Tiwa's dad looks after her for a moment, before he, too, slips out the door.

Amina Auntie shakes her head with displeasure, then hurries back to her auntie clique to report this whole affair, no doubt. Leaving Tiwa and Safiyah to deal with the fallout of her words.

"I hate that woman. This is why her kids all moved to Europe and don't speak to her anymore," Safiyah says, eyeing her best friend's low expression and demeanor. "There's some really good biryani here. I'll go get you some." She pulls Tiwa into one more hug before rushing away.

Tiwa stands there for a moment, watching the aunties and uncles gossip, and the kids running around playing. She feels like an outsider looking in.

She turns away and walks out into the warm evening air. Her parents are nowhere in sight; nobody is.

Tiwa shuffles to an empty bench and sits down. The sounds of the party seem too far in the distance now, almost like they're in another world altogether.

She thinks about Timi, and the funeral, and how she's yet to shed a single tear. How she's a monster for not crying for her own brother.

How her parents have been too busy with their own grieving and fighting to notice her grief at all.

How she's been left on her own to piece together the remnants of her family.

She remembers the Eids *before*, when they'd celebrate with the rest of the town. Eids where they weren't the black sheep of the town because of their grief. When they had no worries in the world. Or at least none like they do now.

Eids when Tiwa still spoke to Said, when they were best friends.

She wishes he were here now, and that they were still friends. Said would know the right thing to say. He always did.

"There you are! I've been looking all over for you," Safiyah says, emerging from the side of the Islamic Center with a steaming bowl of biryani in her hand, her purple salwar kameez blowing in the wind as she nears Tiwa.

"I needed to get away," Tiwa says, looking up at the Walker Center on the other side of the road now, where a very familiar ginger cat wanders about aimlessly.

"Don't blame you," Safiyah says, sitting down next to her on the bench. "I hate at least a quarter of the people in there. Here's your biryani."

Tiwa accepts the bowl but doesn't touch the food, not having much of an appetite as of late.

"I don't think I hate them; I just don't want to be around them. I don't want to bring down the mood. Eid is meant to be this huge celebration and I feel like I'm ruining it for everyone," Tiwa says.

Safiyah takes her hand and squeezes. "You're not ruining anything at all."

Tiwa finds that hard to believe. She saw the way the mood in the room immediately dampened when they'd walked in. The grief clinging to them like an unshakable scent, making everyone around them uncomfortable.

She watches the familiar ginger cat amble back into the Walker Center.

"Do you think it would be rude if I skipped out on the Eid celebrations and went to see Ms. Barnes in the library?"

Safiyah shakes her head. "I won't tell anyone your secret. We can even do a blood oath?"

"A pinkie swear is stronger. You know if you break it you'll get thirteen years of bad luck," Tiwa says.

"When have I ever broken a pinkie swear?" Safiyah asks.

Safiyah *had* never broken a promise in their many years of friendship; the two were like sisters at this point.

"I know, I was just giving you the terms and conditions," Tiwa says.

Safiyah sits up straight, offering her pinkie to Tiwa. "I pinkie swear," she says earnestly.

Their pinkies interlink, sealing the deal.

MEANWHILE, IN A LAND NOT SO FAR AWAY (ALSO KNOWN AS St. Francis Academy for Boys, located in the state of Virginia), Said sits in his English exam prep class, pretending to listen to his teacher Mr. Peters go on about Shakespeare while shading in a picture on the card he'd been working on for the past few days: a dinosaur in a pool of mishtis.

The bell goes off and Mr. Peters screams something about homework or a pop quiz or some other thing Said can't bring himself to care about right now. He just wants to go back to his dorm and sleep. He folds the card back up and places it in his pocket.

"Mr. Hossain," he hears as he tries to leave the class.

Said turns back to Mr. Peters impatiently.

"Is everything okay? You seemed a little distracted during class," he says.

"Everything's fine. I'm just worried about my art exam tomorrow," Said lies.

Mr. Peters observes him closely for a moment before nodding. "I'm sure you'll do well. After all, didn't you win the school art prize last semester? I pass your piece in the staff room all the time and we all love it, so try not to stress over it too much," he says.

Said has no plans of stressing over the art exam. He has other things on his mind.

He nods at Mr. Peters, smiling tightly before hurrying out of the classroom and over to Trinity House, climbing up to the dorm he shares with Julian. When he gets inside, he's relieved to find the room empty.

He remembers Julian mentioning something about a late exam practice, which means he'll at least have the room and the quiet for a few more hours.

He throws his things on the ground by the door, not bothering to take off his uniform. Instead he slumps down into his desk chair, the heaviness of the past few weeks weighing him down.

He takes out the card from his pocket, now a little crumpled, and looks at the message he'd begun writing.

I'm sorry for your loss. Sending my duas.

It all seems so empty. He barely even prays anymore, though he had done so a few days after he'd heard the news. When all else seemed lost he thought it couldn't hurt to try doing that again.

He looks at the black screen of his phone. It also wouldn't hurt to simply call *her*.

What would he even say? *I know last Eid was terrible with the cake incident and everything, and I know we haven't been friends in years but I'm sorry your brother died?*

Was it worse to say nothing at all or to face Tiwa again after everything?

Probably the former, he decides.

With a sigh he scrolls down to a number he hasn't called in years. It is Tiwa's house phone, since she didn't have a cell phone when they used to talk.

He closes his eyes and presses the call button, waiting for the ringing and then the inevitable sound of a familiar voice on the line. But instead, a different sound comes out.

"You have dialed an incorrect number, please try calling again."

His eyebrows scrunch, confused. He tries again and gets the same response.

The number he is calling doesn't work anymore. *Maybe they changed their phone number?*

He decides to call his mom since she would definitely know what their number is and also because he hasn't called her for Eid yet.

"Said?" his mom says.

"Hi, Ammu, Eid Mubarak," Said says.

"Eid Mubarak, shona," she says. "How are your exams going? We're really missing you here. Your abbu made you a scarf, he's sent it in the mail. Make sure you check to see if it's come in."

"He *made* me a scarf?" Said asks. He couldn't remember his dad ever making anything before.

"Yes, didn't I tell you? He decided to take up knitting during

Ramadan. It was all knitting and reading the Quran. You know your abbu, always picking up random hobbies," Said's mom says.

"Oh, right. I'll check the mail later today," Said says. "But . . . can I ask you something?"

"Go ahead," she says.

"I wanted to call the Olatunjis but I don't have their number anymore. Could you text it to me?" Said asks hesitantly.

"Of course," Said's mom says softly. "I've been praying for them every day this Ramadan."

"Me too," Said says. "Thanks, Ammu. I'll call them now, so I'll talk to you later."

"Don't forget to light the incense we sent over. It'll make your dorm room smell just like home," Said's mom says.

"I'll do it," Said says. "Bye, Ammu."

He finds the Olatunjis' new number in his text messages and dials it into his phone.

He waits for the phone to ring once more, drumming his fingers against his desk while his heart beats faster with each passing second.

"Hello," a familiar voice rings out. Said sits up, gripping his phone tighter. He's about to reply when the voice of Tiwa's mom continues. "You've reached the Olatunjis. We can't come to the phone right now, but please leave a message at the beep."

The phone emits a loud beep, and Said sits there in silence, unsure of what to do or say. He ends the call and tosses his phone onto his bed.

He pulls out the pack of incense sticks on his desk and the matches his mom somehow got through the school's mail security and lights them up, focusing on the smoke filling the room instead of the increasingly heavy feeling inside.

Though in separate states, Said and Tiwa both spend their Eid sharing the same feeling of loneliness, despite being surrounded by others.

Dickens put it best: "A multitude of people yet a solitude."

Said and Tiwa were alone, together.

22

YOUR FUNERAL

Said

"HOW MANY SETS OF CLOTHES DO YOU NEED FOR ONE WEEK?" Safiyah asks when she sees me carrying in my backpack full of stuff. I put it down on the mattress that I set up on the floor and dragged in here this morning.

"I wanted to be prepared," I say, a little defensive. "And I don't want to disturb Chacha and Chachi once they get in."

Safiyah still doesn't look very impressed at the fact that between the mattress and the stuff I've dragged in here, half her room has been overtaken by me. Not that anybody would know, considering her room is a mess.

"I thought Ammu told you to clean up in here," I comment, picking up a dress on the windowsill and tossing it to Safiyah. "She's not going to be happy when she comes in and sees the state of this place."

"This *is* clean," Safiyah says. "It's an organized mess."

I glance at the unmade bed, the clothes tossed in random corners of the room, the stack of books about to topple over on Safiyah's bedside table, and shake my head.

"Your funeral." I shrug.

Safiyah sighs, folding the dress in her hands. She doesn't have time to do much more tidying up, though, because the bell rings sharply. The next moment, Ammu's voice calls up.

"Safiyah, Said, they're here!" she says.

The two of us slip out of Safiyah's bedroom and down the stairs where Abbu's cousin, Munir Chacha, and his wife, Shazia Chachi, are exchanging hugs with our parents. Their eyes brighten when they spot us.

"Said!" Chacha says, slapping me in the back so hard that I stumble forward. Munir Chacha always does this whenever he sees me, yet somehow I block it out of my memory. Probably some kind of a trauma response.

"I swear, you grow more and more each time I see you," Shazia Chachi exclaims, pulling me into a hug.

I don't point out that I'm pretty sure that's how puberty works.

I grin and say, "As-salaam-alaikum, Chacha and Chachi, it's good to see you again. How was the drive?"

"Oh, you know how it is, long and tiring as always," Chacha says with a sigh. "Safiyah." He pats Safiyah on the back and kisses the top of her head as a greeting, while Ammu ushers them into the kitchen.

"Sit down. I'll get you something to drink," she says. "Said will take your bags up."

Chacha and Chachi follow Ammu and Abbu into the kitchen. I glance from the two suitcases and the backpack that Chacha and Chachi brought, to Safiyah still standing by the stairs.

"Go on, Said," Safiyah says. "Take the bags upstairs."

"You could help," I say, while grabbing the first suitcase with a grunt. Chacha and Chachi definitely do not pack light.

"I'm here for moral support," Safiyah says cheerily. I roll my eyes

240

and hurry up the stairs, while little tidbits of the conversation from the kitchen follow me up to my room. Chacha tells everyone about his brand-new car, and the move to Ohio, before swiftly moving on to grilling Safiyah about her studies. I tune most of it out, but as I'm carrying the last of their bags on my second trip upstairs, my ears perk up at the sound of my name.

". . . and if Said gets into Johns Hopkins, Amir would obviously be able to get him the lay of the land. Though I'm sure Said has a different specialization in mind than Amir," Chacha is saying. I feel my stomach sink. Even Munir Chacha is making plans for my future, it seems, dreaming of pairing me up with his son once I get to university.

The sinking feeling in my stomach quickly gives way to a simmering anger. My parents and I have never sat down to discuss my future career; nothing about Harvard or Johns Hopkins were ever discussed. It was only ever assumptions. And now they're going around telling everyone. If Munir Chacha knows about my supposed plans for Johns Hopkins to the point of preparing his son for my arrival, I wonder who else knows. I can guess all my parents' siblings, my grandparents, and everyone in my extended family.

I toss Chacha and Chachi's backpack on the floor of my room, and it hits the carpet with a thump. I wish I could just close the door to my bedroom and draw, but the dawat is about to start and there's no way Ammu and Abbu would let me get away with not attending at all.

Instead, I'll have to put on a smile and act like everything's all right. Act like I'm about to pack my bags for one of the universities my parents have been dreaming about me attending for years.

I hover at the top of the staircase, listening, but the conversation topic has changed swiftly from me attending Johns Hopkins, all the way to the Islamic Center and the fire. I take a deep breath and descend the stairs, pasting on a polite smile as I re-enter the kitchen.

Abbu and Munir Chacha are setting up the house by placing plastic chairs all around the kitchen and dining room, while Ammu is getting Chachi to taste every dish she has cooked for the dawat.

"Said, can you go help your sister in the living room?" Ammu asks.

"Sure, I'll help her," I say. I make my way over to the living room where Safiyah is cleaning up the dirty mugs from this morning and fluffing the pillows to perfection.

"Ammu sent me over to help," I say.

Safiyah barely glances up as she hands me the dirty mugs. "Just clean everything."

It doesn't take long before the bell rings and the first guests arrive. After that, we leave the front door unlocked as we always do, and Bengali families from New Crosshaven and surrounding towns begin to pour in and take up every corner of the house. Pretty soon, every room is filled with uncles and aunties discussing everything from politics and property prices, all the way to the latest gossip surrounding the Bengali community in Vermont.

Abbu reintroduces me to every single family with a proud smile and a clap on my back. And even though he never says it out loud, I can almost hear what's going through his head: that I'm bound for Harvard, or Johns Hopkins, or any of those other universities that he dreams about for me. That I'm the future doctor, and how this time next year when my college acceptances have rolled in, I'll be the talk of the town. If he only knew that it'll be for all the wrong reasons.

* * *

FINALLY, AFTER WHAT FEELS LIKE HOURS OF SMILING, NODDING, and saying salam, Ammu calls everyone into the dining room to eat. I sigh, leaning back against the banister of the stairs, tired from all the socialization.

From my spot by the stairs, I can see the uncles hovering over the dining table filled with food, complimenting Ammu's cooking even though they have yet to take a bite of it. Next, it'll be the aunties and their little kids, and finally Safiyah and I will get a chance to eat.

Considering I've been stealing bites since Ammu started cooking this morning, I'm not all that hungry. I decide to take advantage of the fact that everyone's busy to hurry up the stairs and into Safiyah's room. Maybe a chance to work on my sketches will finally help me calm down.

When I enter Safiyah's room, everything looks different. The bed is made, and all the clothes and books that were scattered everywhere just a few hours ago are gone. Including my backpack, which I had left on top of my makeshift bed.

Of course, the first time Safiyah cleans her room in who knows how long would be today. And of course it means she relocated my backpack, which has all my clothes, my sketchbook—basically everything that's important to me.

My jaw clenches as I begin opening up drawers, looking for my sketchbook. I wouldn't be surprised if Safiyah took things out of my bag. I don't find anything inside either of her bedside tables. I move toward the wardrobe at the back of the room, flinging the doors open. Inside, it's even more of a mess than Safiyah's bedroom was earlier. Obviously, she stuffed everything in here in her attempt to clean.

My breathing becomes uneven at the sight of it. I don't know if it's

243

even worth it to dig through it all, when I know Ammu's going to be calling me back downstairs any minute now. But it's not like Safiyah won't make me dig through it later anyway.

So I begin to comb through the mess, past Safiyah's clothes, books, and knickknacks. I know my backpack has to be in here somewhere. At the very back of the wardrobe, I feel a cardboard box that's filled to the brim. I pull it out, trying to make sure none of the clothes inside the wardrobe spill. Finally, I find my backpack. I grab it and check that everything is still inside, but then I notice that underneath it is a stack of familiar-looking envelopes tied together with an elastic band.

I pick it up, shuffling through the envelopes only to see Tiwa's old address on them. In my handwriting. There are others with Tiwa's familiar scrawl, addressed to me at school.

Letters we sent to each other. Unopened. Gathering dust in Safiyah's wardrobe.

For a moment, I can only blink at them. There are a million thoughts running through my head as I run my fingers along Tiwa's handwriting on the back of one of them. All those years ago, she wrote me back. But somehow the letters ended up here—both of ours did.

The answer to why they're here is obvious, but it's like my mind is trying to suppress it. Trying to live in denial.

But there's only one thing these letters could mean.

As if acting on their own accord, my feet carry me out of Safiyah's bedroom and to Ammu and Abbu's room next door, where all the kids are gathered. Some of them are playing a game on a tablet, while others are watching a finger puppet show Safiyah is putting on for them at the front of the room.

"Safiyah," I say. My throat feels dry. The kids barely notice me, but Safiyah looks up with an annoyed expression.

"I'm a little busy here, Said," she says. She holds up her pinkie finger with the elephant sock puppet and says in a deep voice, "I know exactly how to save everyone. I'm going to use my mighty trunk!"

The kids watch with awed expressions, like this is the best show they've seen in their entire life.

"Safiyah, I really need to talk to you. It's important," I say through gritted teeth.

Safiyah must realize something is wrong because she quickly glances over at me again, worry coloring her features.

"All right, kids, now it's your turn with the finger puppets," she says, sliding the puppets off each finger and handing them to different kids. "See if you can come up with a good ending to the story."

She follows me outside the bedroom, closing the door behind her.

"What's going on?" she asks.

I don't answer. Instead, I hold up the stack of envelopes, gripping them so tight that my knuckles are white.

"Why do you have these letters?" I ask, even though each word feels more difficult to get out than the next.

Safiyah's eyes widen, flickering between the letters and me. "Said, it's not what you think."

"So you didn't keep these letters hidden away for the past four years?" I ask, my voice rising. "You didn't destroy my friendship with Tiwa? You didn't lie to me?"

"I didn't, I can explai—" Safiyah's voice is trembling, but I cut her off before she can finish.

"Four years. You lied to me for four years. Then you watched what happened with Tiwa and me, and kept lying over and over again," I say.

"Said, I promise it wasn't—I wasn't—I was just trying to help. I did it because . . ." But Safiyah's words wash over me in a wave. Heat prickles my skin, and it feels like all the air is being sucked out of my lungs. My blood is pumping so fast in my ears, it feels like I've been running a marathon.

"I can't listen to this," I say, turning away from her.

"Said, wait!" Safiyah calls, but I don't wait to hear her explanations. She basically admitted to hiding the letters. That was all I needed. The only truth I'm interested in.

"Said, are you okay?" Ammu is by the front door, putting away a coat into our closet. She peers at me closely and I step away, looking for some kind of a way out from her sharp-eyed gaze. Ammu is able to read me a little too well, and I'm not interested in having a conversation with her about Safiyah or the letters.

"I'm fine," I say, when I spot Laddoo's orange tail peeking out from underneath one of the armchairs nearby. "I just have to take Laddoo out for a walk." I pick him up and cradle him in my arms, ignoring his meows of protest.

"I didn't think cats went on walks," Ammu says thoughtfully.

"Yes, Laddoo . . . loves them. I'll see you later," I say. I quickly step out before Ammu can ask any more questions. Like why if Laddoo loves walks so much nobody has ever taken him on one since I brought him home.

I breathe in the fresh air outside, and the rush of angry thoughts in my head feels a little less overwhelming. I walk a little ways from the house, trying to make sense of everything. Of all the things I expected, I would have never thought that Safiyah would betray me like this. Worse, that she would betray me and lie about it for years on end.

I walk far enough away that I can't see our house anymore. I know I should go back, but the thought of going into that house and smiling and laughing with the aunties and uncles feels like torture.

Instead, I slip my phone out of the pocket of my jeans and dial Julian. He's the only person I can really talk to about this.

The phone rings twice before his familiar, comforting voice sounds on the other line.

"Said!" Julian exclaims in greeting, like he usually does when I call. But the excitement in his voice doesn't make me feel better this time.

"Hey," I say.

"Everything okay?" Julian asks. "I thought you were supposed to have your Bengali thing today? Don't tell me. One of the uncles got too heated about politics and your parents had to break up the party."

"No." I sigh, wishing that was what had happened. "It's . . . Safiyah." I hesitate for a moment. If I tell Julian, the letters and Safiyah's betrayal become real. Then I have to tell Tiwa. I have to deal with the situation.

"Did she relegate all your stuff to a dark corner of the room? I mean, you *are* a guest in her bedroom, so you can't expect that—"

"I found letters in her wardrobe," I spit out. "Letters I tried to send to Tiwa. I don't even know how Safiyah got them. All this time, I thought Tiwa was ignoring my letters, ignoring me. That she forgot about me as soon as I left for school. That she didn't want anything to do with me. But now I know what it was—Safiyah. She somehow got the letters and then watched as Tiwa and I stopped being friends over them. She lied to me for years, Julian! For four years!"

Julian is silent on the phone line for a beat.

"What did Safiyah say?" he asks, his voice suddenly stoic.

"I don't know, she just kept saying she promised she had a reason and she could explain. But she basically admitted it, she stole the letters. All this time, I thought Tiwa was to blame but really it was my own sister," I say, my voice wavering. It was my own sister who betrayed me. My own sister.

"Said, I'm . . . sorry. Maybe you should let Safiyah explain. She could have a good reason for what she did," Julian says.

"Are you serious?" I ask angrily. "Are you really defending her right now?"

"I'm just saying that . . . I mean, this sucks. And I'm sorry, Said," Julian says slowly. "I'm sorry. I thought that you hated Tiwa, and that she was bad for you. That Safiyah was trying to protect you. She *was* trying to protect you. That's why she asked me to take the letters and give them to her. I didn't know that it was going to be this huge thing or that—"

Julian. It was Julian too. Of course it was Julian. How else would Safiyah have even gotten those letters? Somebody needed to steal them out of my mail slot at school, and Julian was the only other person who had access to it since we share a room. Safiyah needed help, and Julian was there to help. To betray me.

"You could have talked to me!" I say. "Why would you just listen to Safiyah? She's not your friend, I am!"

"I know, Said. I was just—I thought I was protecting you."

"By betraying me?" I spit out.

"I wasn't trying—"

I don't let Julian finish his shitty explanation. I hang up the call and turn off my phone, putting it in my pocket. My head is pounding, and my thoughts are chaos. Only one thing registers properly: Julian and Safiyah both betrayed me. They both lied to me. The two people I trusted most in the world.

It feels like the ground beneath me is unstable with this new knowledge in my head. I hold Laddoo close to me and let my legs carry me farther away from my house. I'm not sure where I'm going or what I'm going to do. All I know is that I think Laddoo may be my only friend left in the world.

Somehow, I find myself in front of the Islamic Center, staring at the spot where I had envisioned my mural would go. The mural that'll never happen now, thanks to Mayor Willy. Still, I set down my backpack and sit down on the ground, staring up at the blank wall that could have been my canvas.

And suddenly, I have an idea. Mayor Williams may have gotten everyone onboard with his plans for a fancy apartment block, but maybe if the mural existed—if I made it real—people would finally see how important the Islamic Center is and try harder to stop the demolition. Wasn't that why Tiwa wanted me to paint the mural in the first place?

I glance around me, but the street is quiet. There are no cars, and no people. Nobody to stop me.

So I put Laddoo down, dig into my backpack for my paint supplies, and get started.

THREE HOURS, HALF A MURAL, AND A LEMON TART FROM ABIGAIL'S later, some of my anger has dissipated. I know there's only so much longer I can keep away from home anyway, especially with my phone turned off. It's evening now and I'm lucky that no cars or people have come by while I deface the grounds.

The house is quieter than when I left it. Most of the cars belonging to the aunties and uncles that crowded our driveway a few hours ago have emptied out.

I slip inside and set Laddoo down. He immediately dashes away and up the stairs, like he's had enough of me for one day. I can't blame him, considering I've been using him as my own personal therapy cat for the past few hours.

"Said!" Abbu emerges out of the living room, a grin lighting up his face. "Where have you been? Why are your clothes covered in paint? So many of the aunties and uncles were asking about you."

"Sorry, Abbu. I had to take care of something," I say, figuring the *taking the cat for a walk* excuse might fall apart under any kind of scrutiny.

"That's okay. It's just that I wanted you to meet Ziyad, but it's fine. I got his contact information for you." Abbu hands me a piece of paper with an email address and phone number quickly scribbled on it.

"Er, who's Ziyad?" I ask hesitantly. Abbu and Ammu know so many people in the Bengali community that sometimes it's hard to keep track of them.

"You know Ziyad." Ammu's voice floats in from the kitchen first, before she appears at the doorway with a smile. "You two used to hang out all the time when you were kids, and you'd go to these dawats together. He's two years older than you, Akhter bhai's son?"

That rings a bell for me, but it doesn't really answer why my parents are suddenly giving me his phone number.

"Well, it doesn't matter. You'll remember him when you see him in a few weeks," Abbu says.

"Why would I—"

"I talked to Akhter bhai about your dreams of medicine at Harvard and Ziyad is pre-med there and he said whenever you're free this summer he'll take us all up there and show us around. Insight that you definitely wouldn't get with just any campus tour," Abbu says. He looks at me like he expects me to thank him for this, but all I'm feeling is that burning rage clawing up my chest.

"I didn't ask you to do this," I say, trying to keep the anger out of my voice.

"You don't have to ask, Said," Ammu says, her smile widening.

"No, I didn't—I didn't *want* this," I say. I crumple up the piece of paper in my hands, and my parents watch as if I'm desecrating something holy. "I don't want to go on a campus tour with Ziyad, I don't want to go to Harvard, and I don't *want* to study medicine." My voice rises with every word. "All of that is what *you* want because you think you know everything about me, but you don't. I wish that you would ask me even once what *I* want!"

When I glance up, my parents are both looking at me in a way they never have before: with disappointment in their eyes. They somehow look smaller too, like my words have shrunk them down into different versions of who they are.

I step back from them, like that'll somehow protect them from the disappointment.

"I'm sorry," I say. "I didn't mean to shout. I just . . . I'm tired. I'm going to go get some rest."

I turn around and hurry up the stairs. Neither of my parents call me back or try to stop me. I'm not sure if I'm happy or sad about that.

Upstairs, Safiyah's bedroom door is closed. I hover before it for a moment, but the last thing I want to do is see or hear my sister. I know it'll just fill me up with rage again. Instead, I turn around and head to the study. Closing the door, I lie down on the small couch and close my eyes, thinking about how this may be the worst day of my entire life.

23

SPEAK OF THE DEVIL

Tiwa

IT BECOMES CLEAR HALFWAY THROUGH DOING MY HENNA THAT I probably should have watched a tutorial first.

The lines I've drawn on my hand are wonky and uneven, and all my flowers so far look like multiple intersecting Venn diagrams.

"Is that meant to be a spider?" Mom asks as she collapses onto the sofa next to me. We're both exhausted after a long morning spent setting up most of the Walker Center hall for the Eid party tomorrow, and yet she still has energy to judge my art. I scowl, looking up at her as she judges my handiwork while eating her plantain chips as though she did not just insult me.

"*No.* They are flowers."

"Oh . . . I guess I can see that," she says with an unsubtle frown. It's clear she's lying.

I look down at the mess on my palms. It looks like someone who secretly hates me has vandalized my skin. I wish henna was easy to start over with; because of how slow I am so much of it has already dried. The damage is done.

"Usually Dad is already here by now and does it for me. I guess I didn't inherit his artistic gene," I say with a shrug, going back to drawing my unshapely *spider*.

"Yup, you got all that lack of talent from me," Mom says with a wide smile. I roll my eyes as her phone rings loudly between us.

"Speak of the devil . . ." Mom mutters as she puts down her chips and picks up her phone. "Hafiz, kilonshele? I'm busy."

"Dad?" I ask, perking up.

Mom nods, looking mildly annoyed in the same way she always does whenever he calls.

"Put him on speaker," I whisper.

Mom puts the phone down on the coffee table and taps the speaker button.

"Hi, Dad!" I say.

"Hello, Tiwa, how've you been? Sorry I missed our call last night," Dad says, and something in his voice is off. He sounds low, and I don't have to ask to know why.

Even with the celebrations and everything, Dad is always weird about Eid because of what it symbolizes in our family.

Timi being gone.

"I'm okay. I'm currently trying to do my own henna *and failing miserably*, might I add. It looks nothing like the reference photo. Mom thought I was drawing spiders."

Dad chuckles. "Well, spiders are good luck in Islam," Dad says.

Mom makes a face, since she is not the biggest fan of spiders or bugs. Lucky or not.

Before I can speak, Dad's talking again. "Aisha, can you take me off speaker quickly? I need to talk to you in private."

Mom grabs her phone from the table and pushes herself off the sofa, placing the phone to her ear now as she brushes the crumbs from the plantain chips from her leggings. "You're off speaker," she says in a low voice. I glance up as she walks over to the dining table, shuffling the letters silently as the soft hum of Dad's voice rings out from the line.

I wonder what they could be talking about that needs to be so private?

"Of course, Hafiz. I'm sure she'll understand . . ."

I'm guessing I'm the *she* in this situation. What do I need to understand?

My phone buzzes with a text notification, momentarily pulling my focus away.

Saf: Can we talk later?

"Yes," Mom says, while I make a mental note to reply to Saf when I have the chance. "Just let me know if anything changes. Okay, bye." Mom hangs up the phone and looks at me with a weary apologetic glance.

My heart thrums in my chest and I worry that it's another family Eid death. Is Dad dying? This is how it happened with Timi two years ago. We got a call that someone had seen him playing outside and had found him on the side of the road. A hit-and-run.

I remember Mom had picked the phone up and her face dropped into this ugly, twisted expression as she'd asked the person *Where is he?*

I ready myself. Waiting to put on a brave face, accept the news, figure out how to go on again.

"Is everything okay?" I ask, even though I know something is wrong. It's just an easy question to ask, I guess.

Mom nods. "Yes, everything is okay, mashallah. It's just your dad . . . he—" She stops for a moment, like she's trying to figure out how to word this. I feel sick to my stomach suddenly. "He wanted me to tell you that he loves you very much and can't wait to hang out again in person—"

"Is he okay?" I ask, feeling tense.

Mom nods. "He's well, don't worry. It's something else."

"What is it?" I ask.

Mom sighs. "He's not coming," she finally says.

My muscles don't relax at the news. Objectively this is better than him or anyone dying, but still I feel my bones stiffen and the knot in my throat grow in size.

"What do you mean?" I ask, even though I know exactly what she means.

He's not coming to Vermont. He's not coming for Eid.

"He can't make his flight. Faiza is unwell and he promised he'd stay there with her. He was going to tell you himself but didn't want to disappoint you."

I feel a burning inside, my eyes heavy and glazed over. I never had a problem with Dad's new girlfriend—or *partner* as he likes to say to make it seem more legitimate since they aren't married yet. Faiza is nice enough to me, never used to get in the way of things. But recently she's the excuse that crops up when Dad can't call or watch movies with me.

And now she's the reason he can't come to Vermont for Eid.

I don't realize I've been squeezing the henna tube until I feel the cold of the paste and smell the pungent earthy scent.

I look down, and right on top of the pattern I'd spent ages trying to do, there is now a pile of discarded henna paste.

"Oh crap," I say. This is all truly a disaster.

"Language," Mom says.

"Sorry," I mumble. I don't bother looking up at her, scared that if I do, all she'll see is my anger and think it's aimed toward her.

"Are you okay, Tiwa?" Mom asks after a nervous beat.

Eid had always been the thing that united my family, reminded us that we had each other, forever and always. And now that's gone. Of course I'm not okay. Maybe it was naive of me to think that things would always stay the same. With Timi and Ms. B gone, I should have known by now that nothing good lasts forever.

"I think I'm going to go and dry my hand in my room and fix this mess before it gets any worse," I say, still averting my gaze and awkwardly pushing myself up from my seat. It really wasn't very smart of me to draw henna on my dominant hand.

"Okay . . . just be careful with the sofa," Mom says. I can basically feel her eyeing the brown paste and the light gray fabric of the couch. When I'm finally up, she adds: "And the walls!"

I make sure to avoid vandalizing my mom's precious sofa and greige walls as I make my way out of the living room. Now away from my mom and her worried prying eyes, I try to calm down.

I should have known he wasn't coming. It's like the Islamic Center burning was an omen all along that Eid this year was going to suck.

In the bedroom, on top of my sheets, I see the Eid gift I'd wrapped for Dad earlier. I also see the box that I always bring out whenever he's here. It contains all our favorite movies, our favorite board games . . . random memories.

We usually go through this box and spend hours recounting old embarrassing things, like the time we went bowling as a family and I ended up slipping and crashing headfirst into the pins.

Instead of helping me up, Dad took a picture of me inside the pin hole.

Dad thought it was hilarious and called the event and the picture *the first sighting of the wicked witch of the bowling alley* since my big bowling shoes were also red.

A lot has changed since then. I can accept that those memories are exactly that, memories. They aren't real anymore. They are some other version of ourselves that died. Maybe I need to let go, accept that my family is really long gone.

I snatch up the present, stuffing it into the box before grabbing the box and trying to haul it onto the top shelf in my closet.

I realize quite quickly that I should have gotten my footstool out to make my life easier. I quickly move to shove everything, but as was established by the botched henna job, I clearly don't like myself very much.

After many shoves and the slam of the closet door, I finally have it inside, waiting for Eid next year when Dad may or may not make another appearance. Maybe this is my new normal. Maybe I'll never see him again.

A little dramatic, maybe, but who even knows at this point.

I used to be so sure Dad would always show up for me, but now nothing is certain. Nothing at all.

My phone buzzes, pulling me out of my wallowing.

It's a message from Said.

Said: Hey, are you free right now?
I have something I wanted to
show you

I remember that I need to message Safiyah back, but I'll just call her later.

In the distance I can hear Mom padding around the apartment, and it makes me think about how I want to escape this small space that reminds me of so many painful things. So with my *good* hand I respond.

Sure, where should we meet?

I MEET SAID AT THE ISLAMIC CENTER, OR RATHER OUTSIDE OF IT on the other side of the street.

He's wearing a shirt that is probably a few sizes too small and what seems to be old sweatpants, both of which are covered completely in bright paint.

"Hi . . ." I say, approaching him slowly.

He turns to me, and I see that the paint explosion doesn't just stop at his clothes.

There's pink and blue paint in his hair—which is pushed back by a black headband—and smudges of paint on his cheeks, his temple, and his chin.

Said smiles brightly and waves me over.

I hesitate for a few beats before I walk over to him. I realize this is the first time I've seen him since the weird *ramen not-date date*. It feels strange seeing him now that there's this unspoken shift in our friendship—if you can even call it that.

"Hey!" he says.

Now in front of him, I take in his appearance again, in all his rainbow glory.

"Did a unicorn piss on you or did something worse happen?" I ask.

He looks down at his clothes, as if he didn't notice the color there before.

"Something worse," he says in a low measured tone. "This is the handiwork of pure unadulterated joy, Tiwa."

I smile at the ridiculousness of it all. "Ew, that *is* way worse."

He shrugs. "Told you so. But anyway, I didn't call you here just so you can stare at me. I wanted to show you this in person. I feel like pictures just don't quite do it justice," Said says, gesturing across the road over to the Islamic Center now.

I gasp when I see it. I'm not sure how I didn't notice it when I walked over to him moments ago. It could probably be seen from space.

In front of us is the Islamic Center, only now a huge blue sky- and sea-themed mural runs all the way up from the ground to the top of the walls.

I take in the details in shock.

I recognize the inspirations almost immediately: Van Gogh's *Starry Night*, elements of the Bengali folk art he showed me. Where the cypress tree was in Van Gogh's painting, Said has a sprawling acacia tree with spiders dangling from the branches and webbing wrapped around the tree trunk. In the background, the bare mountains are filled with people. The houses are brightly colored like the buildings in New Crosshaven, and the swirling sky is filled with birds.

All these elements come together to form something truly magical.

"When did you do this?" I ask.

"Mostly yesterday and some of it this morning," Said says, still smiling, but in a sheepish way. He looks nervous, like my opinion on it matters when it really shouldn't.

"It's beautiful," I say, looking at him. "It really is."

Said's face is a little pink and I can't tell if it's the paint or the sun that is the cause of it.

"Not so bad for a guy covered in unicorn urine. Maybe unicorn piss is good luck," Said says, averting his eyes from me, back to the mural.

I raise an eyebrow at him. "I thought you said it was pure unadulterated joy?"

He nods. "That too."

There's a moment of quiet and I just look at how majestic the Islamic Center looks now, even though the marks of the fire still show.

"Is that the man in the moon?" I ask, pointing at the crescent moon and the boy sitting in the curve and holding a star.

"Mhm, up there in all his glory. I think he's my favorite part of it all," Said says, his eyes shifting closely to my hand and the "art" on it. "Is that meant to be henna?"

"Yes," I say looking up at him. His face screws up.

"Oh . . . it's, um, it's definitely something," he says, ignoring the glare I shoot him. "Safiyah was supposed to practice on me before Eid but we aren't really speaking right now."

I stop glaring and instead my face falls into one of surprise.

"Oh, I didn't know that . . . what did you do?" I ask, folding my arms, in part to take the focus away from my bad henna and also to get ready to judge him.

He looks away from me again, seeming hesitant.

"Is it that bad?" I ask, sensing that something weird has gone down.

He finally clears his throat, but completely looks away from me, so that I can't see his face at all.

"Before, years ago now, I think . . . we agreed to send each other letters. I used to write to you all the time and I always wondered why you never wrote back . . ." he starts, and now I'm confused.

I *did* write back. Until his letters stopped coming, that is. What does he mean? I almost protest, but he's speaking again.

"Well, turns out Safiyah had been somehow intercepting them. I found a bunch of them in her room yesterday. We had a big fight and I came here and decided to make the mural while I calmed down. I still can't believe it, to be honest. I don't know why she'd do that."

I take in his words, all of them whirring in my mind at a million miles per hour.

Safiyah took the letters? Said was writing to me? Why did Safiyah take the letters? Why didn't she tell me?

Maybe this is what she was messaging about earlier. She wanted to come clean.

I feel so many things right now. Hurt, overwhelming amounts of confusion, and a weird ache inside about what this all means.

I was angry at Said all these years because I thought he'd just stopped contact with me. It didn't help that he would act all weird whenever he came back for winter, spring, and summer breaks. I thought it was because he'd made his brand-new rich boarding school friends and no longer needed me. But it was because he thought I was doing the same thing to him.

Said finally looks at me, and I can see a swirl of hurt, anger, and frustration in his eyes. The green paint on his forehead makes him look slightly queasy too.

"I can't believe her sometimes. She's always interfering in things. If she hadn't taken those letters, who knows, we could've—I don't know—I know she's your best friend and everything. I just can't believe her."

She isn't my best friend, I think to myself. She's more than that.

She's like my sister, the one constant in my life at all times. Which is why of all the emotions I'm feeling right now, anger isn't one of them.

Safiyah isn't malicious. There's more to this story.

I wonder what was in those letters. All the things he'd written that I'd never gotten to read.

"What kind of things did you write?" I ask after a quiet moment.

"What?" Said asks, looking at me again.

"Your letters . . . anything interesting?" I ask.

He looks pensive for a moment and then shakes his head, the pink on his face growing more vibrant. "I think just that I missed you or something weird like that . . . How about you?"

He missed me?

I almost can't stop the smile that wants to break through. But luckily I'm able to fight it.

"I used to write to you about really cringey things. I'm almost glad you never got them."

"Cringey like what?" Said asks, his interest piqued.

"I'm not saying," I tell him, not wanting to recount the embarrassing mentions I had in there of accidentally calling my English teacher "Mom." I'm not sure he'd let me live that down. I'm not even fully sure why I told him that. It was probably the result of that really pointless article I'd seen that said in order to get your crush to like you back, you need to disclose embarrassing things about your life to them. That way they feel bad for you and see you as someone who needs protecting from the *big bad world*. So feminist.

I feel my neck warm, remembering that I did indeed once have a crush on Said. Before all the anger and hatred filled in the holes that his supposed betrayal had left behind.

I look at him again and I feel my stomach flutter again. *Do crushes ever really go away?* I wonder.

Besides, Said is objectively a really attractive person; scientifically it makes sense to crush on him. Doesn't mean I want to *date* him. That would be the worst idea ever, I think. Probably. Maybe.

"I can assure you, you weren't as bad as me," Said says quietly, nudging me.

"I hardly doubt it. For an unlucky person like me, I think it's rather lucky those letters weren't seen at the time," I say, feeling even warmer and avoiding his gaze now.

In the corner of my eye I see him reaching down for something.

"I just had a thought," Said says.

"What is it?"

"You said you're unlucky, so I figured we should match, seeing as unicorn piss brings luck," Said says, and I finally turn to him alarmed as I watch him dip his fingers into a paint pot and start bringing them near me.

"Don't you dare, Said. I will murder you in broad daylight—I don't care," I say, stepping back away from him.

He gives me a devilish smile. "I'm just joking. I would never."

I roll my eyes. "Yeah, like I believe you. I'm getting a restraining order."

"It's true! I still need to put finishing touches on the mural. Can't waste any more paint."

"I can't believe this isn't finished. It already looks amazing," I say. "You know if the aunties and uncles saw this, they would definitely eat this up. And not just them, I think a lot of people would love this."

"Too bad they won't get to see it."

"Everyone's coming to Walker for Eid tomorrow; they'll see it then. Maybe it'll actually influence more people to speak up in the community," I say, even though I get his resignation. Seeing the mural, though, makes me angrier; there's no way they can get rid of all this.

"You heard Mayor Willy. There's not enough of us to make a difference in this town. If we had five New Crosshavens it would be more than enough, but we don't. We're outnumbered and the Islamic Center is being demolished in two days, a day after Eid. I guess I'm just glad I got to show you the mural at least. You're probably the only person I really wanted to see it anyway," he says.

My heart stutters again and I try to ignore his face. Instead I focus on his words.

If we had five New Crosshavens . . .

"What if we did have more than one New Crosshaven . . ." I say.

Said's eyebrows furrow. "What do you mean?"

"I think I have an idea on how to save the Islamic Center."

24

SUGAR COOKIES AT ABIGAIL'S

Said

A BIKE FLIES PAST US AS TIWA TURNS THE CAR INTO IMAM Abdullah's neighborhood. She's gripping the steering wheel so tight, you'd think her life depended on it.

"Did you see that? A kid on a bike just overtook us," I say, pointing at the bike still in the distance.

Tiwa barely glances at it, too busy staring straight ahead, or checking her mirrors.

"That bike was going too fast. That's dangerous . . . biking," Tiwa says defensively.

"It seemed to be going at a normal speed," I say, hoping that will urge Tiwa to go above 15 mph.

"Look, we're in a residential area. A cat or something could run out at us at any second!" Tiwa says.

I look around for all of these alleged cats waiting to run out in front of our car, but it's evening so it's already dark out, and the street is essentially deserted.

"I think you need to take a right up ahead," I say, studying the houses we pass by. All the houses look more or less the same, but I remember Imam Abdullah's front lawn had a row of pink rosebushes.

"Are you sure or are you just guessing?" Tiwa asks.

"I'm sure," I say, not sure at all.

Tiwa turns right, and I finally spot the familiar house toward the end of the street.

"There, the one with the rosebushes," I say, pointing it out. Tiwa pulls the car up behind the silver Mitsubishi in the driveway, and we climb out. Unlike last time I was here, all seems quiet.

I knock on the front door twice, the sound reverberating a little too loudly in the quiet.

"What if he isn't home?" Tiwa asks in a soft voice. Her question is answered by the sound of footsteps on the other side of the door. They shuffle closer, before the door finally clicks open.

Imam Abdullah stands in the doorway wearing a white vest, a checkered lungi, and a green face mask that makes him look closer to an alien than our local imam.

"Sorry, are we interrupting something?" Tiwa asks.

"No . . ." Imam Abdullah glances down at himself, like he'd completely forgotten what he was wearing. "I was just . . . doing some self-care before bed. A self-care routine is important to have, you know."

Tiwa and I nod along in agreement, though it's a struggle to stifle a laugh. I've only ever seen Imam Abdullah in his thobe, or when he occasionally wears panjabis or sherwanis for special occasions like Eid. He's always the height of composure and even now, while we're interrupting his self-care routine, he manages to look pretty composed.

"Is something wrong? Why are you both here? Maghrib prayer was over a little while ago," Imam Abdullah says.

"Well . . . it's about the Islamic Center," I begin, sharing a glance with Tiwa. We probably should have spent less time during the car ride bickering about Tiwa's driving speed and more time deciding on how exactly we were going to explain our plan to Imam Abdullah to get him on board.

"I was there at the town hall meeting," Imam Abdullah says in a grave voice. "It's hard to believe that we're losing yet another mosque in the area."

"That's just it, we don't have to lose the Islamic Center," Tiwa says. "Said and I have a plan for how we can save it. We remembered you mentioning all the mosque closures around Vermont, and I think that if we could get all the Muslims from the surrounding towns here, we could show the mayor that there *is* a need for the Islamic Center. He keeps saying that the Islamic Center doesn't serve the community because it's just been a few of us going to him with our concerns. There's only a few of us in New Crosshaven. But the Muslim community in Vermont isn't small, and we deserve a place of our own where we can build our community. We just have to show the mayor that!"

Tiwa seems a little out of breath as she finishes her speech.

"You know the Muslim community around Vermont," I add. "We thought if you contacted some of them, maybe they'd come."

Imam Abdullah just blinks slowly for a moment, like he's trying to make sense of everything. But then he heaves a sigh. "Okay. I'll make a few calls."

ABIGAIL'S IS ALMOST COMPLETELY DESERTED WHEN WE SLIP IN through the front doors a half hour later, which isn't surprising seeing as it is near closing time. The cashier gives me a weird look as I collapse into one of the seats by the window. Tiwa sits on the chair opposite me and frowns.

"You should have changed," she comments.

I glance down at my shirt still covered in paint. I'd almost forgotten that I was still wearing it, and that it's not exactly appropriate attire.

"When would I have changed? Should I have borrowed Imam Abdullah's lungi?" I ask.

"Hey, I always thought lungis were pretty fashionable," Tiwa says. "I mean, your dad always makes it look very chic."

"Bangladeshi casual chic."

"Exactly." Tiwa smiles.

I look over the menu, even though I know exactly what I'm craving. When I glance up at Tiwa again, she quickly looks away like she had been watching me. I try to ignore the flutter in my stomach and lean forward instead.

"So, do you know what you want?"

Tiwa shrugs, not quite meeting my eyes.

"I was thinking . . . sugar cookies," I say.

Tiwa turns to me this time, her gaze holding mine for a moment. "The pineapple-shaped kind?"

"That kind exactly," I say with a grin. "I can't remember the last time I had them."

"The day before you left," Tiwa says softly. "Remember? Ms. Barnes gave you fifty dollars as a farewell present and you decided the best way to spend it would be to buy as many sugar cookies as you possibly could."

"And we ate so many of them that we nearly got sick after," I say. "I remember. You . . . didn't have any after that?"

Tiwa shakes her head, and the butterflies in my stomach seem to increase. Of course, I haven't had any pineapple-shaped sugar cookies since that day either. How could I, when it was mine and Tiwa's thing every time we came to Abigail's? I just had no idea that Tiwa might have felt the same way.

"Because I didn't want to get sick from them again, obviously," Tiwa says, making a face. "The stomachache I got that day was probably the worst one I've had in my entire life."

"Yeah, I felt like I was dying the whole ride down to Virginia," I say with a small laugh. "So, our first pineapple-shaped sugar cookies in three years, then. I'll go order."

I slip out of my seat and up to the cashier, who is still eyeing my shirt with disdain.

"We'll have a plate of your finest sugar cookies," I say. She puts in the order on the machine and I slip her five dollars. She arranges a batch of the cookies onto a plate, which has the Abigail's logo printed on it. I carry it back to our table, all the while thinking about how this could have been our every summer for the last three years if Safiyah hadn't messed everything up.

But I don't want to talk about Safiyah and ruin my mood.

I place the cookies on the table between us. Tiwa reaches for one at the same time that I do, our fingers meeting in the middle. A spark of electricity seems to pulse between us, rushing from her fingertips all the way to mine.

We both withdraw our hands, and heat rises up my cheeks.

"Sorry, you first," I mumble.

"Thanks," Tiwa says, reaching her hand out again and taking one of the cookies.

I take one too, biting into it. It's just the right amount of sweetness and crumbliness, and it melts in my mouth.

"I'm pretty sure this is the best cookie in the whole world," I declare.

"And we've been deprived of it for three years," Tiwa says, nodding in agreement.

"Maybe we should order a box for the Eid party," I say.

At that, Tiwa's face falls. She tries to rearrange it into something like a smile again, but it's clear that something is wrong.

"I know the Eid party won't be the same if it's not in the Islamic Center, but . . . it'll still be good. And if our plan works, maybe next year, we'll be back in the Islamic Center again," I say.

"It's not that . . ." Tiwa says. She tears off a small piece of the cookie in her hand—the top of the pineapple. "My dad told us today that he isn't coming home for Eid this year."

"Oh . . ." I say. I know I should say more, but I don't even know what I can say that'll make things better.

"It's just not going to feel like Eid without him," Tiwa says with a sigh.

"I'm sorry," I say. It's really all I can offer.

"It's okay. These cookies are helping." She nibbles at the end of the one in her hands.

I reach for another cookie on the plate that's swiftly emptying. Except this new cookie in my hand barely looks like a pineapple. I look at Tiwa to see if she's noticed, but she's staring down at the table with a forlorn look on her face instead of up at me.

"I found a bald pineapple," I say. That gets her attention. She looks from me to the cookie in my hand. Without the three spikes at the top, it looks more like an egg than anything else, but the first time Tiwa and I had found one of these in our box of cookies, we had dubbed it a bald pineapple. And it had stuck.

"Here." I hand the pineapple to her, and Tiwa accepts it hesitantly, eyeing me like I have some kind of a nefarious plan up my sleeve.

"Why are you giving it to me? I thought we'd have to have a fight to the death over it," Tiwa says.

"Nah, no fight to the death this time. You need the luck more than me," I say. "Besides, it's not like your luck won't rub off on me. If the bald pineapple makes our Islamic Center plan successful, we both reap the rewards."

Tiwa grins. "You've really thought this through."

"I mean, it's not every day that you find a bald pineapple."

"And it's not every day that you have sugar cookies at Abigail's," Tiwa adds.

I nod slowly, like this is sage wisdom. But really, I'm thinking that maybe if everything works out, this *could* be our every day.

Act 4

A DARK AND
STARRY NIGHT

25

A HOSSAIN FAMILY EID

Said

EID MORNING

I wake up to the scent of Ammu's porota and korma—the smell of a Hossain family Eid morning. I slip off the couch in the study that I've been sleeping on for the past couple of days in my attempts to avoid Safiyah, and stretch out my limbs. The couch barely fits me, and I saw Ammu giving the room a skeptical look yesterday as I was crawling onto it.

But none of us have really spoken since everything that went down at the dawat. I'm dreading breakfast as I bound down the stairs. Everyone's already there, picking at their food in a sleepy haze: Ammu, Abbu, Safiyah, even Chacha and Chachi.

"Said, there you are," Ammu says. She's smiling but there's a tiredness behind it that I don't think has to do with the fact she woke up earlier than everyone to make us breakfast.

I take my usual place at the table, picking up a porota and spooning chicken korma onto my plate. We're mostly silent as we eat, with Abbu occasionally making chitchat with Chacha and Chachi, but even they seem exhausted.

"What time is the Eid prayer again?" Chacha asks finally.

Abbu glances down at the clock on his phone. "One hour, we

should start getting ready. We don't want to be late and miss the Eid khutbah."

I shower in the guest bathroom and change into the new clothes Ammu bought for me before I even arrived home for the summer: a light blue panjabi with gold accents. But the study has no mirrors, so I have to go all the way downstairs to the full-length mirror outside the living room to actually see if the panjabi looks okay.

I adjust the collar and pat down my hair, trying to make it look neat—but not too neat, as my hair has a mind of its own. I can't get it just the way I want it to be.

"You look nice!" Safiyah says from a distance. I turn around, and the sight of her coming down the stairs with that sorry smile on her face is enough to make some of that simmering anger return. I don't respond, instead moving away from the mirror and walking into the kitchen, hoping Safiyah won't follow me there.

"Said, do you want a snack before we go? You barely ate during breakfast," Ammu says. She flings open the fridge, barely looking at me, and takes out a box of mishtis one of the aunties had brought over for the dawat. "Roshogolla?" she offers.

"No thanks," I say.

"You're right, not very healthy, especially after porota and korma. How about I cut up an apple for you?" Ammu asks.

"I'm not hungry, Ammu. Let's just go, we're going to be late," I say.

"Okay, I'll go get your abbu," Ammu agrees, though her voice sounds deflated. It's been like this ever since the dawat: Ammu trying to feed me any chance she gets, Safiyah trying to corner me into a conversation with compliments, Abbu mostly avoiding me. At least I had the mural to take my mind off everything and keep me busy before. But now the idea that everyone is going to see my mural makes me a little nauseous.

I walk outside, waiting by Abbu's car as everyone slowly finishes getting ready and shuffles out of the house. They lock the door behind them, and Chacha and Chachi slip into their own car, promising to meet us in front of the Walker Center. The four of us pile into the car, Ammu and Abbu in the front, Safiyah and me in the back.

"Did you hear that Anaan's son is set to get married this winter?" Ammu asks as soon as Abbu pulls out of our driveway. "The engagement is next month; they invited all of us. You'll still be home for the summer then, right, Said?"

"Maybe," I say, glancing out the window instead of at anyone in the car. I know Ammu is trying to relieve some of the tension, but the only person who seems interested in Anaan Auntie's son's engagement is Abbu.

"Isn't he too young to get married? He hasn't even graduated university yet. How's he going to support a family?" Abbu asks, sounding slightly stressed.

"I'm sure they've thought about it, maybe Anaan and her husband will support him," Ammu says.

"That's no way to start a family," Abbu says sternly.

"Sometimes people need help," Safiyah cuts in all of a sudden. "I mean, what's wrong with his parents helping him set up his life? They just want what's best for him."

Abbu exchanges a quick glance with Ammu, while I glare at the trees passing by the window.

"I didn't know you were so invested in their lives," Abbu says.

The conversation comes to a stop as we turn onto the road for

277

the Walker Center. Instead of the usually deserted road, cars are parked across both sides of the street, what seems like all the way from the top to the bottom.

"Why are there so many cars here already?" Ammu asks with a frown. "We're on time!"

"See if you can spot a parking space," Abbu says, glancing around intently from one side of the road to the other. I look too, but almost every single spot on the side of the road is taken.

"There!" Safiyah calls when we're still a few minutes away from Walker. She points to a narrow space between two cars, and Abbu pulls up to it, somehow managing to squeeze in.

The first thing I see when I climb out of the car is a yellow bulldozer in the distance. There are workers with hard hats and uniforms guiding the bulldozer somewhere. Before I have a chance to think too much about that, though, a familiar form appears in the distance. Tiwa is rushing from Walker toward us.

"Tiwa, it's nice to—" Ammu begins as Tiwa approaches us.

"Hi, Auntie, it's nice to see you. I just need to talk to Said for a moment," Tiwa says.

"Okay, sure," Ammu says, looking a little confused. Safiyah gives Tiwa and me a sidelong glance as Tiwa pulls me away.

"I've been calling you and messaging you," Tiwa says. There's a strangeness in her voice that I can't quite put my finger on.

"Why? What's going on?" I ask.

Tiwa takes a shaky breath. "It's . . . the Islamic Center. They moved the plans to demolish it up to today. We're too late."

26

SHAITAN HIMSELF

Tiwa

Said blinks at me, a confused look on his face. "What do you mean we're too late?"

I'm still trying to catch my breath. I really shouldn't have run here, but time is of the essence. "I got here an hour before the Eid prayer to help Imam Abdullah set up the prayer rooms and to begin welcoming the guests from the neighboring towns and I see Mayor Williams talking with these builders. At first I don't really think much of it, and then I see one of the builders ushering a huge monster truck over to the Islamic Center site and Mayor Williams is talking about *starting the process*, which is obviously really weird. So I go and confront him and he tells me they've moved the plans up. They're starting today," I say, not stopping once to pause or breathe.

Said's eyes turn into saucers and he looks ahead, seeing the truck on the other side of the road in the distance and Williams in a gray suit next to it laughing at something with the builders like a cartoon comic book villain.

"I can't believe him. He thought *Eid* would be a good time to do this? I swear, he is shaitan himself," Said says, glaring at him.

I see Said's mom's head whip around at the mention of the *devil*.

Auntie must think we are secretly conjuring something. I smile tightly at her to reassure her that nothing dodgy is happening but she still looks concerned.

"What are we going to do? Everyone's here. We gathered them here to show them the mural and what the Islamic Center's future could look like and Williams is crushing that future right in front of us," Said says.

I nod in agreement. It's like Williams has some weird sadistic love of crushing dreams, not just buildings, at this point. How is it even safe to be starting construction when there were so many people and cars? Yes, everyone was in the Walker Center, but still . . . "Wait," I say, looking at the groups of people slowly entering the Walker Center for Eid prayer.

"What?" Said says, looking back with me.

"I think I know how we can stop the demolition momentarily, but I'll need your and Safiyah's help."

Said makes a face at the mention of his sister. "What do you need us to do?"

"We need an audience. If we can gather everyone that has already entered Walker for Eid prayer back out here, then I think we can get the mayor's attention."

I find Safiyah and tell her the plan and the three of us get to work.

We gather all the guests for the Eid prayer outside on the road. Soon, the whole walkway and street is filled with confused people. It feels like there are a thousand of us even though there's probably only a quarter of that.

I spot Mayor Williams trying to usher people back inside, but per my instruction along with Safiyah's and Said's, they have been told to stay put and ignore the white man in the suit. I'm kind of surprised they listened.

"It's for your own safety. We are starting some very important construction and need everyone to clear the area so we can block off the building and protect you all from harm," I hear Williams explaining to a large crowd of uncles through an obnoxiously loud and unnecessary megaphone. The uncles ignore him and stay put.

Safiyah rushes over to me. "All done. I had to bribe some of the kids with mishtis but everyone's out."

"Thank you, Saf," I say, still feeling awkward about everything. I'm not as mad at her as Said is, but we haven't really had the time to talk about it and I no longer know where we stand.

"Anytime," Saf says with a smile I don't return, and then moves to stand next to me. We watch the chaos unfold. The confused builders, the equally puzzled guests, and the frustrated mayor rushing about. The rise of voices in the air, forming a loud humming.

In a weird way, it's kind of nice, all of us here together. It's what Eid is about after all: community.

"So what now?" Safiyah asks quietly.

"I'm not sure. I didn't think this far. I'm hoping this buys me time to figure something out. I just had to stop Mayor Williams first," I say.

"Well, you should probably think fast: My brother looks like he's going over there to fight Williams, which can't be good," Safiyah says, nodding over at the front of the crowd where a pissed-looking Said is heading over to Williams as he stands on the Islamic Center grounds with a group of fearful builders.

I watch, shocked, as Said takes the megaphone from Mayor Williams, who looks just as astounded, and moves to stand over in the middle of the grounds beside the dust sheet currently covering the mural.

"Attention, please, I want to say something," Said says, his voice loud and immediately silencing the audience.

Williams storms over to Said. "Listen, kid, you need to back away from this area, there's a machine right behind you. This is a health and safety ris—"

Said ignores Williams and steps closer to the machine, audible gasps reverberating throughout the crowd.

What is he doing?

"I'll be quick, and then you can have your giant speaker thing back," Said says to Williams, and then turns to the crowd of curious onlookers.

"Salam, everyone," he says with an awkward wave. There are salams said back in the crowd, rippling around. "I'm Said, and I grew up here in this town. Specifically between these two locations. The Walker Center where I went to the library, like, every weekend to see my favorite librarian and to escape the world, and the Islamic Center where I spent years, going to Arabic school, learning how to read the Quran, countless Eid parties, so many memories . . . all here—" Said is cut off again by Williams.

"The builders are contracted for a certain amount of time. I'm sure you can make this *speech* inside," he says, his lips upturned. He looks like he wants to wring Said's neck. If there weren't so many witnesses, I'm sure he would.

"Let the boy speak!" one of the uncles yells. And others hum in agreement.

Williams scowls and folds his arms.

"Where was I . . . um, yeah, the Islamic Center means a lot. I'm not here much anymore because of school, but I always looked forward to coming back here during my breaks. If I'm being really honest, I struggle a lot with being close to my religion and everything when I'm away, but when I'm here, I always find my way back to it because of the community, and I didn't want to see that gone, so I painted this," Said says, pulling aside the dust sheet and unveiling the mural at last. He gestures at the huge swirl of colors and images that has lit up the walls and ground around him. The mural looks more refined since I saw it, like Said came back here to go over lines and add more depth. And again, it takes my breath away.

People move closer, much to Williams's dismay, taking it in. It is clearly a crowd-pleaser.

I smile, catching Said's eyes briefly. He looks happy.

"Even if you're not from New Crosshaven, you might have heard how important murals are to our town—and seen, as you drove here today. We have murals on nearly every public building, murals on the sidewalks, murals painted onto trees. It's kind of our thing," Said says.

"As much as I'll always love a mural—this one included," Mayor Williams interrupts once again with a grimace. "I told you and your friends countless times, this building can't stay here. And besides, you didn't get permission to paint this in the first place . . ."

I zone out, Mayor Williams's words echoing inside.

As much as I'll always love a mural. My eyes widen as realization hits me. How could I not have thought of this before?

I quickly take my phone out, going to the town's website and scrolling quickly.

"What are you doing?" Saf whispers, looking down at my phone's screen.

I scroll to the section I've been looking for and I almost jump. "Got it," I say.

"Got what?" Saf asks, but I have no time, I'm already moving.

"WAIT!" I shout from the crowd, and I see people turning toward me, including Said and Mayor Williams, who seem to have been bickering before my interruption. Said's eyebrows are furrowed as I squeeze past the bodies of people, my phone held up in my hands.

"You can't knock that building down," I say, breathless. Pushing past people is harder than it looks.

Mayor Williams sighs for the umpteenth time.

"I feel like I am living in the *Groundhog Day* movie at this point. How many times do I have to say that it has been decided—" Mayor Williams starts.

"Yeah, well, the decision is not valid," I say.

Mayor Williams looks like he wants to laugh or cry or both. "It is valid. You were at the town hall meeting; you had a fair chance."

"Not according to the town's regulations." I hold up my phone to him and put on my best *future senator* voice. "Right here in paragraph D subsection C: Any building with a mural attached to the site is protected in the town of New Crosshaven under the 1987 Mural Rights Act. Therefore, it can't be demolished," I finish with a wide, triumphant smile. I see Said's confusion dissolve, replaced by something lighter.

"What she said," Said says, moving to stand next to me with his arms folded.

The mayor's face turns a little pink as he reads and rereads the section, looking for errors or mistakes. Not that he'd find any. It is *his* rule book after all.

Williams finally clears his throat and looks away from the evidence and back to the crowd of onlookers.

"It's not an official mural, so unfortunately that rule does not apply," he says.

"There's nothing in the bylaws about it being an official mural, Mayor Williams. Just a mural of any kind," I say with a shrug.

Williams glares at me, like actually *glares*.

"Mayor Williams, do you really want to disappoint all of these people? Especially people who might have business in this town and who might want to come back frequently to visit?" I hear my mom's voice rise up from the crowd. I turn to her and she's looking at Mayor Williams with her arms crossed like she's issuing him a challenge.

Williams looks furious and for a moment I think he's going to fight my mom in front of everyone here, but instead he puts on his go-to chilling plastic smile.

"I can't argue with that, it seems. What a marvelous mural too, wish I'd commissioned it myself. I guess it just goes to show the brilliance and intuition of the townspeople in New Crosshaven." He claps Said on the back and I hear Said mutter *ow*. Then Williams turns to the builders. "I have decided to overturn the demolishing of the Islamic Center. It's clear that this beautiful mural will surely attract plenty of visitors, especially during our Mural Festival in a few months, therefore driving just as much business as the apartments— which was my goal anyway. Putting the people of this fine town first."

I can't believe it. We actually stopped him.

I turn to the gathering of people, who watch silently, but then, prompted by an extremely loud cheer from Safiyah, the crowd begins to cheer too, applauding much to Mayor Williams's dismay.

I look at Said. He's already looking at me, the biggest smile on his face, and I can't help but throw my hands around him. He immediately hugs me back, and in this moment, I find that I missed hugging Said more than I thought.

A few moments pass and I realize that one, we have been hugging for longer than is socially acceptable for friends (or whatever the hell we are), and two, there are people watching us.

I almost forgot that everyone else exists. It felt for a moment like we were the only two people left in the world.

I pull away, even though I'd stay in that position forever if I had the choice, and awkwardly nod at him as though this was some kind of business partnership. He nods back at me, still smiling.

I look away, feeling my skin warm, and pretend to find interest in the still cheering crowd. I spot my mom near the back. She's on the phone and turned away, probably talking to one of my aunts in Nigeria, wishing her a happy Eid. Nigerians don't have a concept of day and night.

"We did it," I say to Said after the crowd dies down and everyone begins to enter the Walker Center again for the morning Eid prayer with Imam Abdullah. I'm still not looking at Said directly in the eye for fear he'll see right through me, all my thoughts, feelings, and wishes.

He nudges me as we walk toward the center.

"No, you did it. I just stood here and looked pretty."

I roll my eyes, nudging him back. "Yeah, sure," I say. "Your face clearly helped save the Islamic Center."

"Clearly," he replies.

I'm about to make an embarrassing comment about his potential career as a model when my mom saves me.

"Tiwa!" she shouts from the entrance of Walker, her phone still gripped in her hands and a bright smile on her face. "Come and help me inside. We need to put the food coolers in the kitchen before the prayer."

"Okay, I'm coming!" I shout back at her, and then I turn to Said. "I'll see you later?"

He nods. "See you."

As I turn to leave I hear my name again. "Tiwa," he says, and I look back at him.

"Yeah?"

"Eid Mubarak," he says, staring at me strangely.

I feel my heart beat faster as our eyes lock.

"Eid Mubarak, Said."

27

THE MISCONCEPTION

Said

EARLY EID AFTERNOON

A FEW HOURS LATER, THE EID PARTY IS IN FULL SWING. I STAND BY the food and drinks table, filling up my plate with the different dishes each of the families brought in: everything from spicy chotpoti to sweet chin chin.

The Eid festivities around me seem even livelier than usual. Kids are running around everywhere, aunties and uncles are laughing and chatting loudly. There's exchanges of presents, hugs, and kisses throughout the entire center. In a corner I even see Safiyah and Ishra talking with Ammu and Abbu, Abbu laughing at something one of them must have said. It's like the promise of our Islamic Center being rebuilt alongside Eid has rejuvenated the entire Muslim community both inside and outside of New Crosshaven.

"Said, Eid Mubarak!" Munir Chacha's voice booms from behind me. I turn around, my eyes wide. I'm definitely not ready to be ambushed by Chacha today. But he's by my side before I have a chance to escape. He claps me on the back as his usual form of greeting—so hard that I stumble forward slightly, and one of the shomuchas carefully nestled on the edge of my plate goes flying.

"Hey!" an auntie cries in the distance, where the shomucha hit her brand-new sharee. She glances around for the culprit so I turn to Chacha, trying to appear deep in conversation.

"Eid Mubarak, Chacha. I hope you're enjoying the Eid party," I say.

"This is what an Eid party should be," he says, nodding his head as he observes the space, filled with Eid decorations, food, and most importantly, our community. "And we can have many more of these celebrations because of what you did out there, Said. We're very proud of you, I hope you know that." At this, he looks at me with pride in his gaze and I feel a little guilty for wanting to escape him before.

"Thanks, Chacha," I mumble.

"I know your ammu and abbu were beaming with pride when they saw you up there, giving your speech," Chacha shares, while swiping a jilapi from my plate.

I give him a tight smile. After everything that happened between us a few days ago, I seriously doubt that. Chacha is clearly not great at reading the room, though, because the next moment he's waving my parents toward us.

"You have to try these jilapis, bhaiya, they're amazing," Chacha says. "Best jilapis I've ever had, but don't tell Shazia that." He begins to load his own plate with jilapis, leaving me alone with my parents for the first time since the dawat.

"Eid Mubarak, Said," Ammu says.

"Eid Mubarak," I say, my eyes downcast.

"Your mural on the Islamic Center is beautiful," Abbu says unexpectedly.

"And so was your speech," Ammu agrees. I look up to meet my

parents' eyes and I'm surprised to see they don't look disappointed or angry, or even hurt like they had the night of the dawat. If I didn't know any better, I'd think they looked proud.

"Said, why didn't you ever tell us that you didn't want to study medicine?" Abbu asks.

"I don't know, I guess . . . I didn't want you to be disappointed. Especially after you sent me to St. Francis. I know it was expensive and I was supposed to be a doctor at the end, but—"

"We didn't send you to St. Francis because we wanted you to become a doctor," Ammu interrupts. There's a confused expression on her face, like she doesn't know why I ever thought that. "We want both you and Safiyah to have the best education that you can. We have always wanted that. In Bangladesh, your abbu and I didn't always have the opportunities you have here, Said. We want you to have opportunities, and the best education gives you those opportunities."

"And we don't care if the opportunities are studying medicine at Harvard or . . . something else," Abbu says. "We've always just wanted you to be happy. We just thought studying medicine was what would make you happy. You never said otherwise."

If I stop to think about it, I can see why Abbu and Ammu might have had the misconception. When I first got accepted into St. Francis, spending all that money on a fancy boarding school, being away from my family, from Tiwa, all of it had felt terrifying. Somehow the solution to my fears seemed to be studying medicine, becoming a doctor. It was the one field that Bangladeshi families seem to admire above all. Witnessing all my cousins pursue these traditional routes, it was all I thought I could do. It's like for so many years I was chasing an expectation that was never demanded of me by my parents, but was instead something I felt I had to do because it was all I could see.

By the time I realized that my passion was actually in art, my parents had already run away with the doctor stuff I'd told them. Every Bangladeshi auntie and uncle from New Crosshaven to Dhaka knew all about it.

"I should have said something. It just felt like it was too late, and the decision was already made for me," I admit.

"The decision has always been yours, Said," Ammu says.

"So what *is* your decision?" Abbu asks with a raised eyebrow.

I hesitate for a moment, but I know that I need to tell them the truth now. "Art. New York School of Animation is my top choice, but I have a few backups. I know it's not practical, but—"

"Your Anjana Auntie knows one of the professors there," Ammu says excitedly before I can even finish my explanations. "I'm going to call her. After all the mishtis I feed her, she has to help us."

"You need a portfolio for art school, right?" Abbu asks with a frown. "Do you want us to hire a professional photographer for the mural outside? It's a great piece of art; just because it's on the walls of the Islamic Center shouldn't mean you can't use it."

I blink back tears at the familiar behavior of my parents. Always leaping to support me, before I've even asked anything of them. Maybe Julian was right all along about them, and I haven't been giving them the credit they deserve.

"You're really okay with art school instead of medicine?" I ask.

"We're okay with whatever you want to do, shona," Ammu says, beaming. She leans forward and wraps me in a hug. It's my first hug from her this whole Eid and it makes me wish that we had made up earlier. Usually, my Eid day starts with a hug and an Eid Mubarak from Ammu.

"Bhai, bhabi, come here! We're taking a picture!" one of the uncles shouts over at Ammu and Abbu, interrupting our conversation.

I glance over to see a huge group of Bengali aunties and uncles, all dressed up in their fancy new Eid clothes. There's a kid who can't be more than ten years old awkwardly balancing multiple phones to try to take the photo.

Ammu gives me a final kiss on the cheek before hurrying over to the group with Abbu in tow, while I quickly make my escape out the back door of the Walker Center, worried they'll rope me in to take their photo when the kid inevitably fails.

I breathe in the fresh air outside, feeling like the weight of the world has been lifted off my shoulders after that conversation with Ammu and Abbu. And strangely, there's only one person I want to speak to about the whole thing: Julian. He's been by my side as I've struggled to figure out how to break the news of art school to Ammu and Abbu.

He's been my best friend for years, and maybe I haven't given him the benefit of the doubt, in the same way I was wrong about Ammu and Abbu.

I take out my phone and type my first text to Julian in days:

hey julian, I know we have some
stuff to work out, but we'll talk about
it once you get here for the eid
party at our house.

I don't have to wait for long before my phone pings with a reply.

are you sure you still want me to
come?

I don't hesitate before replying: yes.

28

FOOD THIEF

Tiwa

LATE EID AFTERNOON

I'D BEEN SEARCHING ALL OVER FOR SAFIYAH, WANTING TO FINALLY talk to her about the letters, but that all disappears from my mind when I see him.

At first I think I'm imagining things.

It would make sense that my brain has started to hallucinate due to the exhaustion of planning this whole event, but when I blink, nothing changes.

He's still there. In the corner next to my mom and Safiyah, my dad is there, waving at me.

I walk quickly with a skeptical expression on my face, waiting for the cracks in the mirage to show themselves. But when he opens his arms and I run into them, he's solid.

My dad is actually here. He's actually real.

"You're real," I accidentally say out loud, feeling a rush of emotions hitting me at once. Probably again due to exhaustion.

"I am real," Dad says.

I realize that our daily phone calls are not enough; seeing him in person outweighs anything else.

I pull away from him, still in shock. "But how? You said—"

"I know, I really thought I couldn't make it, but we managed to figure it out at the last minute and we thought it could be a nice surprise for you. It was your mom and Safiyah who planned it—mostly Safiyah, but your mom loves to take credit for things." Dad says the last part quietly, but still loud enough for Mom to hear him and whack him lightly on his shoulder.

"I heard that," Mom says, and Dad laughs.

"Hey now, I thought we weren't supposed to lie during holy occasions?"

Mom rolls her eyes. "Don't mind him. He is full of it."

"By it she means Allah's blessings," Dad says with a wink and then the next moment he is looking ahead. "Oh, are those doughnuts?

I nod. "The pink dino-shaped ones are from Abigail's, your favorite. I figured because you weren't coming we'd just enjoy them for you."

That wasn't the only reason, of course. The pink dino-shaped doughnuts were obviously a favorite of the dinosaur connoisseur himself, Timi. He'd always get them as a treat on Eid. I don't even remember Dad loving them so much before Timi died. Having them here was like having Timi here in a sense, and I figure Dad's love for them comes from his love for Timi.

Dad's smile widens. "Well, then, I think I'm going to have to go over and investigate . . . make sure the doughnuts are top-notch."

I nod. "Of course," I say. "We can catch up later. I actually wanted to steal Safiyah quickly," I say, nodding at my uncharacteristically quiet best friend, who is standing awkwardly to the side watching the exchange instead of joining in like she usually would.

"Can we talk?" Saf asks as we step away from my parents, worry weighing her voice down.

"Sure," I say, feeling anxiety rise up inside.

There's a pause, and then as I'm about to break the ice and say *thank you for bringing my dad here*, she's speaking. "I'm so sorry, Tiwa. I never wanted to hurt any of you guys," she says, and I know by *you guys* she means me and Said.

I want to ask her so many things. Like why she did this. Why she thought it was okay to ruin my friendship with Said like that. Ever since Said told me about his discovery, I have been racking my brain for answers.

"I wouldn't blame you if you didn't want to speak to me again. I just want you to know that I didn't take the letters to betray you. I tried to fix things so many times, but the damage was done and everything kept getting worse." Safiyah keeps going before I even have a chance to respond.

I can tell how nervous she is. Her fingers are shaky and she only rambles this much when she's worried.

"I will never stop speaking to you, Safiyah," I finally say. "You're like my sister, and sometimes sisters mess up."

Saf looks like she might cry.

"I still want to understand why you did this, though. I've just been so confused."

Safiyah takes a breath before speaking again. "Remember when I transferred schools in eighth grade and barely spoke to anyone there for like the entire first year?"

I nod. I remember how difficult Safiyah had found moving schools. She'd constantly been picked on and always came home on weekends. She never made any friends there either; I think it's one of the reasons we grew so close over the years.

"Well, I think—actually I *know*—that part of the reason is that I didn't want to get along with anyone at my new school. I secretly hoped my parents would pull me out and let me transfer back to New Crosshaven, but they didn't, and so I spent my entire high school career miserable and alone. It was the worst feeling in the world. Honestly, if I didn't have you or my family I'm not sure what I would have done. I saw Said going down the same path as me. Isolating himself from everyone and everything. I thought that if I stopped him obsessing over New Crosshaven like I'd done, he'd be able to actually enjoy high school and not waste it all away like I did."

I knew Safiyah hadn't had the best experience at her boarding school, but I didn't realize how bad it actually had been. All of this is making sense to me now.

"I'm sorry you went through all of that, Safiyah. I just wish you'd spoken to me sooner. I would have understood. I could've even helped Said."

Safiyah nods. "I know that now. If I could change things, I definitely would have done it all differently."

"I know, Saf," I say, squeezing her hand. "I think you should tell Said that. He would understand too. He's actually probably the only other person who would understand what you went through and why you did it."

"I will, but I just want to make sure that we're okay?" Safiyah asks.

I smile at her. "Of course we're okay. You can't get rid of me; you made a vow, remember? Partners in cookies and crime always."

Safiyah's face breaks out into a small smile at the memory. "You have a point..." she says. "Likewise, I guess I'll need you for when I inevitably have to bury a body."

"Exactly. In the spirit of Eid you are hereby forgiven. Are you going to stop beating yourself up now?"

Safiyah shrugs, staring off into the distance. "I'll consider it. I probably need to speak to Said first before I do."

I follow her gaze over to the back of the Eid party where Said is standing, sneaking treats from the food tables into his hands and looking shifty like he's a food thief and the food police are hunting him down.

It's kind of adorable.

"What a knobhead," Safiyah mutters.

I nod, feeling my heart squeeze in my chest. "Yeah, totally," I say softly.

I suddenly remember the Eid gift I got for Said and the fact that I left it in my mom's car. We're doing the gift exchange in a few minutes, and seeing as Said is not my official Secret Paaro partner anyway, I'll have to give it to him at his mom's Eid after-party in a few hours. It'll be better if I can get him alone too. I'm finding the idea of giving him a present in front of others a bit embarrassing.

I don't want my mom or dad to see and ask questions.

"Wait here, I need to do something," I say to Safiyah, who has somehow gotten herself a shomucha in the time I've clearly been staring off into the distance at Said.

"Sure, I'll be here," she says in a muffled voice.

I make my way through the crowds of strangers and familiar

faces—but community all the same—over to Said, who jumps when I tap him on the shoulder.

"Fuck, you scared me," he says, dropping one of his stolen goods.

I laugh. "Said, were you harboring innocent meat pies?" I say, staring at the two nestled in his hands.

He smiles. "So what if I was? This is a free town."

"So it is," I say in agreement, as I nervously swallow. "Anyway, I didn't come here to arrest you. I came to ask if you were around later . . . I wanted to, um, show you something."

Said raises an eyebrow at me, his interest piqued. "I have to help my friend Julian settle in, but I should be free after seven for a bit."

"Seven is perfect," I say hurriedly, face flushing.

"Where shall we meet?" he asks.

I don't have to think about it. The answer, as though planted in my head by some higher power, comes to me immediately.

"The old tree house."

29

MUFFIN SLUT

Said

EID EVENING

AMMU IS SHOUTING ORDERS AT US BEFORE WE'VE EVEN GONE through the front door of the house.

"Safiyah, help me put out all the food on the tables. Said, make sure all the rooms are clean," she says, unlocking the door. She quickly takes off her shoes and dashes into the kitchen, while Safiyah and I stand in the doorway blinking after her. Nothing drives Ammu up the wall more than having to entertain guests, yet for some reason she loves doing it.

I almost look at Safiyah to roll my eyes at Ammu's antics, but I stifle the urge, slipping off my shoes and hurrying into the living room to make sure everything is tidy. We've been out for most of the day so there isn't much to do other than fluffing some pillows and putting away a few dishes. By the time my phone pings with a text from Julian a few minutes later, declaring he's outside, all the rooms are ready for our guests this evening.

I pull the door open to find Julian standing a few feet away, a half-zipped up backpack on his shoulder and a beaten-up old suitcase in his hands.

"Hey," he says, waving a hand awkwardly in my direction.

"Hi," I say, not sure what else to even say. "Was the drive up okay?"

"Yeah, mostly. Except I almost hit a deer. It just ran out in front of me like the highway was its home or something," Julian says. "I didn't know you guys had wild animals running around everywhere. I would have brought protective gear if you had told me before."

I scoff. "We don't have wild animals running around. I bet even New York has deer."

"I have never once seen a deer in New York," Julian declares.

"Do you need help with your bags?" I ask before Julian can launch into a speech about the lack of deer in New York.

"Sure," Julian says, pushing his suitcase forward. "But wait, I have something for you, I almost forgot." He searches the pockets of his jeans with a frown, before feeling up the pockets on his shirt. "I swear, it's here somewhere. I couldn't have forgotten it. Just as I was leaving, I put it in my pocket because I knew that I wanted to give it you as soon as I—aha!"

He swipes out a card from his pocket, along with a wrapped package that is noticeably shaped like Gengar, and hands them both to me.

"I wonder what this could be," I say, eyeing the present while Julian grins at me. Tearing it open, I find a Gengar plushie the size of my palm, with a little Poké Ball attached to it. The card has an illustration of Pikachu on the front and in a big speech bubble on top of him, Julian has scribbled in *Eid Mubarak!*

"Do you like it?" Julian asks.

"I'll add it to my collection once I'm allowed back into my room again," I say. Julian has gotten me so many Pokémon plushies over the years—many of them Gengar—that my room is already overflowing.

"Don't tell Auntie I gave it to you," Julian says, knowing all too well that Ammu has a dislike of the plushies taking over my bedroom.

I grab hold of his suitcase and roll it inside the front door, while Julian follows behind. He takes in the house with wide eyes. It's been a while since he's been here. "I've never seen your house like this before. Did you decorate it?"

I shrug. "All of us did. We take Eid decor very seriously."

I lead Julian through the hallway and into the kitchen, where Ammu and Abbu are carrying the massive Eid cake to the middle of the table. They set it down and step back to admire their work, before they finally notice me and Julian standing in the doorway.

"Julian, welcome!" Ammu says. She hurries forward and pulls him into a hug.

"Hi, Mr. and Mrs. Hossain. Eid Mubarak," Julian says. He begins to dig around in his backpack and quickly pulls out a blue Tupperware box. "My parents wanted you to have this for the party. It's rice and beans, a Puerto Rican specialty."

Ammu accepts the box with a smile. "I've never had Puerto Rican rice and beans before!"

"We're going to go put his bags away in the study," I say.

"Okay, but hurry down. The guests will start arriving soon," Abbu says.

I turn back toward the stairs, lugging Julian's suitcase in front of me. Thankfully, we don't run into Safiyah as we make our way to the study. I put his suitcase by the wall, while he places his backpack on the couch.

"You've been sleeping here?" Julian asks.

"Yeah, I like it, though. The couch is comfier than you'd think."

Julian eyes it like he doesn't believe me.

"Do you want something to drink? Water?" I ask.

Julian nods. "Yeah, I swear the humidity in this town is ten times more than the humidity in New York. I could use some water."

I leave Julian on the couch and head downstairs to fill up a glass, studying the Gengar plushie and Eid card on the way. I wonder if Julian already had these picked out or if he got them in a rush once I told him that he should still come to the Eid party this evening. Despite what Julian confessed a few days ago, I missed my best friend.

And I realize that I miss Safiyah too. There's never been a single Eid where Safiyah and I haven't spoken, and I'm not sure if I'm ready for this Eid to end without at least hearing her out.

When I get back to the study with Julian's glass of water, I find Safiyah inside. The two of them are sitting together, in the middle of a conversation.

"Conspiring again?" I ask, setting the glass down on the windowsill.

Safiyah and Julian both glance up with wide eyes.

"No, we weren't—"

"I'm just joking," I interrupt.

We fall into an awkward silence, and I have no idea what to say to break the tension between us.

Finally, Safiyah clears her throat. "I just want to say, none of this was Julian's fault. I was the one who came up with the plan to take the letters. Julian had nothing to do with it. I just . . . saw that you were struggling with making friends at school like I'd been, and I figured if you weren't so hung up on New Crosshaven still, you'd find it easier to settle in. Things got out of control, and by the time I tried to fix my mistake it was already too late. I should have never meddled. I just saw how hard the move was on you and wanted to make it easier. I'm sorry, Said."

"It was my fault too," Julian adds as soon as Safiyah's finished talking. "Safiyah asked me to take the letters. I didn't realize she only meant temporarily . . . I should have probably asked more questions about why. I just thought that I was protecting you, but I was wrong. I'm sorry too."

I take in my sister and best friend, sitting side by side, their heads hung low after their apologies. Julian looks a little like a kicked puppy, while Safiyah looks a little constipated after a long day of dealing with my silence.

"You're both doofuses," I say. It's really the only response that seems appropriate.

Safiyah glances up, hope glinting in her eyes. "I got you a muffin from Abigail's earlier," she says, pulling out a chocolate-chip muffin wrapped in cling film and offering it to me.

I reach over and take it from her, unwrapping the plastic and biting off a piece from the top. Like everything at Abigail's, it tastes like heaven.

"Eid Mubarak, Safiyah," I say through my mouthful of muffin.

It doesn't take long for our house to fill up with guests from across New Crosshaven. They eat up Ammu's food like it's the best thing they've ever tasted, and Julian's parents' dish is a hit too.

I'm in the middle of an argument with Julian about who would win in a fight, Arbok or Weezing, when my phone buzzes with a text.

Tiwa: I'm in your backyard. Meet
you in 5?

I try to stifle a smile as I quickly text her back: see you then

"What are you smiling at?" Julian asks, peering close. "A Pokémon battle is very serious business, Said."

"I know, Julian. But . . . I gotta go. Will you be okay here on your own?" I ask.

He nods and waves me off. "Pokémon will always be here," Julian responds in a weirdly prophetic way.

I tell him I'll be back soon before turning toward the kitchen.

I slip in through the door of the kitchen, eyeing the crowd gathered around the dinner table. It's quickly dwindling since Ammu called everyone to grab food about an hour ago, but there are still a few people hovering.

Thankfully, Ammu and Abbu are nowhere to be seen. I casually walk up to the table and grab a paper plate. Quickly glancing around, I note that nobody's paying attention to me. Time to act. Before anybody can call me out I cut two humongous slices of the half-eaten cake and place them on the plate.

Then, as carefully as I can while still hurrying, I slip out of the back door and into the backyard. It's a chilly night for the summer, but there's something refreshing about being out here, away from the crowd.

Balancing the plate in one hand, I climb up the ladder to our tree house. Tiwa's already inside when I open the door. She's holding two boxes of apple juice in her hands.

She eyes the paper plate full of cake I'm balancing in my hands. "How did you manage to get that?"

"I have my ways." I grin, setting it down on the little wooden table I built during my fifth-grade woodwork project. Tiwa sets her apple juice down too, sliding dangerously close to me as she does. My heartbeat quickens again.

It's been so long since the two of us have been in this tree house together, but it almost feels like no time has passed at all.

"I have something for you," Tiwa says. She goes to a shadowed corner of the tree house and comes back with a gift-wrapped parcel, like she produced it out of thin air.

"I already got my Secret Paaro present," I say.

"I know. I saw this and . . . I thought of you," Tiwa says, not looking me in the eye as she hands it to me. Our fingers brush for just a second before we both pull our hands away. I try to ignore the flutter of butterflies in my stomach and focus on the present instead.

"What is it?" I ask, running my fingers along the smooth lines of the wrapping paper. "And who wrapped it? I know it definitely wasn't you."

Tiwa lets out a huffy breath. "My mom helped me, but I did most of the work. Open it."

I carefully tear the wrapping paper open to find a bundle of wool wrapped around a pretty wooden box. First I lift up what seems to be a singular lopsided sock.

My eyebrows furrow. Tiwa looks at me expectantly.

"It's . . . um . . . really nice. Thank you," I say.

"I crocheted it," she replies proudly, and that alone makes me want to treasure it forever.

I nod. "I can see that. I'm going to wear it everyday."

Her face screws up a little. "Don't do that—you'll get athlete's foot. I'm currently making the other sock. Hopefully it'll be ready by next Eid."

Hopefully that one is foot shaped I want to say, but instead I open the next gift.

The box is filled with paintbrushes. They're all different sizes, shapes, and their handles are painted in the most vibrant purples and teals.

"I didn't know what kind of paintbrushes you like but I thought, an artist can probably never have too many brushes, right? So when I saw them I just—"

"They're perfect," I interrupt her. "Thank you."

"You could have probably used them before Eid to paint the mural," Tiwa says. "But you went behind my back to do that, so I couldn't have known."

"I think I'll find use for them, especially if I get into the New York School of Animation."

"You'll get in," Tiwa says. Her voice holds much more confidence than I feel in myself. "Your mural is amazing. I mean, it literally helped convince the mayor of a town to rebuild the Islamic Center. They have to give you credit for that."

"I don't think art school applications take mayoral changes of mind into consideration."

"Well, they should!" Tiwa says. "Did you get a chance to speak with Safiyah?"

"Yeah, everything's good now. She gave me a chocolate-chip muffin."

Tiwa rolls her eyes. "You're such a muffin slut."

"I'm proud to be a muffin slut," I declare.

"Luckily, I like being friends with muffin sluts," Tiwa says.

I smile, and Tiwa and I finally look at each other properly.

"I missed this," I say.

"Sharing secrets and drinking apple juice?"

"Obviously. But also, us being friends," I say. "Though I didn't know you were harboring so many secrets. As rules of the tree house dictate, you have to share one."

Tiwa thinks about it for a moment before answering. "The secret ingredient is mayonnaise."

I look at her, confused. "What?"

"The thing that makes Ms. Barnes's cakes taste so good: mayonnaise—heaps of it."

That is . . . unexpected.

I raise an eyebrow at her. "Are you going to kill me now?"

"I think Ms. Barnes would have wanted you to finally know the secret," she replies, expertly dodging my question about my potential assassination. Tiwa nudges me. "What about you? What's your secret?"

There are a million things I could tell her. We've been apart for so long that there's no end to the things I want to tell her. But there's one secret that I've been holding on to for years, one that I want to share before it's too late.

"Well, the truth is, I think . . . I've been in love with you since that day in the tree house when you promised not to tell anyone about the stolen apple juice," I confess.

Tiwa blinks at me slowly, and I feel a jolt of panic. Suddenly, I'm rushing to get more words out before Tiwa can say anything.

"Not that agreeing to be my accomplice was the reason, I just, um, think that you're the smartest, most amazing person I've ever met. I think all these years I never really hated you. I just—"

"I love you too," Tiwa says, interrupting my rambling. She leans in and says quietly, "I think I have been in love with you since before then."

I smile. "Always trying to one-up me."

Tiwa shrugs, smiling at me. "You snooze, you lose."

I'm suddenly all too aware of just how close we are. My heart is beating so loudly that it's a wonder she can't hear it.

"I don't think I've lost at all," I say, and then I close the gap between us, pressing my lips to hers.

30

MARX WAS RIGHT

Tiwa

ONE AND A HALF YEARS LATER

I'VE BEEN TO THIS VERY BUILDING MORE THAN A DOZEN TIMES and yet somehow I always manage to get lost.

Said's dorm is a confusing labyrinth. I'm pretty sure I have gone past the same mural of Jean-Michel Basquiat ten times at this point.

I sigh, taking my phone out, ready to admit defeat when the device buzzes with a notification.

New message from *the best*
person to ever exist
Are you lost?

Sometimes I'm convinced that Said can read my mind or has some kind of superpower that lets him know things he shouldn't, like the time he told me he could smell burning toast thirty whole minutes *before* I even put the bread in the toaster.

Maybe, I reply, and then add Are there multiple Basquiat murals on campus?

I look up at the buildings around me, praying that the answer drops in my lap somehow. Why is the New York School of Animation built like a maze? Are they trying to trap their students or something?

My phone buzzes once more with a notification.

New message from *the best*
person to ever exist
Nope, just the one :-)

I can imagine his sly smile. The same sly smile he gave me after he'd changed his name on my phone without me knowing at the time.

I haven't changed it back because, well, it's not exactly a lie.

He is one of the best people to ever exist.

Need a clue? he asks.

I almost give in, *almost*, when the answer comes to me in the form of a fish.

Specifically, a fish painted onto one of the dorm windows.

Checkmate.

I rush toward the familiar dorm, up the stairs, and over to the door, where I knock triumphantly.

It isn't long before I hear footsteps and the sound of the door opening, Said's face appearing with a smile on it that contrasts his dark clothes.

"Come in quickly, you're late for the funeral," he says seriously.

"My apologies," I say, stepping inside his dorm. "Your campus is *huge*. Much bigger than Columbia's campus—I got lost in the supply store while looking for a card. Did you know that your school has a supply store on every corner?"

"Yes, it's how they get us to spend our entire allowances. We have no choice when faced with fancy paints and brushes. I'll be broke by the end of the year, but at least my art supplies will be aesthetically pleasing," Said says, pulling me farther into the room and hugging me close, his arms trapping me.

"That's capitalism for you," I mumble as I rest my head on his chest, wrapping my arms around his waist.

"It freaking sucks. Marx was right," he mumbles back, nestling his head into my shoulder.

I don't realize until this moment how much I've missed him, even though it's only been a few days since I last saw him, seeing as Columbia isn't that far from NYSA. I'm definitely starved of his hugs. If I could, I'd hug him forever. But sadly, that isn't an option.

Finally, we sort of pull apart from each other (our arms are still interlocked, which Safiyah says we have a habit of doing).

Said kisses my forehead and I smile up at him.

"How are you holding up?" I ask.

He shrugs. "I didn't think I'd be attending another funeral so soon. Life is brutal like that, I guess."

I nod sympathetically. "Where is he?" I ask, eyes landing on the fishbowl on top of Said's art books on his desk.

"In the bathroom."

"Should we get started? We still need to head back to New Crosshaven for the Eid party—you know how my mom gets when I'm late."

"Good point, my mom would probably yell at me too. Let's get this funeral started," he says in a much more chipper tone than one would expect at an occasion like this.

A few moments later we are in the cramped, old en suite bathroom of his dorm room, which he thankfully only shares with his roommate Roberto.

The dead body of Said's latest goldfish lies still in a large tea mug that he placed on top of the sink.

"I want to make a short speech," he says, sniffing.

I nod, rubbing his arm. "Go on."

He picks up the teacup and holds it over the toilet basin, staring down at the dead fish.

"I didn't know you for very long but you were still a great companion and you will be missed. Thank you for being my goldfish," Said says, before tipping the mug and letting the contents spill out into the toilet.

This would be the second of Said's goldfishes that we are sending to whatever fish heaven is called.

I watch the fish formerly known as Howl the second, named after Howl the first (Said's first goldfish, gifted to him by Safiyah at the start of animation school) as well as the character Howl from Said's favorite Studio Ghibli film.

Said reaches out for the metal handle and tugs it down, the fish flushing instantly with the swirling water.

We watch for a few moments before I finally break the silence.

"This reminds me of our last burial," I say. He looks at me confused and I clarify. "You know, the letters?"

Recognition flashes in his eyes. "Oh yeah, when we buried them in my back garden last Eid. I haven't even thought of them since that night."

"Same," I say.

It's funny how something that once had the ability to make or break us is now insignificant enough to be forgotten.

"Want to head out?" Said asks.

I nod. "Yes, but first I wanted to show you something I got you. It's an Eid present."

"It's funny you mention that. I also have an Eid present for you," he says. "But mine is back at home. I accidentally ordered it to my parents' place."

I smile. "Mine's right here," I say, holding up a gift bag and handing it to him. "Eid Mubarak, Said."

He takes the bag, his eyebrows shooting up when he sees what it is. He reaches in and pulls out a little see-through bag with water in it and a blue-and-white-striped fish inside.

"It's a zebra fish," I say. "Easy to look after."

Not so easy to kill, I think, but I don't say it out loud. With the amount of fish Said has gone through, I sometimes worry that he is secretly killing them on purpose, but I don't say that because I figure accusing him of first-degree fish murder at a funeral would be insensitive.

"I love you, Tiwa," Said says, leaning in to kiss me.

"I love me too," I say when we break apart and exit the bathroom. "And you too I guess . . . sometimes . . . mostly . . . always."

I feel my phone buzz angrily in my pocket and I already know who's texting before I even take it out.

"We have to go," I say, reading my mom's request for updates on my whereabouts.

"Was just putting Howl the third in the old fishbowl," Said says, before joining me.

I raise an eyebrow at him.

"What? I cleaned the water out yesterday," he says as he picks up his luggage by the door and we exit his dorm hand in hand.

"Not that . . . Do you not think that Howl is like a cursed name at this point?"

He looks up briefly like he's considering it. "What about Laddoo the second?"

"Our cat isn't dead yet, Said, astaghfirullah."

"Laddoo doesn't have to be dead to be named after," Said says as we walk out of the dorm building, past the Basquiat mural.

"I think zebra fish should have its own legacy," I say.

"You're right. It needs a name as good as Howl and Laddoo . . . I'll think on it," Said says as we walk over to his car in the parking lot. He loads his things in the trunk and we both get inside.

"Good idea," I say, settling into my seat.

Said starts to pull out of the parking lot, and for a moment I think the name game has ended when suddenly he brakes hard and I almost fly out of my seat.

"Wait, I've got it!" he says, hand on the wheel and eyes wide.

"What?!" I say, my heart racing, slowly recovering from the suddenness of it.

"I'll name it Abigail, like the bakery because it looks sweet."

I look at Said seriously, searching his expression for signs of jest, but as expected, there are none.

"Just drive, you knobhead."

SAID AND TIWA'S FIRST EID TOGETHER

"So much can change over the course of four Eids. Strangers become friends, friends become enemies, and enemies turn into nauseatingly cute couples . . ."

Said's eyebrows furrow as he looks at his sister, who is sitting on a stool in the backyard of the newly built Islamic Center, talking to a group of kids while the other adults inside set up for the Eid party.

"Is Safiyah . . . gossiping about us?" he asks Tiwa, who wears an identical puzzled expression.

". . . I think so . . ." Tiwa replies. "Although maybe she's just—"

"Excuse me," Safiyah says, glaring at Said and Tiwa standing at the back of the small crowd. Everyone turns with Safiyah to look at them. "If you want to listen to the story, you have to sit down and be quiet like everyone else."

"Is she serious?" Said mutters, which doesn't sit well with one of the neighborhood kids, who shakes her head and shushes him.

Said and Tiwa comply and quickly sit down on the grass.

"Where was I? Yes, the end. In the end, after the burning building, the many Eids, the many funerals, *and* the unfortunate cake incident, everyone in the town of New Crosshaven finally came together, and that's why we have this beautiful new Islamic Center to celebrate Eid every year!"

There is a round of applause for Safiyah, who bows her head while stroking the traitorous ginger cat nestled on her lap.

"Now I'm happy to open the floor to any questions," Safiyah says with a bright smile, holding her phone in her hand like a mic as dozens of little arms shoot up in the air.

"Does she think this is a TED Talk or something?" Said mutters.

"Knowing Saf, probably," Tiwa replies.

"Okay, Saira first and then Mohammed," Safiyah says, passing the "microphone" to a little girl with light brown skin and missing front teeth.

"Are Said and Tiwa still together?" Saira asks.

"Last time I checked with them they *were.*" Safiyah glares at them both in the crowd. "Inshallah they stay that way and don't make family dinners awkward by breaking up. Mohammed?" Safiyah says, passing the phone to a boy wearing green overalls this time.

"Did you ever find out how the Islamic Center burned down? Did the evil mayor do it?" he asks, looking excited at the thought of a heinous crime being committed.

Safiyah laughs. "No, of course the mayor didn't burn the Islamic Center down. Actually it was laddoos that did it in the end."

This makes everyone gasp and turn to the ginger cat sleeping on Safiyah.

"The cat burned the Islamic Center down?" another girl in the audience asks, looking horrified.

Safiyah looks confused for a moment, staring down at the feline and then back up at the shocked faces of her listeners. "Oh, sorry, I should have been more specific. I meant laddoos as in the sweets. Turns out Nadia Auntie was cooking them in the Islamic Center's kitchen and forgot to switch the gas off. A tragedy, really, both because the laddoos got burnt and also because we almost lost the center."

More hands shoot up, including Said's, who has a lot of questions for his sister.

"Safiyah," a voice calls from the back door. Safiyah looks up at the auntie who called for her. "I've been looking for you all over. You need to come inside and help your mom." Then her eyes lower to Said on the grass. "You too."

Safiyah sighs. "I guess that's it for today, sorry, kids," she says, placing Laddoo on the ground.

There are groans as the kids start to stand and walk away, back to whatever they were doing before Safiyah's story time began.

Said and Tiwa stay behind. Said's arms are crossed and Tiwa's eyebrow is raised.

Safiyah stands up and startles a little, pretending she just noticed them there.

"Oh, hi, guys. Eid Mubarak!" Safiyah says casually. "When did you guys get here? How was the drive up? I heard the highway was super busy this morning."

Said doesn't answer any of her questions—instead he asks the only one that matters. "Do you do this often?" he asks.

"What?" Safiyah says.

"Tell stories about us?" he clarifies.

She *ohs* and shakes her head. "Don't be silly. I just needed to entertain the kids while everyone was setting up."

Tiwa and Said exchange a glance. Somehow her answer makes her seem even more suspect.

But there are more important things for them to focus on, like finally celebrating Eid in the newly rebuilt Islamic Center. So, Said and Tiwa link arms, and together with Safiyah they go inside, ready for another Eid party.

Now here's where it all ends. In the town of New Crosshaven, known for its colorful murals on every street corner, the best pastry shop in the entire world, the newly rebuilt Islamic Center where Muslims from all over the state gather, and of course, the now famous love story of Said and Tiwa.

The end

Acknowledgments

Four Eids and a Funeral is a product of a chaotic trip to Amsterdam, many cups of breakfast tea, countless Zoom conversations, seven years of friendship, and an endless supply of morbid humor. It is also the product of an amazing team of people without whom this book would not exist.

Thank you to our editors Foyinsi, Rebecca, and Becky. Thank you to our agents Uwe, Molly, and Zoë. Thank you to Jean Feiwel, Dawn Ryan, Samira Iravani, and Allene Cassagnol. Thank you to Ursula Decay for illustrating this wonderful cover!

Faridah: Thank you, Adiba, for being an amazing writing partner and friend. This has been the best experience working on a book I've had and I can't wait to write more books with you! Thank you to my mum and my siblings for all your support. Thank you, always, to my kettle, Steve, for all you do for me.

Adiba: Thank you to Faridah for being the best coauthor that anyone could ask for and also for being a supportive friend throughout everything. I hope we can work on many more books together. Thank you to all my friends who helped me be the best version of myself, as an author and a person: Priyanka, Tammi, Alyssa, Gavin, and Gayatri. Thank you to all my family for supporting me, especially my siblings and my cousin, Nazifa Nawal.

Last of all, thank you to Allah for bringing us together and guiding us down the path to writing this fabulous book (if we do say so ourselves).

Thank you for reading this Feiwel & Friends book.

The friends who made

FOUR EIDS and a FUNERAL

possible are:

Jean Feiwel, Publisher

Liz Szabla, VP, Associate Publisher

Rich Deas, Senior Creative Director

Anna Roberto, Executive Editor

Holly West, Senior Editor

Kat Brzozowski, Senior Editor

Dawn Ryan, Executive Managing Editor

Allene Cassagnol, Associate Director of Production

Emily Settle, Editor

Rachel Diebel, Editor

Foyinsi Adegbonmire, Editor

Brittany Groves, Assistant Editor

Samira Iravani, Associate Art Director

Follow us on Facebook or visit us online at fiercereads.com.
Our books are friends for life.